Jenny 2

Carolyn Sanderson

Jenny 2

Copyright © 2023 Carolyn Sanderson

All rights reserved.

ISBN:

In memory of Muriel

Jenny 2

The characters and events portrayed in this book are fictitious. Any similarity to real persons, living or dead, is coincidental and not intended by the author.

No part of this book may be reproduced, or stored in a retrieval system, or transmitted in any form or by any means, electronic, mechanical, photocopying, recording, or otherwise, without express written permission of the publisher.

CONTENTS

Part One

Chapter One	1
Chapter Two	14
Chapter Three	24
Chapter Four	30
Chapter Five	40
Chapter Six	53
Chapter Seven	61

Part Two

Chapter Eight	73
Chapter Nine	79
Chapter Ten	90
Chapter Eleven	99
Chapter Twelve	107
Chapter Thirteen	120
Chapter Fourteen	133
Chapter Fifteen	139

Chapter Sixteen	150
Chapter Seventeen	163

Part Three

Chapter Eighteen	170
Chapter Nineteen	185

Part Four

Chapter Twenty	195
Chapter Twenty-One	202
Chapter Twenty-Two	213
Chapter Twenty-Three	222
Chapter Twenty-Four	230
Chapter Twenty-five	243
Chapter Twenty-six	250
Chapter Twenty-seven	261
Chapter Twenty-Eight	271
About the Author	272
Also by this author	278

PART ONE

Chapter One

1982

Rachel - Dave

I watched her as she slept. Soon, she would be sleeping right through the night. She was so perfect, my baby, with her tiny fingers, fingernails like miniature pearls, her sleeping face so peaceful, so beautiful, so still. Then, as the weeks went by, her cheeks filled out; I saw her first proper smile, the gurgles of delight when I picked her up.

Night-time was when I saw her most clearly. Waking up was such a disappointment.

Jenny 2

Rachel

Sister Stevens was kind; they were all so very kind, but there was nothing they could do. After the scan they wheeled me back to my room. There were two doctors and a couple more nurses: the room felt very full.

'Rachel,' said the tall one with the rimless glasses.

'I'm so sorry, but we've been unable find your baby's heartbeat.'

It seemed as though my own heart stopped beating. On no, please no, not again, not when we'd got so close this time.

'Where's Dave? Where is he? Where's Dave?'

I could hear someone wailing, the sound of a wounded animal.

'Dave…I want Dave.'

I realised the wailing voice was mine.

Sister Stevens took my hand. 'We've called him. He'll be here soon.' Everything about her was soft and gentle, but I wanted to kick and bite. She nodded to the others, and they filed out solemnly, while she stayed there, still holding my hand.

'Do you understand what's happened, Rachel?'

'My baby's dead.'

'Yes. I'm so sorry.'

'What's going to happen?'

'We'll need to get you delivered.'

Delivered? Give birth to a dead baby? Perhaps she saw my panic, because she went on in that calm voice of hers.

'Don't worry: we'll make you as comfortable as possible: no need to make this any harder than it already is. We'll induce labour and give you all the pain relief you need. It'll be over very quickly.

Jenny 2

The rest of that day hangs around in my memory in fragments. Dave arrived at some point. He didn't seem to be finding words either. He just held me tight and I could feel his tears wet on my neck. He hadn't shaved or combed his hair; it was all tight little curls and tangled knots; I guess that's how he was feeling inside.

Afterwards - after the baby came - they took me back to the room, with Dave hanging on to the side of the trolley as though he thought someone might steal me; or perhaps he was just holding on because otherwise he'd be nothing but a heap on the floor. They left us alone for a while, and we just looked at each other. Then he seemed to have an idea.

'I'll be back in a minute,' he whispered.

I must have drifted off, because the next thing I knew he was sitting there, upright in the chair, and Sister Stevens was coming in, very quietly, carrying something.

'Would you like to see your little girl?'

In those days it wasn't routine to give a stillborn child to the parents to hold. It's a regular thing now, I believe, but back then the idea was to get rid of it, act as though it had never happened; there had never been a baby. Least said, soonest mended.

And so I sat there, holding her. She was beautiful. Perfect. All her fingers and toes were as they should be, so tiny, so delicate. But her eyes were closed, and her chest was still; there was no breath in her.

Dave

My heart started going like the clappers when the phone rang. It had to be the hospital: I just knew. We were about to be parents, at last! All those years of trying and waiting, doctors' appointments, clinics, investigations, procedures, hoping and being disappointed, time and time again. Then,

Jenny 2

at last, *this* time, she got to seven months before they took her into hospital. Everything was fine, just a precaution. They did regular ultrasounds; we saw our baby moving on the screen, heard the little heart beating... So when they phoned from the ward I wasn't fazed: the baby had come a bit early, that was all; I was sorry I hadn't made it in time to be with Rachel, but it must have happened too quickly.

Then the words at the other end of the line began to get through to me.

'I'm so sorry, Mr. Daniels. There really wasn't anything anyone could have done. Your wife is going to need you here. You will have to be strong for her.'

Why do they always do that? Why do they assume the man - the father - knows how to be strong? I had lost my baby too, my hopes, my dreams, just as much as Rachel had.

It was awful, seeing her like that, her eyes dead-looking, just staring, not really seeing me at all. I tried to do the manly thing, but really, when I put my arms round her and held her tight, I was the one holding on, needing comfort. I found myself thinking of all the things I'd have to do when I got home, like phoning her parents. They would be the same as me, thinking the phone was ringing with good news. How could I tell them? How could I break their hearts too? Then I'd have to phone *my* parents, our friends, her colleagues...

After a bit I had an idea. I went to find Sister Stevens. She'd been so kind and helpful all the time Rachel was in hospital. She helped me dress the baby - *our* baby, our tiny, perfect, baby daughter.

I think Rachel was sort of glad I'd done that. She sat for ages, just staring down at her, holding her tight. I had my camera; it was in the bag I'd kept ready for when... Anyway, I took some pictures of Jenny. We'd already agreed that's what we'd call her if it was a girl. Then it was time; time for

Jenny 2

Jenny to go. They gave Rachel something to make her sleep.

I made my way home slowly, like someone with weights in their pockets. The world had turned once on its axis and now I was in a different universe. Everything was wrong, unreal. I almost walked straight past our house. It was a stranger to me now. Then I saw the roses, supernaturally white in that grey dawn, and I stopped and opened the gate. Roses in April! Yesterday they were an omen, a symbol of new life. Now I kicked and tore at them; I wanted to destroy them. I felt the thorns biting into my skin, and I welcomed the pain.

Opening the front door I imagined, just for a second, that I heard a child's laughter. It brought me to my senses: time to get a grip. Somewhere inside me I could still hear the echo of the laughter we shared the day Rachel told me the news. *Are you sure? Has it really taken this time?* I remember gazing at her belly with wonder, almost afraid to touch her. I tried to imagine the tiny creature inside, made up of her and me together, the seal on our love, the dream finally made flesh.

The stairs creaked as I climbed. In that other life, the one before yesterday, I worried about the noise waking our sleeping child. If only it could wake her now. The thoughts kept going round in my head: *you've got to deal with the nursery. Rachel mustn't come home to an empty cot.*

I found myself in the room, somehow. I didn't want to be there. The cot still stood where I'd left it, after the struggle to get all the pieces in the right place. It's not as easy as you might think. Above it, that garish plastic mobile that Rachel had been so keen on, drifting eerily in the strange light. I ripped it from the ceiling, and a lump of plaster came down with it. Even though I was dog-tired, I picked up the screwdriver from the corner where I'd thrown it down, with such a sense of triumph. Was that only last week? In some sort of frenzy I got to work, and found I couldn't stop until the entire cot was no more than a pile of poles and slats.

What next? The clothes, of course: all those tiny garments. We'd been collecting them for weeks. A lot of them were presents, some of them knitted by Rachel's mum. My mum wasn't much of a knitter, but she'd bought a great stack of tiny vests and booties. I couldn't think what to do with them at first, but then I went into our bedroom and dragged out the suitcase from under the bed. I just tipped everything in, but then what? The Oxfam Shop? The Children's Home? A bonfire in the garden? And what about the changing mat? And the little chest of drawers?

It must have been midday when I finally noticed the sun creeping across the floor. With a mighty effort I picked myself up from where I'd been lying. The tears had dried on my face and my nose was running. I'd been dreaming, or maybe just daydreaming: Jenny's first steps; Jenny's first day at school; even, God help me, walking her up the aisle on her wedding day.

Well now it was time to put all that aside. What had they said to me on the phone? I had to be strong for Rachel's sake. She was going to need my support.

Rachel

They made me get up the next day. I didn't want to. I wanted to hide under the covers, hide away from the world. I kept remembering that other time, when they took me in, screaming in pain. Afterwards they said there was no reason why I shouldn't conceive with just the one ovary.

'I know you won't believe me now, Rachel,' said Sister Stevens. 'But you will feel better if you get up and start moving around.' She gave my shoulders a gentle squeeze.

'Life *will* go on, I promise you.'

Jenny 2

They must have warned the others, because everyone was so nice to me, so careful. But that made it all so much worse, because what I wanted above everything else was to be one of them, one of the mothers in the dayroom, complaining about the difficulties of breastfeeding, or that my baby had kept me awake all night. Oh, if only! But it was *their* babies that kept me awake; the crying of all the babies who weren't Jenny. The night my milk came in, I thought I might kill myself.

Then, when Dave took me home that day, and I saw what he had done, I was so angry. I don't know where all that fury came from. I just felt that I had had everything taken away from me. I didn't even have the chance to say goodbye to my hopes. The cot, the clothes, everything, as if our baby had never been, as if we had never planned for her, never talked about what it would be like when we had her, never prepared for her coming. And then he was back at work the next week, as though nothing had ever happened. His life just carried on as normal.

The first morning he hung around in the doorway.

'I'll be in my office all day,' he said. 'You can phone me at any time, and if I'm not there, speak to Susannah and she'll come and find me.'

But why would I do that? What could he do? What could anyone *do*?

'Rachel?' He sounded so clueless. 'I thought your sister was coming round for coffee?'

Was she? Whose idea had that been?

Dave sighed and looked at the clock. I could see he couldn't wait to get out of the house. He gave me a quick peck on the cheek, picked up his briefcase and then he was gone.

Jenny 2

Dave

I hated leaving her that day, but what could I do? I still had to earn money, and it was just expected in those days that a man would go to work as normal. Perhaps seeing Laura wouldn't be such a good idea anyway, although surely her sister would have the sense not to bring the baby with her? I took a deep breath and left the house. It was raining, but I didn't bother going back for my umbrella. The roses near the gate were drooping; the overnight rain had rotted the new buds, and they hung there, crumpled and grey; they would never open now.

I had been so convinced that I was doing the right thing, getting rid of all those reminders before Rachel came home and saw them. Perhaps I needed to do it for myself, too, to make the loss real. I could see my mistake now, of course. Rachel had expected that it was something we would do together. More than that, she had *needed* it to be something we did together. But I couldn't undo it, just as I couldn't undo that awful moment when they'd phoned from the hospital, when Rachel had already faced the terrible news alone. They say that shared grief draws people closer together, but we were already being pulled apart by it.

The train was crowded. I was almost glad of the familiar discomforts of the journey: I knew where I was with all that. In a strange way I enjoyed being jostled as I left the station, by people whose lives hadn't been touched by tragedy. When I reached the office building, I headed for the stairs and found myself on the third floor without knowing how I got there, trying to marshal a few facts and figures to prepare for a day of analysing statistics, hoping that would crowd out every other thought. Female colleagues murmured their sympathy, some laying a hand on my arm; the men made gruff remarks about the weather.

Jenny 2

Susannah was waiting when I reached my own office. I was grateful that she didn't do the murmuring thing. She just got on with filling me in on significant events during my absence, and then she put a file in front of me that contained a list of all the things I needed to do that day.

Lunchtime was difficult. I bought a sandwich in the canteen and brought it back to my desk to avoid conversation with colleagues. I wasn't hungry. It was then I realised I hadn't thought about Rachel for over an hour. I dialled our home number and let it ring and ring. If she'd gone out, she hadn't set the answering machine. I wondered where she'd gone. Long before mobile phones then, of course, so no way I could contact her. If she'd gone out, that could be a good sign. Or was she still so angry with me, so distressed, that she was sitting there listening to it ringing and ringing and just not picking it up? I couldn't even leave a message.

I pushed the sandwich to one side and filled my head with cold hard facts and figures again. At least there was something in this changed world that I could deal with. The ever-tactful Susannah came in at five o'clock to point out it was time to go home, and I saw her discreetly drop the sandwich into the waste basket beneath her own desk. I had a quick look at the papers she'd given me that morning. Only three of the things on the list were ticked off.

There were a lot of evenings like that first evening. I would half-heartedly attempt to cook a meal that we would half-heartedly attempt to eat, and then scrape most of it into the bin. Rachel would sit in front of the TV, not really watching, dozing off and on, and I would go upstairs and try to complete some of the tasks I hadn't got round to during the day. I don't know why I decided to try to work in Jenny's room. I hadn't managed to dispose of the chest of drawers, and the table where the changing mat had been worked quite well as a little desk. There was a kind of comfort in being there.

The first time I did it I was so deep in thought I didn't hear her come up the stairs.

'What are you doing?' Her voice was so angry. 'What are you doing in here?'

'Oh, just some things I didn't get done during the day. Are you ready for bed? Would you like me to help you …?'

I didn't get to finish the sentence. Rachel twisted away from me; her breath was coming in little gasps, and she looked close to collapse. I got up and tried to hold her, but she pulled away and I saw, too late, that I had made another bad mistake.

Rachel

My Mum had been to visit, but she didn't stay long because my dad couldn't cope on his own. I understood, but I wished she'd been here all the same, especially after that first day when Dave went back to work. Mum and I used to talk on the phone. One day I must have been on the phone to her for at least an hour and a half.

'I just don't know how he could do it. It's *Jenny's* room. How could he? Sitting there, calmly working away, as if nothing had happened…'

I heard his key in the latch and finished the call; I didn't feel strong enough for any sort of scene. He paused in the doorway for a bit before coming into the room, so he must have heard me talking about him. Next thing, he was down on his knees beside me, trying to hold my hand. I flinched; it was still all bruised from the cannula.

'Why didn't you tell me how you felt?'

'I shouldn't need to.'

Jenny 2

He sighed. 'Come on, budge up.' He tried to fit into the space beside me like he used to, but it was different; our bodies didn't fit together any more.

Dave

I watched as she heaved herself painfully up off the sofa and headed for the stairs. Our bedroom door closed with a thud. Eventually I got up too. I climbed the stairs but didn't follow her into our room. Instead, I went into Jenny's and sat down again at the little table. I'd been holding my own tears back, but now they were falling freely. I just sat there, slumped in the place that should have been her changing table, and then I reached in my pocket for something to wipe my face. What came out was a tiny vest. I must have been carrying it round with me all day.

I went with Rachel for her six-week check-up. The hospital was treating her like anyone else on its system: she'd delivered a baby, so she had to attend the post-natal clinic. Never mind that she didn't actually *have* a baby. Of course, my rational mind knew that she needed a physical check-up, but it seemed so cruel that she had to sit there, alongside all those mothers fussing with their babies. You'd have thought they might have made other arrangements for someone in her situation.

Anyway, there we were, sitting side by side on the creaky black plastic chairs, waiting. The six-week check-up is apparently known as the moment when the mother is given the all-clear to 'resume marital relations.' That's what it said in the pregnancy book we'd read together; back then, back in a different lifetime, when we *were* together. Now, although our shoulders almost touched as we sat there on those narrow chairs, we could have been several thousand miles apart. Would we ever make love again? Already I was missing the tenderness, the touch of her soft, warm skin. I thought about the way her hair tickled my face as we cosied up together in bed before going to sleep. I didn't mind so much about the sex, but I was missing the closeness so much it was like a physical pain. I can even tell you where it's located: there's a place, right there, in the middle of my ribcage. I ached to be close to her again.

New-born babies have a special cry all of their own; it's loud and reedy and piercing and repetitive, and I could see it was driving Rachel nuts. It must have been hell on earth for her in the hospital after... after Jenny, surrounded by that sound. No wonder she was twitchy that day at the clinic.

So we sat there, not speaking, not quite touching. Women came and went, some alone, some with their partners, and a few with older children in tow, but every single one of them was carrying a baby. I wished again that there was a special clinic for someone like Rachel; I so much wanted her to be spared the sight of what might have been, what so nearly was. I cleared my throat to stop the tears: if Rachel could remain dry-eyed, so must I.

It seemed ages that I sat there, watching, hardly seeing. One by one, names were called and the mothers shuffled awkwardly to the consulting rooms with their tiny bundles in the crook of their arms. I thought we might survive the morning - just - so long as we could stay tightly insulated from the world beyond. We were together but separate, in our own bubble of misery.

The clock on the wall moved with agonising slowness. Mother after mother entered one of the mysterious doors, and came out, smiling, relieved. I could feel myself growing more and more tense on Rachel's behalf. What Rachel was feeling was unimaginable.

One of the mothers passed right in front of us. She had her baby clasped tight to her chest. Did she think we were going to snatch it? She nodded to Rachel and seemed about to say something, but then apparently changed her mind.

I growled something along the lines of 'Why can't they see us at some other time?' and then couldn't find the right words to express my outrage that Rachel was being subjected to so many reminders of her loss. I tried again. 'Why do we have to sit here with all these...all these...'

'If you don't want to sit here, why don't you go home?'

'Oh, Rachel, you know that isn't what I meant...' There was an awkward silence then.

I tried to change the mood by asking a question. 'So, who was she...?' I nodded in the direction of the consulting room. "Do you know her?"

'She was in the room opposite me on the antenatal ward. We were due on the same day.' She grimaced. 'We *had* our babies on the same day...'

I so desperately longed to gather Rachel to me, to wipe her tears and shed my own, but the stiffness of her body made that unthinkable, as she sat there, staring ahead, not looking at me. I heard her draw breath to speak again, as though the effort was almost too much.

'There were ... problems, when her baby was born.... didn't breathe for a while or something...' Her tone was heavy as lead. I understood. For a moment she turned and met my gaze, and I knew that, for this brief moment at least, we were thinking the same thing: that woman may have had problems at the birth, but in the end she had taken home a healthy baby.

Chapter Two

Rachel – Dave

She'd been crawling for months, one of those lively, inquisitive babies, into everything, gurgling and giggling with delight. I saw the room lighting up with her smile, the sweet little dresses I'd put her in, the cute little socks with frilly tops. Perhaps her birthday would be the day she took her first steps? It was all so vivid: the little friends invited round for a birthday tea, my niece and nephews, Laura so envious of Jenny's development. I'd wondered about inviting the woman at the hospital, the one who had a baby the same day as me, but I hadn't kept in touch.

Rachel

I was sitting, staring at the row of cards. *Sincere Sympathy*. Dave was arranging the flowers in water, and not making a very good job of it.

'Leave them, Dave.'

He called through from the kitchen, 'No, it's all right, Rachel, I'll do it.'

When he came in with them he set them down on the coffee table right in front of me.

'There you are. You'll be able to get the scent from there.'

I made no response; couldn't think of one.

'Look, Love, you will want to go back to work eventually. It'll help…'

'Not back to the Council Office, though…'

He took my hand. 'No, but…'

Jenny 2

'I couldn't face them, Dave. Surely you can see that?'

He made soothing noises. They didn't work.

'You know what? They'd have sent flowers if I'd come home from the hospital with a living baby. They must have thought it would be a pity to waste the gesture.' I felt like a jilted bride. Was I supposed to return the gifts: the babygros, the toys, the blankets with bunny rabbits on?

'Oh, Rachel...' He was as lost as I was.

I was fighting back the tears now. They'd told us, at the antenatal sessions, that new mothers often felt tearful, but I couldn't for the life of me see what they had to cry about. I had left the office to start my maternity leave, all round and rosy and full of excitement. How could I go back with no bump and no baby, dark circles under my eyes and misery in my face?

I did go back to work eventually, but not to the Council Office. Dave kept saying it wasn't doing me any good sitting at home, and once I was more or less physically back to normal, he pushed me to do something, so I did. I took a series of anonymous jobs, shelf-stacking, filing, anything where I didn't have to face people. And I did something else, too.

He came home that evening and went upstairs to get changed. Then he came down again.

'Rachel? What's happening? Where are your clothes?'

'In the spare room...'

'Because...?'

'Because the spare room is my room now.'

I don't know, even at the time, why I was so cruel to him, but all he said was, 'Oh,' and went into the kitchen to fill the kettle.

Jenny 2

After that he sort of tiptoed round me, for a while, and then we settled into the sort of domestic routine that two strangers might have if forced to share a house. I made an effort, once in a while. On our wedding anniversary, the following year, I cooked a special meal, but he was late home from work, and when I finally put my burnt offering on the table, Dave couldn't eat more than a few mouthfuls. I don't think the not eating was because it was overcooked; I don't think he even noticed that. It was just that he seemed to have no appetite any more. Looking at him, as he sat slumped in his chair, I noticed for the first time how thin he had become. I even wondered if he was anorexic, but that's ridiculous, isn't it? Men don't get anorexia.

In his way, Dave made an effort too, sometimes. He brought me flowers, or cleaned the bathroom when it wasn't even his turn. For some reason, that made me really angry. Was that supposed to make it all right? Was that all our daughter's life was worth – a bit of an extra scrub behind the U-bend?

At first I thought about Jenny pretty much all the time, even when I was asleep. I would wake some mornings with tears running down my face. As time went on, I found myself dreaming during the daytime, too. Her first birthday was probably the worst moment.

I thought about that woman, at home with her baby daughter and her perfect little family. I'd seen them when they came to visit, the smartly-dressed husband, the well-behaved little boys with their blond hair and blue eyes. I hated her.

I took Jenny swimming when she was still a toddler; she loved it right away, giggling and squealing with delight as she kicked her little arms and legs in the water. I

Jenny 2

daydreamed about how it would be when she was old enough to go to nursery. I already knew what it was like there – I'd taken my nephew for a while when Laura was expecting...

I watched her when she didn't know I was looking, in the little home corner, making pretend tea parties; her speech was very advanced. With parents who took care to talk to her so much, she learned early. And the dressing up corner... It occurred to me that I should have a dressing up box at home, but somehow I never got around to it...

Yes, I know it's all fantasy, but some days it was more real than my real life. Jenny got bigger, and older; she learned to ride a bike. It was a big day when we took the stabilisers off...

'Rachel,' Dave said, one evening, as we were sitting pretending to watch TV. 'It's not doing you any good, you know.'

I moved away from him. He made me so angry all the time now.

'How would you have the faintest idea what is or isn't good for me?'

'Whether you believe me or not, it still hurts me too, you know.'

I doubted that.

'We will always mourn her, of course we will, but Rachel, we have to let her go.' His expression was so serious it was almost funny. 'There is no Jenny. She didn't live and you cannot bring her to life.'

He had no idea.

Jenny 2

The job at the supermarket was okay to begin with; at least I didn't have to talk to people, except the dozy ones who interrupted me to ask for things that were right under their noses. Sometimes they would raise their voices, and ask to speak to the manager, and I would stand there open-mouthed that they could attach so much importance to such trivial things. What did it matter if the store no longer stocked their favourite brand of breakfast cereal, or if there really wasn't any demand for root ginger? What did it matter if the whole building fell about their ears? What did anything matter in the whole world when my Jenny was dead?

It really came to a head when Laura's little girl started school; I found myself thinking: that's what Jenny would look like, in her royal blue uniform, with her big brown satchel. That's what little schoolkids had in those days.

I did her hair in plaits each morning, and she squawked if I pulled it too tight. I used to tell her to eat up her breakfast, most important meal of the day...

'Come on, Sweetheart, how are you going to do all those sums if you don't have a good breakfast inside you?'

Jenny giggled and began blowing noisily into her cereal bowl. The Rice Krispies and milk went flying in every direction. I tried to sound cross as I mopped it up, but really all the time I thought it was funny.

Dave heard her from upstairs where he was having a shave and came thundering down the stairs so as not to miss out on the fun, shaving foam still clinging to his face. Jenny squealed and rushed away from him as he pretended to be a monster, and chased her across the kitchen...

I found it really hard, some days, working in the supermarket; it made me ache inside to see how impatient some mothers were with their children. And slapping them!

Jenny 2

Dave and I would never once have laid a finger on Jenny. Well, we wouldn't have needed to: she was such a happy little thing, and we loved her.

I watched a woman one day with a beautiful toddler, a really sweet little girl, almost as sweet as Jenny; she was clearly tired. Her mother had dragged her round the shop; she wasn't even talking to her, just yelling at her to 'Come on!' and then when the child sat down in the middle of the aisle, this awful woman yanked her to her feet and gave her a ringing slap on the leg. Several people looked round. I could see the red mark. It ought to be illegal to hit a child. Probably is, by now; I wouldn't know, would I?

The manager called me in.

'We've had complaints, Rachel.'

I looked at her. 'Complaints?'

'Yes, Rachel, several. People asking you for things and you ignore them.'

I had no memory of ignoring anyone, but I didn't really have the energy to argue. I just looked at her. I was still thinking about that awful woman.

'Rachel, your colleagues are complaining too. They say you're not pulling your weight, that you're in a daydream half the time, you're too slow...'

That's what they call a verbal warning. The next stage is a written one. It wasn't long in coming. They'd put me on the baby products section; how cruel was that?

Jobs were becoming harder to find. I signed on with an agency and they sent me all over the place for a few days at a time: backroom offices where I photocopied endless reams of papers, packed stuff in boxes, made cups of tea for the work force... It was an existence, of sorts.

Dave

I was finding it hard just being in the house where it had all happened: the hopes, the false alarms, the visits to the special clinic; and then, finally, the pregnancy that was almost carried to term. I was going to be the best Dad ever, fully involved in our son's upbringing (those were the days before it was possible to know the baby's sex in advance) I diligently painted the baby's room in neutral shades, put together the furniture, made endless trips to Mothercare with Rachel, asking stupid questions like what breast pads were for and why did we need to buy so many terry nappies?

Afterwards, I simply didn't know what to do. Rachel wasn't Rachel any more; it was as if she had travelled far, far away, and I couldn't reach her. She kept telling me that it was all right for me, going off to work every day, but what did she know? My workplace was suddenly bursting with proud Dads and pregnant women, and it was impossible to concentrate on anything. What did a job matter, now that I had lost not only my daughter, but apparently my wife too? I wanted to hold Rachel, protect her, comfort her, but she wouldn't let me; she was covered in thorns, and there was no way of approaching her.

I found some comfort sitting in Jenny's room. I told myself I was finishing the work I was too debilitated to complete during the working day, but most of the time I simply sat there at the little table, thinking about what might have been.

And so we drifted on, separate from each other in the same grief and loss. Months became years. Rachel had eventually gone back to work, although not to her old job: she needed to get out of the house, get away from all the reminders. We avoided the anniversary, of course – Rachel referred to it as 'Jenny's birthday'– and on the day itself we were scrupulously careful not to mention it. We used to organise a trip or an outing, never admitting, perhaps not even to

Jenny 2

ourselves, that the things planned for April 20th had anything at all to do with our lost child.

One evening, I was sitting in Jenny's room. It had become an entrenched habit, especially after Rachel moved into the spare room. I suddenly found myself utterly overcome with grief, and, when I went downstairs I discovered that Rachel had gone out without telling me. Something gave way deep inside me and before I knew it, I was lying prostrate, sobbing into the carpet. I've no idea how long I lay there. I didn't even hear the front door open, didn't notice how dark it was getting…

Suddenly the light snapped on. I sensed rather than saw Rachel standing over me. Her voice was cold and distant.

'What do you think you're doing?'

I had no idea how to answer. What did I think I was doing? Thinking didn't come into it. The carpet was wet beneath my face.

'I can't do this any more, Rachel,' I finally managed to mumble. I turned my head and looked up at her. 'I love you, but you shut me out. You seem to think you're the only one who's grieving. I wish we had our Jenny too, you know.'

She watched in silence as I gathered myself up, slowly, as though every bone and muscle had forgotten what it was for. When I was finally on my feet, I just stood there for a moment, looking at her. Then I heard myself say: 'Do you want to try to make our marriage work, or is it really over?'

And that was that. Or rather, it wasn't, because it felt unfinished, and went on being unfinished, for a long time.

Jenny 2

Rachel

I was a bit dubious when the agency sent me to the primary school, but there was nothing else in the offing, and I didn't want to go back to sitting at home. Besides, I needed to earn money, now that Dave and I were separated. With perfect irony, the job was to cover a maternity leave.

The office was just inside the main entrance, with a sliding window where people coming into the building could sign in or ask questions. I didn't have to do any of that: there was a lot of photocopying and filing, which I was used to, and checking of registers and dinner money, dealing with lost property, and occasionally I had to take a message to a classroom. Sometimes it was a child's lunch box or pencil case that the scatty mother had brought in at the last minute, or an excuse note they'd forgotten to bring for PE. It was usually the same ones. I watched them, thinking about how organised I'd have been with Jenny.

I told Diane when I arrived that I wasn't good at dealing with people – it sounded better than saying I didn't *want* to talk to anyone - and she said that was OK, there was lots of other stuff needed doing anyway, but I might have to cover for her on reception sometimes when she was on a break or if the Head needed her to do something else. Nine times out of ten I just sat there, in a world of my own as usual.

After a while I found myself wondering about the woman whose job I was covering. There was a picture on the desk: a pretty young woman and a small child, and under the desk a bag with a pair of old shoes in it. Some of the things in the drawers looked as though they might be hers, too: a fancy key ring with no keys on it, and a shiny zip-up pencil case. I started to feel I knew her, and as her due date drew closer I found myself thinking about her. Was she going to be one of those mothers who sails serenely through pregnancy and childbirth? Had her scans been all right? I wondered if she was worried, and if she was seeing the

Jenny 2

midwife, and whether her ankles were horribly swollen like mine had been. I found myself getting more and more anxious about her and her unborn baby, and some nights I even dreamed about her.

And then one day Jenny walked back into my life.

Chapter Three

Rachel

She stood there, golden hair tumbling around her sad little face.

'My Mummy's forgotten to pack my lunch.' There were tears in her eyes.

I looked round desperately for Diane, who normally dealt with things like this, but I was alone in the office. I had made it absolutely clear that I didn't want to deal with children directly.

'Er, just a moment,' I said. 'Can you tell me your name, Sweetheart?' (*Sweetheart!* Where on earth had that come from?)

'Liz'beth.'

She said it with a sweet little lisp. I noticed that her shoes were on the wrong feet, and her little cardigan was all buttoned up wrong. It did something to me, and that something hurt.

I pulled myself together and asked for her surname. She looked at me blankly.

'Your other name,' I prompted. 'Elizabeth what...?'

'Oh.' She paused, looking at me with those big, blue eyes. 'Mary?'

'Elizabeth Mary what?'

I was standing there uncertain. I needed her name to look up her emergency contact details. Did she really not know her surname? What were her parents thinking of?'

Diane breezed in just then, a sheaf of papers in her hand.

'Problem?'

Jenny 2

'Oh, Elizabeth has come without her lunch and I need to contact home, but she doesn't seem to know her surname.'

'Hmmph! I know it well enough. I'll phone them for you – I just about know the number off by heart.'

She ran her finger down one of the lists pinned to the corkboard and went over to the phone. All the while, Elizabeth stood, shrinking on the other side of the sliding window.

Diane slammed the phone down with an impatient gesture. 'Recorded message. And...' She returned to the list, 'I'll bet there are... No, as I thought. No emergency contact details.'

Another child's head appeared at the window.

'Miss! Miss!' She was addressing Dianne. 'Mrs. Andrews says come quickly. There's a dog in the toilets...'

Dianne rushed off, leaving me uncertain what to do. What sort of family has a lovely child like this and fails to look after her? I made a quick decision.

'Do you like ham sandwiches?' I asked. She nodded, tentatively. 'And chocolate biscuits?' Another nod. I reached into my bag and pulled out my own lunch.

Of course, I got a telling off when it came to light.

'Did you check for allergies? Parental wishes?'

I pointed out that the parents didn't seem particularly concerned about the child's welfare, and then Diane conceded that the forgotten lunch business had happened more than once. Marion, the head of Early Years, spoke to the parents and wrested some emergency contact details out of them, and I was let off with a warning and that was that.

Only it wasn't. From then on, I spotted her each morning as she arrived, dragging her little feet, her hair

Jenny 2

neatly combed and tied up, her clothes more or less in order. By lunchtime she was dishevelled, and if she'd had PE her shoes would be once again on the wrong feet. If I looked out of the office window I could see her in the playground, hanging back, watching the other children, never joining in, never being noticed. My heart began to ache for her.

Then she was in my dreams. Jenny was always there, of course, but now she took on a definite physical form. I felt the soft golden curls under my hand as I brushed out the tangles, saw the clear blue eyes looking up at me as I wiped away the tears...

The business with the lunch wasn't an isolated incident, either. The mother turned up a couple of days later with something she said the child had forgotten: something she'd forgotten to give her, more like! Her clothes marked her out as a professional, and her entitled manner as someone I could never like. She stood out like a sore thumb from most of the other mums; some of them turned up at the school gates in a shell suit over their pyjamas, but somehow, I found it easier to forgive them. You could see they found life hard.

This one wore expensive perfume, too, and understated gold jewellery that must have cost a pretty penny. You'd think someone like that would be well-organised, but there was always something breathless about her, as if she spent her life running just to keep still. I almost felt I knew her - I certainly knew her type well enough. She'd brought Elizabeth's PE kit and I told her she could go to the classroom with it. That was in the days before security and safeguarding.

'Oh, I'm so sorry, but could you take it? I'm already late and I need to drop off Miles' sports kit at the senior school and then I need to call in at the shop for milk and I'll never make it in time for my meeting at 9.00, and ...'

Jenny 2

I glanced up at the clock on the wall behind me. She was quite right: she wasn't going to make it in time for her meeting.

'All right, but I can't leave the office until my colleague comes back. Now, which class is she in, and what's her name?'

'Elizabeth. She's in...'

She was already halfway out of the door, heels clicking on the tiles as she replied, so I didn't catch the name of the teacher. When Diane came back she knew immediately who it was by my description.

'Why don't you take it, Rachel? It's time you found your way around the school a bit. Miss Pringle's classroom, third on the left down the Early Years corridor.'

Miss P wasn't all that pleased to be interrupted.

'Elizabeth Brown, come and collect your PE kit. Hurry, child, Mrs Daniels hasn't got all day.'

I was feeling really sorry for the child, what with that mother and now Miss Pringle. She was sitting at a table near the back, a little apart from the others, but as she looked up she gave me a tentative smile and came shyly forward. Hard to imagine that this tiny waif was the daughter of the smartly dressed, impatient woman with the clickety clackety heels.

Everything about her made me ache inside, from her wrinkled tights to her untucked shirt, the misbuttoned cardigan and the ponytail flopping over one ear, the fine gold curls escaping to form a kind of halo around her little face...

She stifled a sob and did her best to apologise, and my heart hurt for her. Miss P gave her a little lecture about taking responsibility for her own things now she's a big girl at school... The tiny waif sank visibly into herself. Miss P gave me an impatient nod.

'Thank you, Mrs Daniels...' and I was dismissed.

Jenny 2

Little Elizabeth wasn't the only child with problems. I had found myself getting more and more involved with the children, the one thing I had absolutely not wanted when I took the job. Diane complained that I was getting behind with my real work, and I said sorry, will do better, but I didn't.

At playtime I saw Elizabeth in the corridor on my way to the staff room.

'How was PE?' I asked.

She told me that she hadn't been able to do PE because she didn't have her plimsolls.

'But your mum brought your kit…'

Elizabeth gave a sigh. 'My plimsolls weren't in the bag. I had to sit out. Again.' She looked down at the floor, and I wondered whether she ever noticed that her shoes were on the wrong feet. Today they weren't even a matching pair. Then I knew what I had to do.

Dave came round to look at the boiler. He was still paying the mortgage until I could 'get back on my feet' enough to face selling the house. I'd forgotten how responsible he was. I told him what I was considering doing. He took some time to think before responding. I didn't tell him directly about the little golden angel; instead, I talked about how some of the children needed more attention in school to compensate for being neglected by their parents. I explained how the teaching staff needed more support, too.

He grilled me for a bit on my motives and asked whether I'd really thought about spending one-to-one time with individual children, whether I'd really thought about my own feelings… I say grilled, but that's not quite fair; in truth he was very gentle. I'd forgotten that about him too…

In the end, he said, 'I do know how hard these last few years have been for you. You know I always thought you would make a wonderful mother.' He looked away, blinking. Tears?

Jenny 2

Then he turned back to me. 'Maybe this is a way you can draw on all that maternal instinct, to do some good...

He even gave me a hug when my own tears came. And he was right. At some barely articulated level I did think that, although Elizabeth's mother might not be very maternal, I would be able to compensate for that. One day I would see those sad blue eyes smiling at me.

Mrs. Grainger was surprised when I asked about training as a Teaching Assistant.

'Well, I'm always pleased when someone expresses an interest in special needs, but I had understood that you joined us as admin. only. In fact, I believe you were quite insistent on that. I'm wondering what's changed your mind?'

Chapter Four

Rachel

Rachel

It worked out well, at least for a few years. I was able to do my training on the job, supported by the more experienced TAs. They were good years, the time at the primary school. I loved the atmosphere in the staff room; the teachers all seemed to care so much about the children. Most of the younger ones didn't have children of their own, and that only seemed to lend them extra energy for the job.

I especially loved the routines. The children, even the smallest ones, learned to line up for everything. A finger to the lips indicated the need for silence. When the teachers counted down from three, the children scurried to do what they were told. I asked Miss Fawcett one day what would happen if they didn't, and she admitted she had no idea: no child had ever failed to obey before the count was over!

During my training period I got to sit in all the classrooms and observe. I really enjoyed that, squashing myself into the tiny chairs, getting down to the children's level, trying to get to grips with how things are taught nowadays. It's certainly different from how it was when I went to school. I'd had no idea. Of course, if Jenny…

Then they said they wanted to designate a child as my special responsibility. Perhaps they decided on Elizabeth because they'd already noted the bond I was forming with her. I had to work with other children too, of course, but the little blond-haired, blue-eyed angel was by far my favourite. She had dyslexic tendencies, they thought, and that's what made her so difficult to manage. I thought 'difficult' was the wrong word; unhappy, more like. But, whatever the case, she needed help. She couldn't seem to control her pencil to make the letter shapes, so I made it into a game. We stood in the playground, sometimes, making great big letter shapes in the air, swinging our arms. Then I would challenge her to make the shapes smaller and smaller, until she could make them on the page.

It was the same with the reading: we turned the letters into animals, or familiar household objects, and then they didn't seem so unfriendly to her. We always seemed to be laughing together, but sometimes, when she wasn't laughing, she looked far too sad for a five-year-old.

Mrs. Grainger, the Special Needs Co-ordinator, seemed pleased with what I was doing. She sent me on some courses, so I could learn more about behaviour issues. It was just as well, because, as time went on, there was less laughter. My little angel became increasingly unwilling to attempt her reading, and I felt I was no longer getting through to her.

One day - it was the end of lessons and she should have been getting her coat on ready to go home - she hung about near the classroom door. Her long blond curls had escaped her hairband, and she had a smudge of crayon on her face.

'Mrs. Daniels?' It was a question. It meant: will you listen to me if I talk to you? I had felt for some time that there was something not quite right at home and I wondered how much attention she got there.

'Are you all right there?' I said, in the bright and brisk tones, designed for maximum reassurance, that I was carefully honing as part of my professional armoury. 'What can I do for you?'

The child looked down at her shoes. I thought I saw a tear glint.

'Why can't I have green band books like Milly?'

Jenny 2

So that was it. She had noticed that she was falling behind the others.

'Oh, Elizabeth, I'm sure you will soon, just as soon as you're ready to move on. How many purple band books do you have to go now? It can't be many.'

Her voice came out as a strangled whisper. 'My brother says I'm stupid. He says when he was in Reception he had finished all the books and his teacher had to get more books for him from Class 1.'

She was still looking at the floor, and the tears were falling freely now, splashing onto her little blue shoes. I noticed that they were yet again on the wrong feet. I wanted to hug her, to reassure her.

'Jenny,' I wanted to say, 'It doesn't matter which books you're on. You are a lovely, warm, funny child, and I love you very much...' but I remembered myself in time. Instead, I said, 'And what does your brother know? I'll bet he can't paint beautiful pictures like you? Or dance and sing like you?'

I omitted to mention that she'd been left out of the Nativity Play because her singing and dancing were a bit too spontaneous, and that the beautiful paintings were so thick with paint that it was impossible to peel them off the easel. And I really didn't care about the paint she'd put on my umbrella: she was right, it was a very pretty colour, and looked much better than boring old black.

While I tried desperately to get her to smile, I heard the rapid tap-tapping of smart court shoes - not the sort of things teachers wear to work - and the mother gusted in, a mixture of apology and exasperation.

'Oh there you are! So sorry I'm late. I got held up at work. Shall we sort your shoes out? Have you got your reading book?'

She turned it over, frowning at the back cover, and sighed.

Jenny 2

'Oh dear! We really need to get you moved on, don't we? See if we can get you to catch up with the others?'

Clearly it wasn't only the brother who was making the child feel inadequate. I made a tactical withdrawal.

Another day I found the little one weeping in the toilets. It took me some time to persuade her to come out. She hated school, she said. She had no friends, everyone laughed at her. And she was never, ever playing rounders again. It seemed her team had lost, and for some inexplicable reason they had blamed her. It was all too easy to scapegoat a vulnerable child.

I talked to Mrs. Grainger about her. The parents were called in yet again. Nothing much changed.

Dave came round that evening. He used to do that. I guess he still felt some sort of responsibility towards me. I noticed he always found some excuse during his visits to go upstairs, to look into Jenny's room. He accused me of not 'letting go,' of not 'moving on,' but he was every bit as bad. I told him about the child at school. He made some practical suggestions, but he knew nothing about children, and his ideas were rubbish. Then he said something that really hurt me.

'Don't get too attached, Rachel.'

'What do you mean? It's my job!' I was blazing.

'You're not her mother. She's already got one, even if she isn't making a great success of it. You've got to stand back, be objective...be professional.'

I was beyond fury. Had I ever told him how to do his job? Before I knew it, I was lunging at him. He held my wrists, and kept making these annoying, soothing noises, like I was a child myself. Then I just went limp - all the anger and energy went out of me, and he caught me just before I hit the floor.

Jenny 2

'Come on, sit down. It's time we talked - really talked.'

And so we talked, and he stroked my hair, and he somehow talked me into 'giving it another go' even though he was the one who had left.

Things looked up for a while. Then it was the start of the new school year. I loved the familiar new paint smell all along the corridors; the notice boards empty and waiting; the piles of exercise books clean and ungrubbied by little fingers. There was expectancy everywhere. I felt better than I had for ages. I could see that Mrs. Grainger noticed it too. She came past just as I had opened my locker and was energetically sorting through the contents. I called a greeting.

'Morning! Good holiday?'

'Good enough. Ready for the fray. And you?'

'Lovely thanks!' I knew I was beaming; I couldn't help myself. 'We went to a Greek island – lots of sunshine and blue seas and golden sand!'

I felt a bit self-conscious when I said 'we' and I could tell that Mrs. Grainger had noticed it, but she let it go. She clearly had other things she wanted to discuss as she ushered me into her office.

'I'm afraid we're a TA down this term - Myra's on long-term sick leave, and there's no money for a replacement, so you're going to have your work cut out a bit, I'm afraid.'

'Oh, I don't mind. I'm ready for anything!' I was too, full of energy.

'I've worked out a timetable that will allow us to share you out a bit more evenly around the classes where you're needed.' She handed me a sheet of paper.

To tell the truth I was a bit disappointed once I realised that I would be spending so much less time with my

Jenny 2

sweet little girl but, remembering what Dave had said, I had to accept that it might be for the best.

I saw that I had also been timetabled to run some group sessions, with three or four children at a time withdrawn from their classes. Mrs. Grainger explained that it was a more efficient use of my time.

We started the sessions the following week, and I found the sessions lively, and to be honest, a bit challenging, although on the whole I enjoyed them.

A few weeks later I was sitting with a small group around one of the tables in the library.

'Why do we have to learn all these letters?' sighed William. I already knew William: he was a boy who wrote very laboriously and usually backwards, and I wasn't making much headway with him. The child next to him, who was mildly dyspraxic but overfull of self-confidence and always ready with a put-down for children like William, was already pointing out in her bossy voice that William hadn't actually learned any letters. William looked near to tears. I hastened to calm things down.

'Sharon, everyone learns at a different pace. Some of us are good at writing, but rubbish at catching a ball.' I realised belatedly that this was a bad example: Sharon was particularly hopeless at any sports activities and the other children knew this. However, they also knew that I was pretty rubbish myself. I did an imitation of me dropping a ball and the children laughed. It broke the tension and cheered them up, especially William, who, while so slow when seated at a desk, was a different child when out on the field. I found myself laughing inordinately.

Everything seemed to be making me laugh these days, even Dave's rather feeble jokes. I was just bending

Jenny 2

over the third child in the group, silent little Lucy, encouraging her to hold her pencil more comfortably, when a wave of nausea swept over me. Goodness: I was getting like the children, sick with excitement at the start of term! For some reason it was at that moment that I realised that I hadn't seen the little blond girl, my angel, my not-Jenny, around the place for some days. I was so distracted by anxiety that I failed to notice, until it was too late, that the unfortunate William was jumping from foot to foot, a sure sign that he was desperate for the toilet.

I pulled myself together and put my head round the door of the next classroom. What I needed was a spare body to accompany William as far as the boys' toilets, or maybe keep an eye on my little group while I took him. What I saw filled me with fury. Miss Fawcett, the class teacher, was bending over a table where a group of children were counting bricks as part of their maths lesson. She was clearly oblivious to the classroom assistant at the back of the room, crouching on the floor next to the little blond girl - my little blond girl, my golden angel-child.

'How many times?' the TA was muttering, quite savagely. 'Are you stupid, or what?'

I stepped further into the room. The woman -- it was someone I didn't know -- was engaged in wrapping something round the girl's feet, over her shoes and round her ankles.

'Now will you learn?'

As I opened my mouth to say something, I became aware that William had followed me, and that a warm trickle was splashing my ankles.

My initial energy level began to wear thin as the term crept on: I was no longer leaping out of bed before the alarm. One morning I arrived slightly late and very out of breath, to find the packaging tape woman in the corridor just outside my classroom. The little blond girl was backing away from her,

Jenny 2

and her head collided with the row of pegs behind her at child height. She put a hand up to rub the sore place and tears welled up. I can't be a hundred percent sure, but I thought I heard the words 'Cry baby' come from the woman. She glanced at me sideways and bundled the child off in the direction of the staff room.

I finally crossed paths with Mrs. Grainger at playtime. 'Grace?' I said. 'Can I have a word?' She seemed a bit harassed, but stopped to let me catch up with her.

'I'm a bit bothered about the classroom assistant who's been working with Miss Fawcett.'

'Oh?'

'I'm a bit bothered about her manner with some of the children.'

'Well, she's only temporary, of course, but she came from the agency with very good references, and she clearly enjoys working with children. Yes dear?'

This last was addressed to a small boy in a back-to-front jumper who was timidly tapping her elbow, and I knew I wasn't going to get more of a hearing just then. Inevitably the bell rang, and the day rushed on, and at the end of the afternoon I decided to go straight home instead of staying on to plan for the next day as I usually did.

It was on the Friday before half term that things really blew up at school. I was between classes, thinking about some of my children, when I became aware of such an uproar in one of the classrooms that without even stopping to think I just opened the door and charged inside. The room was full of children; they were laughing uncontrollably, shrieking, calling out, pointing to something - to someone, as it turned out - in the far corner. A rather panicky-looking Miss Fawcett was trying to quieten them, without the slightest success. I took one look and moved on auto-pilot, marching straight up to the tall teaching assistant, and wrenched from her hand,

Jenny 2

none too gently, the roll of tape she'd been using. I was beside myself.

The only words I could manage were, 'You bully! You bully!'

Next on the scene were the Head and Mrs. Grainger. In one smooth pincer movement they had the children lined up at the door and heading off to the school hall, while I was left to try, with shaking hands, to release the little blond girl from the layers of tape that bound her to the chair. Some of the tape covered bare skin, so that it was impossible to remove it without hurting her. I steeled myself for the yelps of pain, but little Goldilocks just sat there, mutely enduring, tears running in silent streams down her face. A large piece of tape covered her mouth.

'I'm sorry, Mrs. Daniels,' she said, when all the tape had been removed. 'I'm sorry for not sitting still…'

With the TA from the supply agency gone, it was harder than ever to keep track of all the children with special needs, and it was clear that there would be no replacement for some time. When I returned after the half term holiday, during which I found myself snapping at Dave pretty much all the time, it was a few days before I noticed that my little blond angel was missing.

'Yes, I know. She was a real favourite of yours, wasn't she?' said Grace Grainger when I asked about her. 'She didn't have a very happy time here with us, though, did she? Even without that awful incident…'

It had been announced to the staff, in confidence, that the bullying TA was to be prosecuted on grounds of child cruelty.

'Anyway, her parents were having a lot of behaviour problems with her at home before that, and they were thinking of taking her out of school. I don't think we'll be seeing her again.'

Jenny 2

'So what will happen to her?'

'They'll home school her, I expect. Probably for the best! Now, I have an appointment with William Green's parents. Better hurry - they're always so annoyingly early.'

I drove home slowly, a sense of loss and foreboding settling on me. It was as though I were losing Jenny for a second time.

Chapter Five

Rachel - Dave

Rachel

The Indian summer gave way to autumn, and as predicted by Grace Grainger, my little blond girl did not return to school. I continued to feel sick until I could ignore it no longer. Indeed, having to rush out of the classroom to throw up in the staff toilets was now interfering with my work to a considerable extent.

'Do you think there's any chance you could be…?'

Dave clearly couldn't bring himself to say the word; I'm not even sure if it was because he hoped that I was or hoped that I wasn't pregnant. As for me, I refused to allow myself to hope and dismissed his suggestion as nonsense. Then I made a doctor's appointment.

Dave

So we didn't sell the house after all, at least not then, not now we were back together and about to become a family. A small warning voice inside me told me we had been here before, but somehow this time it really did seem different. While Rachel was busy making lists of all the things we would need for the new baby, I got on with sorting out the garden. It had been badly neglected over the years. The white roses near the gate were blooming again, and I planted a crazy quantity of spring bulbs to greet our new child in the spring. Rachel scolded me when I walked into

Jenny 2

the kitchen with muddy boots, but it was all good-natured: she had started to relax again. I cut the last of the Michaelmas daisies to make a posy for her, and then presented it to her with a flourish. She laughed. It was just like old times.

I went with her to all her hospital appointments. They were reassuring and said she would receive special care and attention because of her previous history and her age. Sitting on the plastic chairs in the waiting room, I remembered our last visit, and it seemed to me a miracle that we were here again, holding hands, once more planning a future that would see us become a family.

In the evenings we sat together on the sofa, just like in the old days. Rachel allowed me to draw her head down on to my shoulder, and I stroked her hair and dropped kisses on her hairline. It felt almost as if we had just met.

'So, let's see your lists, then,' I said one evening. 'What do we need to buy this time?'

She stiffened. '*This time?*'

I had obviously chosen my words badly.

'What do we need to get, you know, for the early days? To get us started...'

'Well, of course, we had all the things for a newborn, before...'

'Before I heartlessly got rid of them. Yes, I know!'

'So now we'll have to start again...'

'Perhaps it's for the best.' I tried to soothe her. 'We'll be buying them specially for this baby and not...' Too late to bite my tongue.

'And not for Jenny.'

There was an awkward pause. 'Isn't that for the best?'

She didn't reply, and I hurried on. 'I brought a catalogue home, you know, for cots and prams and things...' I reached over to get it out of my bag, and thankfully her eyes lit up at the pretty pictures. After flicking the pages back and forth we identified a cot we both liked, a completely different design from the one I had struggled with seven years previously. The moment of tension was past, and as we talked further we agreed that this time we would buy only the bare minimum of baby clothes. It still seemed unreal; sometimes we found ourselves just chuckling with delight when we thought about it.

At work, I was careful to keep the news to myself; but I overheard Susannah remark to her friend Sandra that her boss seemed more like his old self these days. I started socialising a bit with my colleagues at coffee time, and discovered that I liked their company after all.

There was one awful evening, though, when we had the fiercest row of our married life. Rachel had been shopping after work; even though it was such early days, her waistline was beginning to expand, and she had decided she needed to invest in some baggier clothes. For once, I was home before her. In fact I was in the kitchen, just putting on the kettle, when she walked in with her shopping bags. I took them off her, and pulled out a chair; she looked as though she needed it.

'I could get used to this kind of treatment,' she laughed, as she flopped down. 'Oh, what's this?'

She'd noticed the book I'd bought on the way home from work. It was an A-Z of babies' names. She picked it up and started scanning the pages.

'Well, I thought it was about time we started thinking. There are some amazing names in here. Look!'

The kettle boiled but we ignored it, absorbed in the list.

'Aaron? Adam? Alexander? Arthur? Oh no, not Arthur - that was my uncle's name. Too old fashioned.'

'Benjamin? Bernard? Bradley?'

'I couldn't have a child called Bradley - there's one at school with a squint and he smells of wee...'

Jenny 2

'OK. Let's look at the Cs. Carl? Christopher? Clifford?'

'Clifford? Sounds like an undertaker!'

We carried on like this for some time, until I suggested we might name the baby after Rachel's father, Richard. His health was deteriorating, and there was an unspoken fear that he might not live to see his grandchild.

'It could be a middle name if you don't want it as his first name,' I said. 'It would be a nice tribute.'

Then the question of girls' names came up.

Rachel

We'd been getting on so well, as we began to make cautious preparations for the baby. I wasn't really starting to show, but my waist had thickened a bit, and I allowed myself the indulgence of buying some looser clothes, ready for the months ahead. I was so excited, but I tried very hard to keep a lid on it. We both did. Dave was being really supportive, not letting me carry things and running round after me. He made me endless cups of tea, plumped up the cushions, fetched my slippers. It was really touching to see how much he cared.

And then he brought home that A-Z of baby's names. We were amusing ourselves going through it, and finally settled on Richard if it was a boy, in honour of my dad. Then suddenly, out of the blue, Dave said 'Of course, it might not be a boy. We'd better start looking at the other section…'

I was stunned. 'What do you mean?'

'Well,' he said, and his tone of voice changed, as if he thought he needed to tread carefully with me. 'It might be a girl….'

'Yes. And?'

'Isn't she to have a name?'

Jenny 2

'But... we have a girl's name.' What need was there for further discussion?

'But...'

'We always said we would call our daughter Jenny. How can we go back on that?'

He gave me a strange look. 'We did call our daughter Jenny. Our *first* daughter. We couldn't possibly call another one by the same name.'

I don't know why I turned on him the way I did. Even then I knew I was being irrational, but I was beyond reason. I felt my face crumple, and then I was like a toddler, completely out of control.

'I want a daughter called Jenny. I want my Jenny.'

I was sobbing and struggling for breath, and Dave moved protectively to cradle me in his arms, but I fought him off. The deep sense of loss that had suddenly resurfaced was something he could never protect me from. Jenny was the name we had chosen, together, for our daughter, the daughter who still lived somewhere within my imagination. I wanted her to be real.

Dave was adamant that it was unreasonable to expect a child to bear such a burden, to be named after a dead sibling. A lot of things were said that night, and it only came to an end when I threw the A-Z book at him. He ducked and it landed in the sink with the dirty dishes. We laughed then and agreed to leave the subject; after all, the need for a name was still nearly six months off.

I was late for school next morning, something that never happened normally. I was assisting in Mr. Edwards' class that day, and I could tell he kept sneaking little glances at me: I knew that my eyes were all puffy. He said nothing though, and I just got on quietly, focusing all my attention on the children under my charge. At lunchtime I ate my sandwiches in a corner of the staffroom, and then found

Jenny 2

myself suddenly overcome with nausea and faintness. Grace Grainger took one look at me and insisted I should be at home.

That evening, Dave was solicitous in looking after me and sorry we had argued, although I know he was still privately adamant that we could not name the new baby Jenny if it was a girl.

A few days later I set off for work in my car. I hadn't said anything to Dave, but I was continuing to experience waves of dizziness and nausea, and now there was a nagging little pain in one side of my tummy. I told myself it was indigestion. I started to remember all the discomforts of late pregnancy, and that made everything worse because it brought back memories I didn't want to have.

At the junction of Elm Vale and Lime Avenue, just as I was poised to turn right, I felt a sharp, stabbing pain. It made me gasp. How I made it across the busy junction and into the staff car park I will never know. The pain was getting worse by the minute, and there was no way I could get out of the car by myself. I'm not sure how long it was, but after a bit Grace Grainger appeared, a gaggle of small children tugging at her elbows, yelling unhelpfully.

'Mrs. Daniels is lying in her car.'
'She's stuck!'
'She can't get out!'

Grace said afterwards that she had to make a quick decision: should she call an ambulance? How severe did it have to be? What about A&E? Her timetable was clear until playtime, and she thought about driving me there in her own car. But then, she started to think about how long we might have to wait. And, having once got me there, could she

Jenny 2

leave me on my own? Apparently the school secretary was still trying to track down Dave, but without success.

Grace decided to take me to her own GP practice. They would be able to see me as a temporary patient or some such – it was immaterial to me. By this stage I was groaning out loud, clutching my belly, hardly conscious of what was going on around me. I vaguely remember Grace shooing away the remaining children, wide-eyed with innocent curiosity, and then she cautiously began to manoeuvre me out of the car and into her own.

At the surgery we were shown into a consulting room, where the nurse practitioner asked a lot of questions and demanded a urine sample. I clutched the wall as I staggered to the toilet. Even in the throes of the most extreme pain I could ever remember, I wondered how anyone could possibly have deliberately chosen custard yellow for the walls. Perhaps it was a job lot that had been going cheap. Funny how the mind works...

By this time, Grace was convinced that I had appendicitis. I heard her and the nurse whispering. She was worried, I think, that my appendix might burst. The pain was getting worse and worse as I writhed about on the examination couch, and Grace gave me her hand to hold on to. She was lucky I didn't break several bones with my frenzied grip. The nurse was methodically following some prescribed procedure, and Grace kept turning away to shout at her.

'Can't she have some pain relief?'

'I can't give her any. We'll have to wait for the duty doctor. She'll probably give her an injection.'

'But when? She can't go on like this.'

'Soon. I promise you, soon.'

The door opened and a bright, brisk doctor appeared, making Grace jump. She asked some of the same questions that I'd already answered, and then picked up the phone.

Jenny 2

'Can you put me through to the surgical registrar, please.'

There was a buzz of voices at the other end, and then I could hear the doctor describing my condition.

'Yes, pregnancy test positive,' she was saying.

I could see that Grace was surprised. I had told her, or at least let her believe, that I was unable to have children, after Jenny. Well, it's what I believed myself. We didn't often talk about personal things; that was a one-off. Grace was a cheerful and no-nonsense mother of four, with her first grandchild on the way. She couldn't really imagine how it was for me, although she did her best.

Finally, the phone call finished and the doctor produced a syringe. The injection had no effect on the pain, but the doctor kept assuring me that I would soon be in hospital and in good hands.

'No, I don't know exactly how long, but we'll have you there super-fast. We've requested a blue light ambulance.'

Even as she spoke we heard the siren and within seconds the paramedics were in the room and rolling me gently onto a trolley.

'Don't you worry,' said Grace, squeezing my hand. 'I'll get hold of your husband. He'll be with you before you know it.

Dave

So that was the second time in my life that I found myself summoned by an urgent telephone message to attend my pregnant wife in hospital. The first time my heart had been beating with hope, at least at first, but this time there was no room for hope at all.

I repeated what they said to me on the phone in order to remember it. 'Ward 14. Surgical assessment unit. Yes, I'll be there. I'll be there.'

Jenny 2

The car seemed to carry me magically to the hospital, as though some unseen presence was driving me. It felt as though my body was in a different place from my mind, and all the while my mind hammered, in rhythm with the blood beating in my ears: *No! Oh no! Not again. Not again. Oh no! Oh no! Oh no!*

The corridors were like a labyrinth. I was running, but my feet didn't seem to be taking me anywhere, like one of those nightmares when your legs won't move but your life depends on running as fast as you can. The more I tried to find my way, the more lost I became. How did the nurses do it? Cheerful porters cruised past me with their trolleys, drip tubes swinging as they rounded corners, wheels squeaking as they avoided collisions with oncoming trolleys.

I finally came to rest by the desk at the entrance to the fearsomely named Surgical Assessment Ward.

'Sorry. Sorry. I'm....' I was breathing hard, like someone who's run a marathon. 'I'm looking for my wife.'

'Name?'

Like an idiot I started to give her my name.

'Patient's name?'

'Oh, sorry, I mean Rachel Daniels.'

'Mrs. Daniels?' The blue-uniformed nurse behind the desk ran her finger slowly down the list. 'Mrs. Daniels? Mrs. Daniels? Now let me see...'

I somehow resisted the temptation to tear the list from her hands.

'Oh yes. She's in bed four, bay three. That way,' she called, pointing helpfully, a few seconds after I'd begun to charge off in completely the wrong direction.

I burst into the side ward a little more forcefully than I intended, and stopped, embarrassed. It was quiet in there. Three women lay sleeping peacefully. Three women who were not Rachel. The fourth bed was empty. I rushed back

Jenny 2

to the desk at the other end of the ward. A different blue-uniformed nurse now sat there.

'My wife. I'm looking for my wife,'

'Name?' asked the nurse.

'Daniels - no you don't need to do that,' I blurted, as she began to pore laboriously over the list of in-patients. 'It's bed four bay three, but she's not there...'

'What did you say your wife's name is? I can't seem to find a Mrs. Danvers on here.'

'DANIELS, not Danvers,' I could hear my voice too loud in the hushed space. 'Daniels! She's supposed to be in bed four bay three... but she isn't. What's happening? Please tell me what's happening.'

A motherly lady in a beige uniform appeared in my peripheral field of vision.

'Come on sir, I think you'll be more comfortable in the visitors' room. I'll make you a nice cup of tea.'

She led me along the wide corridor, with its peculiar flooring that overlapped the walls. For hygiene. To avoid places where germs can collect. I kept noticing unimportant details; my mind wanted to be anywhere except where I was and what I was about to face.

Several patients were making their way unsteadily towards me, dragging with them drips and tubes swinging from hooks on strange robotic contraptions. My mind wandered again. What was in the bags of fluid? What should I do when I drew level with them? The beige nurse ushered me into a small room full of chairs before I met any of the patients, so it was all right, I didn't have to work out how to pass them. She disappeared with a promise to return with tea 'in a jiffy', and then popped her head back round the door to ask, 'Sugar?' before disappearing again even as I shook my head. The power of speech seemed to have deserted me completely.

When the tea - and the beige nurse - finally arrived, she encouraged me to tell her what had happened.

Jenny 2

'I don't know. I can't get anyone to tell me.'

'OK. Wait there and I'll see what I can find out,' and she was gone again.

I sat there, staring at the tea. I supposed I ought to drink it, but somehow the mechanics of grasping the cup and putting it to my lips seemed beyond me. My mind began to replay yet again the scene when I reached Rachel's hospital bedside all that time ago…

My thoughts were interrupted by the reappearance of the nurse, accompanied by a man wearing clothes that looked as though they were made of J cloths. I realised he must be an anaesthetist, or possibly a surgeon. My anxiety level soared.

'This is Dr. Abdullah. He will be able to explain to you what is happening.'

The doctor held out a hand.

'Mr. Daniels? My colleagues have assessed your wife and, unfortunately, she will need surgery, which I will be performing. Please, sit down. I will explain. As you know, your wife experienced severe pain, accompanied by vomiting and dizziness…'

'No, I don't know anything…I don't know anything. What's happening?'

'Did you know that your wife was pregnant?'

I nodded.

'Unfortunately, it seems that the baby has started to grow in the wrong place. It sometimes happens. Instead of developing in the womb, the baby is growing in the fallopian tube.'

'An ectopic pregnancy,'

He gave a kind smile. 'Just so.'

'So what can you do?'

'Well, in your wife's case, it's a little more complicated. The pregnancy has advanced so far that the fallopian tube has ruptured. There is a risk of internal bleeding. We need to remove the fallopian tube as quickly as possible.'

He paused to let his words sink in.

'Can I see her?'

'No, I'm afraid she is already being prepared for theatre.'

'Just for a minute? Please?' I must have sounded like a small child, but I was beyond caring by that stage.

'I'm sorry. This is an emergency situation. We can't afford any further delay. As soon as I have scrubbed up, I will operate.' His face softened a little. I realised how grateful I was for the surgeon's honesty.

'Don't worry - we'll do everything we can. She is in good hands here, I assure you.'

After he had gone, I just sat there with my head in my hands. The beige nurse returned, removed the cold tea, and brought a fresh one. This time I drank it.

'He's a good doctor, Dr. Abdullah. The best. He'd just finished for the day when your wife was brought in, and he insisted that he would go back into theatre to operate himself. It's his specialism. She'll be fine, you'll see.'

Oh yes, she'll be fine, I thought savagely, if you call taking away our longed-for baby, cutting it out, along with a ruptured fallopian tube and then yes, she'll be fine. My head told me that the surgeon was saving Rachel's life, but my heart was crying out in agony.

I sat beside her bed for a long time, watching her, holding her hand, wondering what to say to her when she came round. What could I ever hope to say or do to comfort her? When she did finally come round, she met my gaze, looking a little puzzled, and then memory stirred behind her eyes. There was no need for either of us to put into words the fact that her only functioning ovary had been removed. There

Jenny 2

would be no more babies, ever. This time we asked no questions about the lost child. Rachel made a full physical recovery. She was up and about in a surprisingly short time after such major surgery. Her body was healed, but that was the end of our marriage.

Chapter Six

Rachel – Dave

Rachel

We had lost the past, because it was too painful to think about; we had lost the present, because we no longer knew how to be with each other; we were treading on eggshells; we couldn't talk. Worst of all was the feeling that we had lost the future too: we'd been given a second chance, but there was no baby, never would be...

We did finally sell the house. It was only on the market for a matter of weeks. The agent assured us that it would sell quickly: it was in immaculate condition...Of course it was, with no children to mark the pale walls or scuff the paintwork.

'Immaculate, yes,' I said, and thought: immaculate, but with no heart.

'A family home in a good school catchment. Any number of people will be keen to snap this up.'

He had an annoyingly jolly manner. I don't think either of us liked him, but we didn't say so to each other. We weren't saying anything much to each other by then, and even when we talked, we didn't really say anything. The words 'family home' and 'school catchment' made us both flinch, though.

The agent continued bustling through each of the rooms. In the lounge he lifted his arms to stretch out the tape measure and there was a stale odour, and as he bent down I could see how the seat of his dark suit had become shiny. Somehow his appearance seemed an insult to us and to the house; it cheapened the whole business.

I couldn't bear the thought of being in the house when the viewings started. Dave volunteered to show the potential buyers around, and I was grateful to him for that. I went to stay with my sister, Laura, the one with the little girl Jenny's age. She was forever saying how well they would have played together. I wished she wouldn't. She had two lively little boys as well.

At Laura's house my niece was moving beyond her sweet little girl phase into something increasingly gangling and boisterous. Her ambition was no longer to be a princess, but a pop star. Her brothers spent their time tearing around with a football, trampling their mother's bedding plants, shouting and yelling and play-fighting like puppies. There wasn't a lot of chance for Laura and me to talk, and I think Laura was secretly glad of that. She'd never really known how to talk to me about the loss of Jenny, and when she tried it was clear she was all at sea. I found myself observing the children, in the same way as I observed the world around me: with detachment.

Gradually the scar tissue healed; my check-up, at the same hospital where I had given birth to Jenny, where I had lost my second Jenny, came and went. There was nothing to stop me getting on with my life, the doctor said. Except everything. I was signed off by the hospital, but it was already the start of the Christmas holidays, and I had resigned from my job as soon as I came out of hospital. The school had shown compassion in not insisting that I work out my notice.

Christmas at Laura's was not a joyful time, certainly not for me, and the gloomy cloud I seemed to be carrying clearly cast its shadow over everyone else. On the surface, though, things followed the usual pattern, as they tend to for everyone during the so-called festive season. Laura has this amazing ability to see things from the children's point of

Jenny 2

view, and normally she loves this time of year, inventing all sorts of silly games for them, and she lets them take a full part in planning the celebrations. She never bothered with a sophisticated colour scheme for the Christmas tree, so the children were allowed to decorate it with whatever they liked, although she did draw the line at the older boy's football strip going on there. The cake was made well in advance, and 'fed' with brandy; on the more stressful evenings I noted that she also fed herself with some. Despite the mess, the children were allowed to help mix the Christmas pudding, and then they stirred it one more time while they made a wish. It was all painfully slow: they kept changing their minds about what they most wanted, so the words, 'I wish... I wish... I wish...' were repeated until even Laura's patience gave out.

On Christmas Eve Tom, the youngest, (Tom Thumb, his father called him - they were so *twee*) hung up his stocking with the others and went in search of a carrot for Rudolph. Unable to quite reach, he pulled an entire vegetable rack over on himself, escaping with a bruised cheek and a mild reprimand, while the vegetables for the following day's dinner rained down around him. His brother Alex burned himself in his eagerness to get his hands on a mince pie for Father Christmas, and Annie, the girl who was just months older than Jenny, took every possible opportunity to sulk and pout and generally make life difficult. And I found myself thinking: *Jenny doesn't behave like that.*

Throughout the evening, as Laura and Derek stuffed stockings and prepared vegetables, and throughout Christmas Day itself, as we all waded knee-deep through discarded wrapping paper, I could feel my own silent misery drawing light and laughter out of the atmosphere. Everywhere I looked, I saw Jenny: Jenny opening presents, Jenny sitting down to write polite thank you letters; Jenny singing along to the carols on the radio. Her presence was more real than that of my niece and nephews.

Jenny 2

One morning, as the days were gradually growing longer, I woke up, not just from sleep but from the kind of dazed state I'd been in for months. February brought a rash of snowdrops and crocuses even to Laura and Derek's trampled borders, and I went out into the garden and took deep breaths of the sharp air, like an infant just emerging into life. My share of the proceeds from the house was sitting in my bank account doing nothing, and I realised that what Laura had been gently suggesting for ages was right: I should at least go and start house-hunting.

So it was that, on a grey afternoon, I found myself outside Mason's, the same estate agency that had sold our old house for us. I scanned the pictures in the window, unseeing, and realised that I had no idea where to start. A man in a shiny dark suit caught my eye from the other side of the window and beckoned me inside. Was he the agent we'd dealt with before? I couldn't remember. I know I didn't warm to him much, but then warmth was no longer something I was familiar with.

'Do take a seat. Mrs....?'

He was waiting. I realised I was meant to supply my name.

'And what are we looking for today, Mrs. Daniels?'

We, I thought; there's no 'we' any more.

'I'm, er, I'm looking for somewhere to live...' I finally responded, rather lamely.

'Can you give me some idea of what it is you're looking for? A family home? Garden? Three, four bedrooms?'

So, I thought, that's what he sees when he looks at me.

No,' I said aloud. 'I don't need much. I'm...on my own...'

'Right.'

Jenny 2

'I'm looking for something suitable for a single, childless woman.'

I thought I saw a look of disappointment in his face. So much the less commission with this customer, then! Looking at him again, I realised he wasn't the same man who had sold our house, but he might have been; he had the same unctuous manner, the same shiny suit. Suddenly, out of nowhere, I felt a wave of sympathy for him. I had pigeonholed him, reduced him to the popular caricature of the estate agent. He was only trying to make a living, just as I would have to from now on until the day I retired. Who knew what his personal circumstances were? Did he have a family? Had he, like me, suffered loss?

'Hmm, sorry?'

I realised he was waiting for an answer. 'Oh, no, nothing to sell...'

Leaving the Estate Agent's half an hour later after supplying various interminable details, I was clutching a sheaf of brochures so tightly that the ink came off on my hands. The thin February sunshine belied the cold wind; it cut into me and threatened to tear the papers from my grasp. I felt suddenly more alone than ever, and I told myself briskly that I'd better get used to it as this was how it was going to be from now on.

I couldn't face going back to Laura's so soon, so I turned in to the first café I saw and ordered a large latte, which sat going cold as I read my way determinedly through the pile of brochures. After a while I began to sort them into two piles, until the rejects pile was so large that it threatened to engulf the little table, and I shuffled the papers together and began again. If what they said was true, then the world was my oyster, full of flats that 'must be seen to be believed.' This was no good: I needed a system. Dave would have been good at this; he would have patiently teased out the priorities. *Where do you need to live? How much space do you need for yourself? Will you want friends to stay occasionally? Do you need a spare room, or would a sofa bed be enough?*

And what about office space? Would he have asked me about that? Or was it a subject he would have avoided? Not for the first time, I wondered how things might have been different if I had held back on my anger, had allowed him to persuade me not to keep Jenny's room as a shrine, to allow it instead to become just another room. Was it all my fault? How much had Dave been to blame? Had it been anyone's fault?

That night I lay in my bed at Laura's listening to my nephews in the room next door, whispering to each other after lights out, and felt myself coming to a series of decisions. The first was that I couldn't actually make a decision about where to live, or what kind of property, until I had decided just what I was going to do with the rest of my life. I had an English Literature degree, which had never seemed of great importance, but now I could see that it might hold the key to my future. I had loved working with the children at the primary school, and would like to continue...but now my sights were set on being the teacher rather than the assistant. I was sure I could do that. I had developed a warm relationship with all the children in my charge, and particularly, of course, with little, golden-haired Elizabeth. One thing was for sure: I was not going back to the shelf-stacking and filing that I had used as an escape after Jenny.

Dave

I think it was just as well I was the one who showed people round. The starry-eyed young couple who eventually bought the house returned for a second viewing and announced breathlessly that they were sure it was the house for them. I was glad to spare Rachel the sight of the young woman and her full, round belly. I didn't ask when the baby was due, but they couldn't help telling me anyway.

    'So, do you have any children?' the husband asked.
    I just shook my head.

While Rachel was recuperating at her sister's before Christmas, I did the small things that needed doing at the house: arranging to have the gas meter read, sorting our smaller belongings into two piles, unearthing the instruction booklets for the cooker and the dishwasher. I was just leaving one morning, on my way to work, when I spotted the tiny green points of the bulbs starting to push through. I was overwhelmed with memory: of how full of hope I had been when I planted them, overjoyed that we'd been given a second chance, a fresh start. For a moment I even considered digging them all up. By then I had found a new little house with a small garden; it was crying out for some planting. Perhaps this was one last memory of our former life I could take with me, a permanent reminder of what might have been. The next moment I told myself I was a fool and flattened the patch of earth with the sole of my shoe. Then I set off for the lonely privacy of my workplace. As I was jostled by the crowds, I felt more alone than ever. Susannah clucked her tongue as I trod mud onto the new office carpet, and I saw her looking at me when I didn't even pretend to eat anything at lunchtime. When it was time to go home, she reminded me gently that she had arranged some annual leave, and wouldn't be back until January 2nd. Then she wished me a cheery 'Happy Christmas' and probably wished very much that she hadn't when I barked at her like a demented Scrooge.

    Contracts were exchanged, completion was successfully achieved; the removal vans took our belongings off to their separate addresses – in Rachel's

Jenny 2

case into storage, since she hadn't been able to make decisions about where she was to live. I was still there when the van full of the belongings and hopes of the new owners pulled up outside what was no longer our home.

Joe, the soon-to-be new father, paused by the gate.

'They've let this go, haven't they, Patsy?' He shook his head as if in disbelief, while his gaze swept appraisingly over the front garden. 'I'm really looking forward to sorting this lot out.'

Patsy gave a derisory laugh. 'Don't you believe it! You'll have your hands full with plenty of other things once this little one's here.'

She patted her stomach affectionately, as if she and the baby had already formed an understanding. Joe agreed, and moved close to her, while I ached with all the unspeakable pain of loss.

'All the same,' he said, with a nod towards the bedraggled rose bush by the gate. 'I can't wait to get rid of that.'

'Yes.' His wife flicked a finger at one of the blackened roses, scattering dead petals as she did so. 'It's seen better days, I suppose.'

I turned on my heel and left the past behind.

PART TWO

Chapter Seven

1993

Hannah

Hannah

I knew, really, that things weren't right. I'd known for a long time: I just hadn't let myself know that I knew...

This mirror that I let Jono persuade me we needed, it's like so much of the *stuff* our house is full of... it doesn't make the hole inside me any less deep or any less black, doesn't stop me wishing I could go back to the beginning, start again, do things differently.

From time to time I did seriously wonder whether Elizabeth had, after all, been damaged by the lack of oxygen at her birth. The first bout of projectile vomiting took me completely by surprise; I'd never heard of it before, and I was ready to rush her off to A and E, but Jono persuaded me to wait and take her to the GP the next day. I hardly slept all night, and must have sounded so desperate on the phone that they gave me an emergency appointment, but then the contrary child smiled and gurgled and wriggled with excitement and the doctor looked at me as though I had made the whole thing up.

Jenny 2

It was the same with the midwife: when I told her I couldn't cope with the screaming colic in the evenings, I got the impression she thought I was making a fuss, that it was somehow my fault. I tried to tell myself I couldn't be a completely useless parent: after all, the boys were doing well. Elizabeth was just...different. And she still wasn't walking at twelve months, but again I was fobbed off.

We'd really been looking forward to the birth of our third, the child who would make our lovely family complete. If I'd known then... but what could I have done differently? Things started to unravel when I became unwell a month or so before my due date and the Consultant insisted I had to go into hospital for bed rest. I felt torn apart: what about the boys at home? And Jono? How would they cope? My mother turned up with her suitcase and took over the household with her usual all-encompassing presence.

They called it bed rest, but it was anything but restful, even in a private room, and when I got upset they just told me to stop fretting about my other children and focus on the one in there. Jono was just as bad. He as good as told me that if I didn't calm down I might seriously harm our baby. The doctors prescribed stronger and stronger sedatives, and eventually asked him to take my clothes away. I think they were afraid I might discharge myself and run sobbing from the hospital. Then someone jabbed a large syringe of Valium into my thigh.

It felt like a relief when I finally went into labour: soon I would be going home. But then there was that awful time after the birth, when our little girl's life hung in the balance.

It took a long time to get over the fear and shock of seeing our baby looking blue and limp when she was born. They whisked her away and I was left with Jono, holding on to my hand so hard I thought I could hear the bones crunching.

Jenny 2

'It's OK, Hannah. It's OK. Everything's going to be fine.'

He kept saying it, over and over, which I didn't find one little bit reassuring. My own body started trembling and I couldn't control it.

'It's all right...they're just sorting her out...she's going to be fine. We have a lovely girl.'

There were tears in his eyes. He brushed them away with his free hand.

'Do you still want to call her Elizabeth after your mother?'

Did I? No, I didn't want to call her after that woman, but if I didn't, I'd never hear the end of it, would I? It would be yet another thing I'd done to disappoint her. I nodded weakly.

Jono squeezed my hand. I knew he was looking over my shoulder at the little huddle of nurses in the corner; I sensed, rather than saw, the paediatrician arrive, and it seemed as though time was standing still.

'Look,' Jono was saying, 'A newborn baby can last longer without breathing than an older person - there really isn't any reason to be anxious...'

After what seemed like hours, a small, warm, and very wriggly bundle was placed in my arms, and I wept tears of joy and relief so profound that I completely missed the sound of Jono hitting the floor in a dead faint.

They wheeled me back up to the ward, but Elizabeth was still downstairs, and I kept asking where my baby was. After all the drama of the delivery, I was frantic. The nurses were very kind, especially Sister Stevens, and they kept on saying that Elizabeth would be up soon, and that everything was fine, just that there was another emergency going on...

And then I heard it: the sound of a mother who has lost her child; the primordial wailing of a soul in torment. I can never forget that sound. How will she ever find comfort

Jenny 2

after that?' They took her down to the delivery suite to deliver her dead baby and they brought Elizabeth up to me.

I still think of that woman every year on Elizabeth's birthday. She lost her baby, and I had mine. I was the lucky one. Apparently.

I'm still not sure about this mirror. Jono persuaded me that a cheval mirror was the most practical for our bedroom, and I do quite like the oval shape: it's elegant, and it does complement the rest of the décor. I like the gilt edging and polished stand well enough... but it's what I see *in* the mirror that troubles me. Amazing how much what you see reflected hides what's really there. I just don't like her any more, this well-preserved woman of middle years, expensively dressed, smart shoes, good posture...

This isn't how I expected my life to be. My hopes weren't even particularly ambitious, in reality: just a happy and successful family, comfortable home, strong marriage, maybe a satisfying career ... the things anyone would want. My mother was right about me: I'm a failure. I was given a chance, a healthy baby. I should have been able to give her a happier life...

I did think about keeping in touch with her, the other mother, because we'd both been in there for bed rest, and used to chat a bit, lying on our trolleys, when we were taken down for our scans and things, but in the end I thought it would be insensitive... I'd have liked to help but I but didn't know how and I didn't want to make things worse.

People used to say things like: you've got your hands full with those three, haven't you? But it was more than full: my hands were overflowing. I had thought having a daughter would be lovely after being outnumbered by the male members of the family: even the cat was a tom. Theo, of

Jenny 2

course, had been an absolute model of a child from the beginning, and that hadn't changed. He did his homework without being told, enjoyed reading and sums, and kept his school uniform spotless; and Miles seemed to be following suit, but Elizabeth... from the moment she could crawl, she was inquisitive to the point of life-threatening, and capable of smearing her breakfast in impossible places; some of our walls began to look like pieces of abstract art, and Jono was none too pleased about that. Her little fingers seemed made for exploring electric sockets, she loved nothing better than redistributing the contents of the fridge - mostly on the floor - and ornaments that had survived both her brothers had to be raised several feet above ground level to avoid a violent end. I'll never know how her first pair of shoes came to end up blocking the downstairs loo.

As she grew, she was forever falling over or bumping into things; she fell over her own feet. We had to keep the boys' homework out of her reach, especially after the episode with the jelly, and how she reached the turmeric I'll never know, but I had to throw away an expensive cashmere jumper.

Dr. Malik sighed whenever we turned up; he didn't exactly say he thought I was an over-anxious mother, but it was clear that's what he thought. Didn't stop him examining her for cuts and bruises though, handling her like an explosive package, and giving me a strange look.

We had started out with such high hopes: Jono was a bright young thing then, a head full of ideas and ambitious to build up the business. I encouraged him. It was incredibly long hours to begin with, but while he was young and energetic, the long hours didn't matter so much. We used to talk about 'when the company gets established' and how we would have more time for other things, but I'm still waiting...

I'd loved my job as a researcher at the University before we were married, but I gave it up, pretty much willingly, to support him in the business, in a more humble

Jenny 2

role as a sort of secretarial dogsbody, and I carried on when Theo and then Miles were born. Once Elizabeth came along, though, I found I just couldn't keep both balls in the air any more, so I resigned, gave up the job - such as it was - that had been my one escape from the messiness of home.

There was that time when I got to the school really late and the TA was with her. Elizabeth was pouring out her heart to her and I behaved badly, I know I did. I was supposed to be the grown-up... But then, let's be fair, she *was* a long way behind with her reading. There never seemed to be enough time in the day to sit and read with her, and by bedtime I was always exhausted.

When we got home that evening, I already knew things weren't right, but I was miserable with myself and didn't want to make things worse by asking her what was wrong. Instead I asked her what she wanted for tea.

She looked surprised.

'Eggs in nests?'

Her voice was so quiet I could hardly hear her. My heart sank. I knew the boys hated what they called 'messy food.'

'And jelly and blancmange.' Her voice was a little louder this time. 'Please.'

I didn't want to risk a scene by refusing, so I set to, making the mashed potatoes. The cat got under my feet and one of the eggs ended up on the floor, and when I swore at it Elizabeth ran out of the kitchen.

I managed to get the jelly to set by using ice cubes, but the blancmange was more of a challenge, so it was only half set by the time we were ready to eat. I had no idea what time to expect Jono.

'What's *that*?' was Miles' first comment, followed by Theo's 'Yeuch!'

Jenny 2

They could probably see the thunderclouds building behind my eyes so after that they meekly accepted what I put on their plates. Elizabeth was very subdued and just sat there without touching her food.

'Elizabeth?'

She just sat there without responding.

'Come on...' I was aiming for an encouraging tone, but it probably came out as anger. I could see the tears starting. I tried again.

'Don't you want to eat?'

She shook her head without looking at me.

'I'm not hungry.'

'This is what you asked for.'

She still didn't respond.

'Come on, Elizabeth.' I was becoming really frustrated by now. 'OK. What about some jelly and blancmange?' I ignored the boys' rebellious looks, as they continued to eat their eggs and mashed potato without enjoyment.

She sat looking at the plate of jelly and watery blancmange.

'Elizabeth...'

The next second she had flung her plate on the floor and left the room.

It wasn't until the next morning that I discovered some of the blancmange had ended up in my handbag. By then it had curdled and smelt foul. Once upon a time I would have laughed at that; this time I cried.

'Thank you for coming in, Mrs. Brown,' said the Special Needs co-ordinator. 'Do take a seat.' I sat down a bit too heavily on the hard chair on the other side of the desk and looked at the alphabet posters on the walls, the low-level bookcase, the row of miniature plastic chairs lined up against the far wall. This was not a room I'd been in before.

Jenny 2

Parents' evenings usually took place in the child's classroom, and once, when I was called in because Elizabeth had been bitten by another child, I'd been ushered straight into the Head's office.

'Is your husband joining us?'

I just shook my head. How many meetings at school have I attended alone over the years? Jono always seemed to have important meetings of his own to attend.

On first acquaintance Mrs. Grainger seemed okay, a plump, jolly woman with a no-nonsense streak. That was probably just right for dealing with five-year-olds, but it didn't make me feel any less apprehensive, not that I showed it, of course. I was well practised at painting on a mask as part of my morning routine.

She looked up from her notes. 'Look, I'll get right to the point. I know you're worried about Elizabeth's progress, and clearly there are behaviour issues. She's a bright child, but she is struggling with her reading and writing. She may have dyslexic tendencies, but it's a bit early to be certain.

I opened my mouth to protest, but she forestalled my reaction. 'Look, don't worry, because there are lots of ways we can help her cope with this. For one thing, we are due some more funding next term, and we should be able to give her some classroom support.'

'What sort of support?' I realised that I was perched on the very edge of the chair, and made a conscious effort to sit up straight.

'Someone to sit with her in class and make sure she's on task and focused. They'll be able to help her when she doesn't understand something, and help her to be a bit more methodical.' She paused, frowning at me. I was still trying to take it all in.

'There is also the possibility of withdrawing her from some lessons to help her practise her writing, and develop strategies for coping. How does that sound?'

Jenny 2

I felt myself swallowing air. 'If you think it's worth trying...'

How had it come to this? The child came from a good home. We'd encouraged her from day one and she had the example of her brothers. Jono and I have good degrees: he has a Masters *and* a PhD. Why would *we* have a child who can't cope at school, who can't read and write properly? But when I spoke, it was calmly; I was well-practised at dealing with people like Mrs. Granger.

'Thank you, Mrs. Grainger. Shall I talk to Elizabeth about the extra support?'

'No, no, you leave that to us. It won't be starting immediately in any case, but as soon as we have the funding and a Teaching Assistant available, we'll introduce Elizabeth to the idea.'

She stood, to show the interview was at an end.

'Did you know, by the way,' she remarked, casually, 'That something's happened to her school jumper? It looks as though someone's cut a chunk out of it.'

Once the children were in bed that evening Jono and I had one of our regular exchanges. It followed the usual pattern, me ridiculously tearful now there was no-one else to see, and Jono soothing me and offering weak reassurances.

'Look, if she needs special help, then the sooner she gets it the better. If she's dyslexic or something it's no big deal.'

I tried to dry my eyes, but the tears kept coming.

'Come on, Love, you know it's a good thing that they've picked this up early.'

'Oh, Jono, when I think of what it was like when she was born, and we nearly lost her. And now this! What have we done?'

'We haven't done anything. It's not anyone's fault. She's still our lovely girl. She's still Elizabeth, full of fun and mischief. And there are masses of things she's really good at...'

I waited for him to enumerate what those were, but he didn't. Still, it was good to have him there, being positive, just as he had been when Elizabeth so very nearly didn't survive.

She only fell off her chair once at breakfast the next morning; unfortunately, her breakfast fell with her, and I had to go and find a clean pinafore dress, leaving Miles, mildly complaining, to sweep up the pieces of broken plates. Theo was harder to placate, though, since it was his project on castles that had taken the brunt of Elizabeth's tumble.

I wondered again whether I should broach the subject of special help directly with Elizabeth, but decided I'd better follow Mrs. Grainger's advice and leave it to the school. I was actually a bit preoccupied that day anyway, as I'd finally decided that my sanity was at risk if I stayed at home full time any longer: so I was filling in a job application.

In the event I snapped at both Miles and Elizabeth, and forgot to thank Miles for helping. Typically, Elizabeth, once her tears were dried and her bruises tended, put her arms sweetly around her older brother, and apologised for 'hurting' his schoolwork, and Theo grudgingly accepted the apology, which was all very fine, but that meant we were going to be even later for school.

I got the job. It was just admin, part-time, and although at least I was back in a university environment, and didn't feel quite so separated from the world, I was always rushing everywhere, always late. The academics looked down on the office staff, and so as well as losing my confidence as a mother I now felt it draining away in my workplace too.

If I'd found being a full-time mother hard, this was even harder. Packed lunches still had to be made: I was so

Jenny 2

focused on making sure the children had what they liked that I often forgot about my own lunch, which was probably just as well as there really wasn't time to eat in a busy office. I forgot Elizabeth's a few times too. I could sometimes get two or three days' wear out of the boys' uniforms, but Elizabeth's clothes arrived home every day stained, crumpled and often torn. Then there was the rush to get them there in the mornings and collect them on time when the schools finished at their ridiculously early time...

There was one evening when Jono was so late that I was seriously starting to worry that something had happened to him, and when he did finally get back I could see the that he was mentally somewhere else.

I hurled a cushion at him to remind him I was there.

'I am *so* sick of this!'

To my fury he looked bewildered.

'What's happened? Is it the children?'

'Yes, it's the children - the children we both agreed we wanted but who seem to have become my sole responsibility.'

He was still looking at me stupidly.

'Jono, you're never here, and when you are, you're not, not really.'

He came across to me then and tried to put his arms round me but I pushed him away. 'That won't do, Jono. There are no simple fixes.'

He went into the kitchen and came back with a bottle and two glasses, the large ones. I gave in.

'Look, is it the job, the house, Elizabeth...?'

'All of it!'

'So what is the first thing you want us to deal with? Do you want to give up work again?'

'No, definitely not. That's the one thing that is mine, where I can be me.'

'OK. So...Elizabeth?

'Of *course* Elizabeth.'

We were both silent for a while. Then he said,

'Why don't we get her assessed properly, by a professional?'

'But Mrs. Grainger is a professional...'

'Well, in a school setting, yes, but I mean an educational psychologist, someone who deals with problem children all the time.'

'Elizabeth is NOT a problem child!' Even I was surprised by my own vehemence. 'She's just taking a bit longer to learn to read and write.'

'And to do as she's told? And to sit still? And to stop fiddling with things until they break? Come on, Hannah, you've got to admit she isn't like the boys.'

'No, she isn't; she's.... she's our Elizabeth.'

'My point exactly.'

In the end I was so weary with it all I just said, 'All right. I'll make enquiries.'

Chapter Eight

Hannah

Hannah

It turned out the educational psychologist was very booked up, even for parents prepared to pay for an appointment. We would have a long wait, it seemed. Having decided to address the problem, I found that it suddenly seemed to loom very large. Elizabeth came home from school day after day subdued and sullen. Sometimes I managed to get some sort of account of her day out of her, but often what had happened at school remained a mystery. The 'nice lady,' who had worked with her on her reading and writing in her first year, was suddenly not so often available after the summer holidays, and Elizabeth didn't like the other one. Miles came home with tales of his little sister standing by herself in the playground at lunchtime, and of other children calling her names. One day she came home with her shoes fixed to her feet with tape; Miles said she was famous at school for never getting them on the right feet.

And then we were suddenly requested to attend a rather hush-hush meeting with the Head. It was a rather delicate matter, Mrs. Knight said, one that could be very damaging for the school.

When Jono heard what had happened, he exploded!

'You mean to tell me that this school has been employing a woman who ill-treats small children? Small, vulnerable children, like our daughter?'

I noticed a vein throbbing in his neck. Seeing him so angry was almost as frightening as what we'd just been told

Jenny 2

by the headteacher. How had I missed the signs? But they'd been there, hadn't they, if I'd looked properly?

Jono was still sounding off.

'And what do you mean by 'discreet'? I don't care who knows about this, this... *disgraceful* affair. I expect to see this woman prosecuted, and if you won't go to the police...' He gave the head teacher a look of pure fury. 'Then I most certainly will!'

I was frankly amazed: it was a long time since I'd heard him so fired up about anything to do with the family.

'And if you think our daughter is spending one more day in this school...' His voice was rising to a dangerous pitch now. I was getting really nervous. At last he made a very conscious effort at self-control, and added:

'Would you please arrange for someone to bring her, and all her belongings, so that we can take her home with us, now, right away?'

This was all very well, but my head was spinning as we drove home with a very puzzled seven-year-old. The question was: what now?

The home-schooling plan at least took away the constant worry that our daughter was being bullied, but it also took away my newly-won independence: I had to give up my part-time job. The theory was that Elizabeth would learn at her own pace, without other children to compare herself with, but in reality I found it harder and harder to motivate her to do anything at all. Perhaps I lacked motivation myself?

Jono was full of ideas about turning the household shopping trips into a maths lesson, by which he meant *my* shopping trips: obviously, since I was no longer 'working', that would be my responsibility now. He made one of his increasingly sardonic remarks:

'Perhaps she can also learn that money doesn't grow on trees.'

Jenny 2

I thought, but didn't bother to say aloud, that while he might know something about money he didn't know the first thing about fighting your way around a supermarket with a young child in tow, or the difficulties of fitting in everything else that had to be done, Elizabeth's education included, between the school run, Theo's music lessons, Miles' athletics trials and my own feeble attempts to keep the house under some level of control. And keep a tighter rein on household spending, apparently.

I worried constantly that I wasn't up to teaching a child with dyslexic tendencies, and spent hours in search of professional advice. I didn't actually consider myself capable of teaching *any* child. Miles and Theo had simply *learnt*. I began to wonder if Elizabeth's clumsiness, which hadn't abated at all over the years, was somehow connected with her reading problems. I even wondered, sometimes, whether there was a problem at all, as Elizabeth seemed able to read and write when she wanted to.

I'd been advised by the local authority person to take her to gatherings of other home-schooled children at the local park. It was a nightmare: the other mothers were so intimidating; it felt like a competition I hadn't signed up for. They were supermums, whipping up fascinating syllabuses that enthralled their offspring for many hours each day, and every one of them claimed that their child was far ahead of where they would have been had they remained in school. With hindsight, I wonder if they might have been exaggerating, but at the time I just felt so inadequate.

The memories of that time are still raw, even after so many years. There was one who said to me,

'I just don't think school suits every child, do you?'

We were standing beside the giant sandpit at the local park one afternoon. Her child was a pathetic little thing, a really scrawny six-year-old; he was about to strike out along the monkey bars, but he looked in terror of his life.

Jenny 2

She called out, 'Come on, Rupert, don't be left behind!' and then she said to me, 'Rupert was so bored at school. I really think they were holding him back. He's so much happier now.' Rupert's grip on the bars finally gave way, and he fell in a crumpled heap as his supermother rushed forward, but it wasn't to help him - it was to tell him off for not hanging on. Poor Rupert looked anything but happy. At least I knew when my child was unhappy, even if I didn't know how to make things better.

I moved round to the other side of the sandpit where I could see Elizabeth sitting alone, sifting the powdery sand through her fingers and singing quietly to herself. She was in her own little world, but she didn't look unhappy. I began to wonder why I persevered with these group sessions: Elizabeth clearly had no inclination to be part of the group, and it was wearing me down.

I used to wander about, smiling and nodding woodenly at the other mothers, wishing desperately that one of them might turn out to be even partially on my wavelength, although to be honest I wasn't quite sure what my wavelength was, any longer. So much of my time and energy was devoted to Elizabeth that Theo and Miles were becoming rather jealous, and Jono had started to grumble when he was at home, which wasn't like him. And as time went on, he was there less and less anyway.

There was no time for me at all.

By the end of the summer I was at my wits' end: I was a failure as an educator, a failure as a mother; I couldn't even seem to manage a few simple household chores. Then one day I simply decided to stop coping. Elizabeth had just thrown down her reading book and kicked it across the floor. On a whim I said,

'Get your coat, Elizabeth. We're going out!' She was so surprised that she did as she was told, without arguing.

Jenny 2

Our day in London was magical. Elizabeth had never been on a train before, and she was completely entranced by the whole process from the moment we got to the station. She chatted to the man in the ticket office, skipped up the stairs, and stopped to gaze through the railings from the bridge to watch the trains passing beneath. She read the information board aloud for anyone who cared to listen, jumped up and down with excitement on the platform as the train came in, explored the entire compartment, examined the other passengers at close quarters, and hopped and skipped every step of the way from the tube station to the Museum. In the main hall she was transfixed by the gigantic dinosaur skeleton; she had seen one like that in a book, she told me. I had no idea she'd ever seen a book with dinosaurs in it. I asked her to tell me about it.

'The one in the book had its meat and skin on, though. It lived millions of years ago, and it ate plants by stretching its long, long neck up to the tops of the trees. Do you think its neck was made of rubber?'

Her eyes were alight. She was interested in something! I'd never seen her like that. We carried on to the displays showing the animals that had once lived in the very place we were standing; Elizabeth was enthralled by the 'big hairy elephants' and the remains of sea-creatures that had been found off the South coast. She pressed buttons and watched videos and marvelled at the blue whale swimming through the air, and when we got home that evening she was tired out and yet glowing with a spark I could barely recall seeing before.

After this, home schooling took off for a while. We visited the costume museum and the Botanic Gardens; we watched some interesting documentaries on TV. When I saw in the local paper that the little theatre in town was offering a musical drama suitable for primary age children, I rang immediately and booked tickets, without even feeling

Jenny 2

nervous. I even began to feel that I might be OK as a mother after all.

But it couldn't last. The boys were moving on through the school, and Elizabeth was going nowhere. The arrangement couldn't have continued much longer. I mean, what sort of future would she have without formal qualifications? I knew I wasn't capable of tutoring her in the full range of GCSE subjects, and Jono clearly didn't have time. We started talking about getting her back into school; not to her, of course: these were late night conversations, over a bottle of Merlot. It was becoming the only time we ever talked, and the only subject we ever talked about.

So we sent Elizabeth to school. There was a bit of a scene when we took her in on the first day, and she absolutely insisted that I stay in the car when I went to pick her up, as if *she* was ashamed of *me*! Once she was in bed I cornered Theo, but he couldn't tell me anything about his sister's first day at her new school, and Miles was out training with his friend Jimbo. For once, I was glad Jono was late home: too late to interrogate Elizabeth and be disappointed by her answers. The poor child was fast asleep when he did get home, and so was I, on the sofa, flat out. I'd fallen asleep with an empty wineglass in my hand.

Chapter Nine

Lizzie - Rachel

Lizzie

The day I started at Hillmore High, all trussed up in the hideous blue and yellow uniform, with its pointless tie and sweaty nylon jumper, was the dreaded end; the beginning of the end, anyway. My parents decided I should start with everyone else in Year 7 so as not to stand out; but I knew I was different, and I was pretty sure everyone else did, too. I hadn't been to school for years… We arrived in the entrance foyer, with me clutching my empty schoolbag and my PE kit, and Dad announced, in his Embarrassing Voice, that they wished to see the Head Teacher. Miles and Theo had scuttled in through a side entrance. They didn't want to be part of a scene in a public arena, with their mates watching.

The Head ushered us into her office.

'It's such a pity Elizabeth wasn't able to attend any of the induction sessions in July,' she said. 'Still, with her brothers in the school I'm sure that Elizabeth …'

She burbled on: something about lack of any evidence of previous attainment, blah, blah… I had been hanging back, trying to melt into the nearest wall. I wasn't looking at any of them: my eyes were fixed on the floor, and right in the centre of my view were the ugly school-regulation shoes.

'I will of course be obliged to place Elizabeth in the lower sets for all her subjects…'

Dad interrupted her. I could see him beginning to splutter.

Jenny 2

'Now, Miss McClure...' he started to say, and then the Head added:

'Of course, once Elizabeth has settled in and started to show what she can do, we can revise that.'

Dad mumbled something, and I saw Mum give him a dig with her elbow.

'Elizabeth ...?'

The Head was trying to get my attention.

'I suggest you go to your form room now and you can start to get to know your peer group.' She went to the door and beckoned in an older girl in the same ugly uniform as the one I was wearing, but with a prefect's badge on her chest. 'Take Elizabeth to Mr. Bridges' room, please, Natalie.'

I followed the prefect. Mr. Bridges' room couldn't be any worse than the Head's. I didn't look at Mum and Dad as we went out. Served them right.

'You'll like Mr Bridges,' Natalie was saying. 'He's really nice: strict but fair. 'Which school were you at before?'

I wasn't quick enough to think of an answer, so I said nothing. Natalie obviously thought this meant I was nervous, and said, reassuringly, 'Don't worry, it's all right here, it really is. So long as you follow the rules and do your work, you'll enjoy it.'

I very much doubted that. Rules! I already felt as though I was choking with the sensation of the tie and the stiff new shirt collar round my neck. Finally, we got to a door with a window in the upper part; through it I could see featureless rows of uniforms seated behind brown tables. Every one of them was facing the front, listening to the youngish teacher, and he broke off what he was saying as Natalie knocked on the door. Twenty-nine pairs of eyes turned in my direction.

'Come in, come in!' The teacher gestured for us to enter, and gave me what was clearly meant to be an encouraging smile. 'You must be Elizabeth. We're expecting you. I imagine Natalie's been telling you all about us.'

Jenny 2

No response appeared to be expected, and I made none.

'Here, we've saved you a seat, next to Samantha. She'll look after you.' There was another encouraging smile. I sat down without looking at the other girl.

Natalie said, 'Bye, Elizabeth. I'll see you later – let me know if you need anything,' and was gone.

'So, as I was saying....'

Mr. Bridges was addressing the whole class. 'In a few minutes the bell will ring, and we'll be going to our first assembly. You will see the whole of Year 7 there. Just like you, they are all new here today, and they are probably all equally unsure about what will happen. You needn't worry about not knowing what to do: there will be plenty of people to answer your questions over the coming weeks...'

'So why were you late, Elizabeth?' the Samantha girl asked, under cover of Mr. Bridges' monologue. 'Why didn't you come in with everyone else, like we were told to do on the induction days?'

Despite myself, I told her. 'I wasn't here for the induction days. My parents only decided to send me here at the last minute....and my name's Lizzie.'

'Hi, Lizzie. I'm Sami.' I looked at her properly then, and we both smiled.

Mum was waiting in the car, just as she'd promised. I'd been half afraid she'd be hanging around the entrance, ready to embarrass me again, and it was a relief to see that she was keeping a low profile. I looked at my feet as I walked; I was scuffing my PE shoes along the ground, and that reminded me that I was supposed to change them before leaving the building. At least they were on the right feet! It used to drive all the adults wild when I was younger. Somehow it just never seemed important to me which foot I put my shoes on.

'Bye, Lizzie!' Samantha – Sami – called as she breezed past. 'See you tomorrow!'

Jenny 2

Rachel

Somewhere in the back of my mind I must have known what I was doing, when I started the teacher training. I wanted to carry on following Jenny. I wanted to be in the classroom with her, see what life was like for a twelve- thirteen- fourteen-year-old girl who could have been my daughter. Should have been my daughter...I knew what I was doing, and yet at the same time, I didn't know. Or maybe I just didn't let myself know.

The room I had been directed to was down a long, brown corridor. I had to keep stopping to peer up at the little brass nameplates, high on the doors, until I found the one marked Dr. Blair, Admissions Tutor. My anxious fingers fumbled the doorknob, and the voice from inside the room called 'Come in' two or three times before I finally managed to turn it. The decision to apply for the postgraduate certificate of education course had not been easy. Dr. Blair did nothing to put me at my ease.

She acknowledged that I had the academic qualifications, even if it was some years since I had used my English degree in any meaningful sense, and seemed moderately pleased that I had experience of working in a school; she went so far as to tell me that what I had was more than most of the people who came 'wandering into the education department in times of high graduate unemployment.'

'I really got a lot out of my time in the primary school,' I told her, 'But I am clear that I want to qualify as a secondary teacher.' Then I wanted to bite my tongue out because I said aloud what I'd been thinking. '*That's the age Jenny would have been.*' She let that pass, and so I went on quickly to reassure her that, having no family ties, I would

Jenny 2

be able to devote all my time to the course and the teaching practices.

Dr. Blair looked at me over her glasses. 'That's just as well, Mrs. Daniels. The teaching profession is a demanding one, and there is no point our training anyone who might not stay the course - or leave the profession when they realise it's harder than they expected.'

So that was me told! I felt like a naughty schoolgirl up before the Head, and was fully expecting a rejection, but in the event she told me there was no reason why I shouldn't apply with every expectation of being accepted, subject to references and so on, of course. It was mid-year, but as an independent, mature student there was no need to conform to the published dates, and she had told me how to go about applying. I was confident that Grace Grainger would give me a good, professional reference. It was a pity about the manner of my leaving, but surely, as a special needs teacher, Grace would be especially understanding, and would not present that as a negative.

Now I was free to get on with the business of finding somewhere of my own to live. I walked down the High Street feeling airborne, hurrying past Mason's. I would try a different Estate Agent this time, one with no connection to my and Dave's joint past. I'd happened to see him once, a few weeks earlier, on a bus, his nose buried in a newspaper. I don't know whether or not he had seen me. It felt so odd, seeing him like that, a stranger, separate from me. I made no attempt to catch his eye, but I felt some relief to note that he wasn't looking quite so thin any more.

Laura tried to persuade me not to move out into rented accommodation.

'It's crazy, Rachel. You could stay on here, rent free, save up some more towards your deposit on a decent house.'

Jenny 2

We were out with the children, one Saturday morning. The boys were running about, chasing squirrels and each other. They hadn't quite shaken off the childish joy of being free in the open air, but I knew that soon they would hit the moodiness of early adolescence. Annie, by contrast, was a solemn little thing, and stayed close to Laura's side. I couldn't tell Laura that part of wanting to get away was the sadness of being in the same house as the child who was only a few months older than Jenny. But the main reason was the desire to begin my new life.

'I've already got enough for a deposit from my share of the house sale. Dave did well with that.'

She gave me a strange look. 'Yes, he was a good man.'

I sighed. Here we go again. 'Laura, I know that. What happened wasn't his fault, but it wasn't mine either. There was just too much...' I felt my voice cracking. 'Too much had happened...we could never have got over that. This way is better for both of us.'

There was an ear-splitting yell from one of the boys.

'Tom!' Laura's shout was equally ear-splitting. She'd always had a good pair of lungs, my sister. 'Stop winding your brother up!'

It's what our mother used to say to us when we were little. Apparently I was the chief winder-upper. If Jenny had had siblings, that experience would have stood me in good stead.

Laura was looking at me. 'Sorry. Go on. You were explaining why this idea of moving into rented accommodation is a good idea.'

I took a deep breath. How to explain, properly? It wasn't really about the practicalities, more about how I felt. And how did I feel? Liberated, on the cusp of a new life, an independent life. Now that I had made my decision, I was desperate to get on with it. A little rented flat would be a first step towards full independence.

Jenny 2

I remembered that day when I'd sat in the café poring over the shiny brochures, before giving in and going to Laura's. This time, the decision was easy. I took out a year's lease on what was really a very basic, student flat. The postgraduate teaching course carried no fees, and so I only had to find living expenses. I could live frugally, and I still had some savings, apart from the money for the deposit. My plans - my future - were all coming together.

Grace Grainger was surprised, but clearly not displeased, to hear from me. She suggested that I come in after school one day so that we could have some time undisturbed, and she made me a cup of tea in the staffroom.

'We were all very sorry,' she began, looking at me with concern over the rim of her mug.

I gave a tiny shake of my head, as if to say, 'No need.' To my surprise I found my hands shaking, and I didn't dare pick up my own mug for fear of spilling it. Instead, I gave Grace my practised smile.

'I'm fine now, looking forward to getting on with my training.'

I stretched out a hand to my mug. It was one of the 'Teachers Change Lives' ones, the lettering faded and scratched with much washing. I risked a try at picking it up, but then withdrew my hand.

'Obviously…' I paused. 'I'll need a reference. It's a bit different if you're not applying straight from college.'

To my relief, Grace nodded. 'No problem. I can get that done as soon as you like.' Then she asked the question that I had no ready answer to. I hoped it wouldn't count against me.

'What are you going to do until the start of term? It's still six months away.'

'Well, I'll need a job to pay the rent, of course, but it could be anything'.

Jenny 2

'Ah.' She gave me a wide smile. 'Well, as it happens, we are in need of a good teaching assistant here; we have a maternity leave coming up. What do you think?'

'Oh!' I was taken aback. It was the last thing I'd expected. 'I...well, thank you, thank you. I don't know...I wasn't expecting...'

'Don't worry. Take a few days to think about it. Come on, drink your tea. It's getting cold.'

Two weeks later my alarm clock rang at an unearthly hour. I reached for it awkwardly and stumbled out of bed and into the still unfamiliar bathroom, with its dingy wallpaper and yellowing paintwork. The shower over the bath just about worked, and as I shivered under its sparse spray my eye alighted on the black mould at the base of the curtain. Laura had been right in a way: this student accommodation was not for the long term. I thought about how, when I was finally ready to buy a place of my own, it would need to be far more suitable. With an effort I supressed the automatic qualifier: *there must be a room for Jenny ... Now she's getting older she needs her own space.*

I was thankful that I'd laid out my clothes the night before, so there were no more decisions to be made before leaving the flat. Breakfast was a cup of coffee, standing up in the cramped kitchen. I did wonder, even then, whether it was wise to be going back to the school where I'd lived through the years Jenny would have been there, and through the traumatic loss of a second child.

Then I pulled myself together: everything was different now. I was setting off for work from my own flat, not the house Dave and I had shared, not the house where we had hoped to bring home our child, not once, but twice.... No, enough! I had to stop those thoughts. Time to move on.

Jenny 2

The flat was near enough for me to walk into school, and as I walked a crowd of young mums and small children seemed to snowball around me. An image of The Pied Piper of Hamelin passed through my mind.

It was odd, entering the gates on foot like one of the children. I tried to imagine how it would appear from two feet closer to the ground; it might be quite scary. I found myself wondering how the approach could be made more child-friendly. How tall would Jenny have been by now?

I skirted the car park, not wanting to think about the last time I had driven here, and how it had ended. I supposed that Dave must have got someone to drive him in so he could retrieve my car while I was in hospital. We had never discussed it.

Days passed, and then weeks. I was kept busy. But it wasn't the same, going back to the primary school. My heart wasn't in it any more. I tried really hard not to get attached to any of the children; Dave would have been impressed. But somehow, not being attached got in the way of doing the job. That doesn't sound very professional, does it? I just ached for Jenny, all the time. I had lost a child, twice over, three times over, if you count the little golden angel. It hadn't escaped my notice that fate had once again presented me with a vacancy caused by a maternity leave. I was glad when the summer term ended.

The PGCE course was demanding: the lectures about how children learn; the sessions on classroom management; the other students. I wrote essays about theories of teaching English, experienced the joy of falling in love with Shakespeare all over again, and the horrors of trying to get to grips with the National Curriculum. It was just what I needed: no time to think about anything else.

Jenny 2

I did genuinely find it interesting. For the first time in a very long time I was focused on things outside myself, outside my own feelings. And our time was not our own, especially when the teaching practices started. I'd never known tiredness like it: so much to do and to think about.

'You must reflect on good practice when you observe others, and above all, reflect on your own,' our tutor used to say. 'And do try to get some rest when you can.'

I wondered in which hour of the day that was supposed to happen!

I remember the very first time I had to take a class all by myself. I was trembling so much my hand slipped from the door handle, causing me to drop all my papers, my carefully constructed lesson plan and worksheets, my evaluation sheets, my copy of the Shakespeare play they were supposed to be studying: all lying in a muddled heap on the floor, and the children - twelve-year-olds - all tittering and gearing up to have fun at my expense.

I wasn't the only mature student on the course, but I might as well have been the youngest as I stood in front of that class and waited for quiet. I felt about thirteen myself, a little girl playing at being a grown-up. The quiet didn't seem to be happening, so I raised my voice to ask for silence, and a pathetic squeak came out. More tittering. I introduced myself, told them I'd be working with them on their study of Romeo and Juliet, and chose a boy to give out the copies of my carefully prepared worksheet. He turned out to be the class clown, and entertained the class with a passable imitation of me dropping the papers. By the time he'd done this a few times, the sheets were pretty grubby and unappealing – a feature that the tutor later remarked on.

Little by little I gained confidence. I managed to get my voice down an octave, to sound more in control, more

Jenny 2

authoritative. I learned how to use the children's names as a tool.

'Gary!' I said one day, with my back to the class as I wrote their homework on the board. 'Why haven't you copied this down?' I smiled to see his surprised reflection in the shiny whiteboard.

In those early days I would wander round the classroom while the children were engaged in some task or other, gleaning all the important knowledge I could: football boots poking out of a rucksack, birthday cards being opened surreptitiously under a desk.

'Come on, Freddie, you don't want to have to stay behind finishing this instead of going to football practice, do you?' was always worth a try, as was, 'Amanda, you need to get this finished. Wouldn't it be a shame to be late home on your birthday?' while Amanda asked in wide-eyed wonder how on earth I could possibly have known it was her birthday. It was a relief to be thinking about something else, something other than the pain. It was like taking a holiday from myself.

They kept me on after my teaching practice. It was a good foundation, but after I'd been there for a couple of years, I felt ready for a change. That's when I got the job at Hillmore High School.

Chapter Ten

Rachel

Rachel

It wasn't itchy feet, not entirely. I thought it would be good to start afresh, somewhere where I wouldn't be seen as the newly qualified teacher. Because of my age, people wouldn't automatically assume I was inexperienced. I thought I could walk in and be seen by everyone, the teachers as well as the students, as an established teacher.

It began well: I felt very happy, settled, as if I were in the right place for the first time in a long time. I loved being in the classroom. It was different from being a teaching assistant, of course, being responsible for a whole class by myself. I even had to direct my own teaching assistants. Having been one myself helped, of course.

The older students… they take up so much more space than the primary children. They're so much louder too. It was wonderful, and a bit terrifying, seeing what Jenny's life at secondary school was like…what it *would* have been like.

Before the term at Hillmore High School started in earnest, I attended a staff training day. I was exhausted at the end of it as I staggered home with a small forest of information: this was before school intranets and the like. There were school policies, exam syllabuses, lists of this and that, but the really exciting piece of paper was my timetable. It was pretty much what I'd expected, with a scattering of most year groups, including Year 9, Jenny's year group.

Jenny 2

I had been allocated a classroom next to Mrs. Rogers, the Head of Department, which offered some sense of security. Francine Rogers was a tiny, feisty woman, with hair piled up on top; it added height, although her powerful presence suggested such outward signs were not really needed.

'Just remember, I'm here, right next door, if you need anything, anything at all.'

Before I could say a word, she rattled on.

'Now, let's have a look at your timetable.' Her eyes scanned the sheet. 'Yes, yes, you'll enjoy that group. Yes, the Year 8s are a lively lot, but I'm sure you'll handle them. Ah!' She paused. 'Yes, Year 9. They're OK mostly, but watch out for Lizzie B. Don't let her get the upper hand.'

I knew that the advice was well intended, but wished Mrs. Rogers hadn't named an individual child. What hope was there now that I could start off in any kind of neutral relationship with her? The more I thought about it, the more angry I felt, although as the new girl, I didn't feel able to risk saying so. From that moment I was determined that this Lizzie girl would receive fair treatment, even if I had to bend over backwards to give it her.

And so term began. There were assemblies in year groups, with the same messages hammered home each time about hard work and preparing for exams; about behaviour; and about respect for other members of the school community. One or two students were removed by their form tutors for what seemed to me fairly minor misdemeanours.

The girl was sitting with her back to the door as I entered, her long fair hair tumbling in a tangle down her back, her shoulders hunched against the world. The rest of the class shuffled, hissed at each other and faced the front when they

Jenny 2

saw their new teacher, but the girl remained obstinately facing the back, enclosed in her own private space.

Right, so you're Lizzie B, I thought.

I made a quick decision: I was not, under any circumstances, going to get into a confrontation with this girl: it was bad enough that my Head of Department had prejudiced the chances of an easy relationship. I put down my bag on the chair next to the teacher's desk, picked up a marker, and wrote 'Mrs. Daniels' on the whiteboard.

'Good Morning!'

Then I paused and made eye contact with twenty-nine students. 'I will have the pleasure of teaching you English this year. I've heard a lot of good reports about you, and I'm looking forward to it.' This was untrue, of course, but there was no harm in making the most positive start I could, and it might win over one or two of them.

'I'd be interested in knowing what your experience of English has been so far....'

There was a brief pause, before the response came: a barrage of noise and shouted comments.

'Bor - ing!'

'Irrelevant!'

'Rubbish!'

I put my hands over my ears. Someone laughed.

'OK,' I said, in a voice soft enough for them to have to quieten down to hear what I was saying. I didn't want to squander the advantage of being an unknown quantity.

'It would be easier to listen to you one at a time, so this is what we're going to do.' The hubbub died down to a whisper.

'I suggest that you begin in groups of about four...That's right, just turn round so you can talk to each other.'

There was a scraping of chairs legs and some calling out to their friends, as they shuffled into small groups.

Jenny 2

I had brought some large sheets of paper and coloured markers, and bustled about laying them in front of each little group, ignoring the looks of incredulity at a teacher who was encouraging her class to talk instead of listen.

'That's right, yes. Talk to each other; compare notes. Think about what English lessons are for; what you like, what you find interesting... Now if one person in each group could be the scribe...'

'What's a scribe when it's at home, Miss?'

'The person who writes things down on behalf of the rest of the group. Do you think you could do that for us, Daisy?'

The rather lumpish girl who had asked the question spluttered with astonishment.

'How did you know my name?'

'Oh, I have my ways.' I smiled, mysteriously, avoiding glancing in the direction of the scruffy pencil case Daisy was holding, with her name incised in smudged blue ink.

The boy next to her grinned, and whispered rather loudly to a boy at the next table, 'Hear that, Wayne? Mrs. Daniels knows all about us. You'd better watch your step!'

I waited a few minutes, and then, passing nonchalantly by the next table, addressed Wayne by name, confirming his and everyone else's impression that I possessed secret knowledge. His little group was making some effort to discuss the subject, and I offered praise. All the time I was wondering how I could begin to win round the infamous Lizzie B. It wouldn't do to use her name, that was for sure; the girl was bound to know that she was notorious.

In fact I sensed that she was just waiting for me to do that, to prove that everyone was against her, and I certainly didn't want to give her any opportunity to feel aggrieved at our first meeting.

An awkward little group had formed round Lizzie, who was still seated above the others, looking fixedly into

Jenny 2

space. They were all girls, and seemed pleasant enough; at least they were attempting to have an intelligent discussion. By this stage I had written some questions on the board and a serious-looking girl with short, dark hair and glasses was reading them out to the others.

'Why do we learn English?' she was saying. 'What is English Literature? Which books have you most enjoyed reading?'

'Well, it's so we can speak proper, in't it?' responded the girl next to her. I wondered if this was intentional irony, and moved on. As I did so, I had the faintest impression that Lizzie's gaze was following me. I felt sure that ignoring her behaviour instead of addressing it had been the right approach. Next time I looked, Lizzie was sitting on her seat.

On the basis that this class were more likely to listen to each other than to me, at least today, I hit on the idea of inviting someone from each group to come out and read aloud their answers to the questions. I gave them fifteen minutes and then positioned myself next to the board to note their responses to the questions. It was clear that very few knew what 'Literature' meant, that they had read nothing that stretched them in the slightest, or if they had, they had not remembered it, and that they had very little intellectual curiosity about the nature of the subject. I rounded off the lesson with a summing up of what they had said, and left the room feeling relatively unscathed.

No-one had warned me that the dark-haired, serious girl was the daughter of a member of staff, but that must have been how reports of my lessons with Year 9 found their way to Mrs. Rogers. The Head of Department called me into her office after school one day to ask how things were going. I was enjoying myself in the first flush of a new job, and responded in positive terms, so I was utterly stunned when Mrs. Rogers asked me pointedly why, two weeks into the

Jenny 2

term, I still hadn't started on any of the set texts. Furthermore, it appeared that I had not been setting homework on a regular basis, there were no spelling tests, and the most challenging girl in the class had not once been reprimanded for her rudeness and surly behaviour.

I just sat in silence, trying to formulate words to explain how I had been trying to win the class's trust and co-operation in order to proceed with the syllabus more effectively. I tried to explain that I had worked, as a TA, with some very difficult and challenging pupils, and that confrontation was a sure way of alienating them. I was trying to be more subtle, I said, but clearly, my reasoning was too subtle for Mrs. Rogers, and from then on my relationship with the woman who, on the first day of the term, had offered unlimited support, became strained.

Talking to other teachers in the staff room during the all-too-brief lunch break (apparently I was expected to supervise the debating society and the poetry club at lunchtime - that was certainly never mentioned at the interview) I began to get a flavour of the school that I had somehow missed on my previous visits. This was a school where Authority and Conformity were exalted; individualism was not to be encouraged. I felt very much on my own.

Most of my classes had taken on board the unspoken as well as the spoken rules of the place, and meekly responded to what was asked of them. I enjoyed attempting to inject a little life and critical thinking into them. Strangely, though, the class I enjoyed teaching most of all was the 'difficult' Year 9 group. And most of all, I enjoyed the challenge of the wayward Lizzie B.

I was happy at the school in the main, although there were aspects of its ethos I disliked. I hated having to inspect the students to check whether their uniforms were correct, and the endless form-filling for minor misdemeanours. It turned me into a bit of a rebel. I wanted to show them that there

Jenny 2

were other ways of doing it. That made it easier to relate to some of the students; it certainly made it easier to relate to Lizzie B. She was a rebel too... oh yes, was she a rebel!

I was thankful to have made a good start with that difficult Year 9 group. Perhaps it was only because I was new to the school and hadn't yet learned its ways; perhaps I didn't yet have the ground-down look of some of my colleagues. Whatever the reason, from that first lesson with them they were taken by surprise. I think they saw me as different, and that was refreshing for a group of thirteen-year-olds who were just learning to be world-weary and dismissive of everything that came from anyone over the age of nineteen. I learned, later, at the first parents' evening, that some of them had told their parents, with amazement, that their new English teacher asked them what they thought about what we were reading, instead of telling them what to think.

'I want you to close your eyes,' I told them at the beginning of a lesson, as I prepared them for a descriptive writing task. 'You are standing outside, over near the trees. There is a soft breeze blowing. You can feel it on your skin. It caresses you, brushes your cheek, ruffles your hair... The air is warm...you can almost taste it. It makes you think of holidays and faraway places...Somewhere, someone is burning logs: you can smell the wood-smoke. It's a smell you like, a smell you remember from another time and place....'

I was deliberately making my voice slow and hypnotic, trying to stimulate their imagination, something I guessed was not usually encouraged at Hillmore High School.

'Now,' I asked. 'What can you hear?' At that point Nathan Carter, slumped as usual against the back wall, his eyes closed and his fleshy features relaxed into an expression of utter contentment, let out a series of gentle snores. The class returned to full consciousness and their

Jenny 2

giggles awoke a bemused Nathan, who never did discover what the joke was.

I wrote the task on the board.

'Remember, when you describe something, you have five senses. Don't focus only on what you can see, but include what you can feel, taste, touch, hear – there were more giggles at this last word - 'and now you have thirty minutes to write your first draft.'

I had moved from the rented flat some time ago, and was now living in a modest little house in keeping with my new status as a 'proper' teacher. There were two bedrooms, but I could never bring myself to use the second, smaller one as a study, so I did my marking at the dining table, where all my books were to hand on the bookshelves I had bought just after I moved in. It seemed I was preserving the other bedroom for another use.

The Year Nines' first attempts weren't bad - apart from the small number of boys who included snoring as part of their descriptions of 'My favourite Place.' Some of them - the girls, mostly - had written about their bedrooms when asked to describe their favourite place, and I was interested to note the kind of décor Jenny's contemporaries seemed to favour. It must have affected me subconsciously when I came to decorate the spare room, because, when an old friend came to stay, she took one look at what I'd done and exclaimed, 'When are you going to do up the spare bedroom, Rachel? Or are you planning to take in a teenager?'

Jenny would have liked it, I thought, later that night as sleep eluded me. I knew how much I would have loved having a thirteen-year-old around the place. I found my mind straying to the actual thirteen-years-olds I knew: the hapless Nathan, with his gormless expression and inability to hold a pen properly; the dark-haired Eve, daughter of my colleague Francine; the sly Samantha – Sami, she liked to be called –

97

Jenny 2

who smelt of cigarette smoke and unwashed underwear; and Lizzie, the girl branded as a troublemaker, who ignored me as much as possible, and whom I ostensibly ignored right back.

It was Lizzie who refused to close her eyes for the imagination exercise; Lizzie whose written work infuriated and puzzled me; Lizzie who wrote a few sentences and then laid her head on the desk, handing in at the end of the lesson an incomplete piece of work on grubby, crumpled paper. Determinedly, I didn't comment in class, but in the evening, when I had read the little that had been written, I couldn't stop myself from exclaiming aloud.

My favrite place doesn't exist on earth, but in my head it is heven. There is no-one there to bullie me or make fun, no-one to tell me Im not good enuff. I have my own door to lock against the world, and I can feel how solid it is. Outside I can hear them, but they cant get in. There is a feeling of ~~saftie~~ safety in my speshal place...

In my dreams I saw Jenny, her long, tangled hair falling about her shoulders as she slammed the bedroom door shut against the world. I thought I heard her crying, and tried the handle, but the door was locked.

'Go away... this is my special place...

Chapter Eleven

Rachel

Rachel

For several days I wondered if I ought to speak to someone about Lizzie, but the mere mention of the girl's name seemed to have such a negative effect that I decided to wait and see how things developed. Should I speak to her directly?

Lessons continued as before, and I returned the written piece to each student with a brief comment.

'Interesting, Adam. I like the way you include the sense of touch… Yes, Jo, good effort. Very polished, Eve – you must have worked hard on this.'

When I reached Lizzie's, I stopped at her desk and spoke more quietly. As usual, the girl resisted my attempts to make eye contact. 'I found what you wrote very moving, Lizzie. You express yourself with real feeling and sensitivity…'

There was no acknowledgement, and I'd expected none. Perhaps I'd overdone the praise. I moved on.

'I like your description of the woods, Jack. It would be good to know a bit more about the sounds you can hear. Sami….' I looked around, but the girl's desk was empty. Again.

Now there was a child I really ought to be mentioning to the Head of Year.

Some weeks later, I was heading home with a head full of restless Year 10s and my thoughts on the evening's marking when I almost collided with a huddled figure in the shadows by the Year 9 lockers.

Jenny 2

'Oops, sorry, Lizzie! Didn't see you there. Are you OK?'

'Goodnight, Miss.'

Well, at least she had acknowledged my presence; but what was she doing there when the others had gone home? She looked so alone, poor kid.

Unsettled, I lingered on the path for a while, but no Lizzie emerged from the building. Finally, I made my way to the car and tipped my bag and piles of papers on to the passenger seat. As I was about to make my way around to the driver's side I heard voices. I recognised Lizzie's slight form, and saw that she and another girl were heading away from the main building, whispering and giggling. The other girl's voice was quite loud, so that it was only seconds before I identified her as Sami. I felt a prickle of anxiety.

Later, beating eggs for a hasty omelette, I realised what it was that had disturbed me so much. There was nothing necessarily odd about the girls being still on the school premises: any number of school clubs ran until quite late, although Lizzie and Sami were the least likely members of a club that anyone could imagine. No, it was the fact that I had heard the withdrawn and usually silent Lizzie giggling. That, and the fact that Sami had been absent from school that day.

Next morning I mentioned Sami's name in the staffroom before briefing. There were several responses of the 'Oh, that one!' variety, before Lawrence, the rather world-weary Head of Year 9, explained that Sami had been spotted as a trouble-maker from the moment she entered the school.

'Lives on the Rivers estate,' someone said, as though that explained everything.

Miss McClure came striding in, and the room fell silent while she issued a series of notices and instructions at her usual lightning speed. Then the bell went, and I

Jenny 2

realised that there would be no opportunity for further conversation until the final bell of the day rang at 3.30.

As soon as last lesson finished, I made my way to Lawrence's classroom. He was hard at work at his computer, surfing holiday sites.

'Ever been skiing?' he asked pleasantly as I entered. 'Edie and I are thinking of going over the Christmas holiday.'

I tried to keep any look of censure from my expression. Was I really such a prig? I still couldn't help feeling, though, that the desktop computers, recently installed to replace the paper registers and provide instant access to banks of worksheets, were not really intended for personal use. I noticed also that Lawrence seemed to have gained an energy that was normally lacking during the school day.

'Right,' he said, swivelling round in his chair as though reading my disapproval.

'You want to know about our friend Sami?' He assumed a more formal expression. 'She came to us in Year 7 with a history of unauthorised absences and an attitude the size of the English Channel. She became pals with that other troublemaker – Lizzie B – on day one. *She's* a mixed-up kid all right,' he added as an aside. 'We know she smokes, they both do; you can smell it a mile off. They're both regulars round the back of the science block.'

I must have looked puzzled.

'Smokers' Corner,' he supplied. 'All the no-hopers and kids who are a waste of space hang out there.'

'That's a terrible thing to call a young person. How can you possibly call anyone that?'

'How long have you been teaching, Rachel?'

I hesitated; I knew the point he was getting at. 'Not as long as you, although I have worked in schools for a long time….'

Jenny 2

'...and when you have taught for as long as I have perhaps you won't be quite so dewy-eyed about the little sods. Tell me something: does Sami make it easy for you to teach? Is she rude and insolent? Does she interrupt your lessons? Aren't you relieved when she's not there?'

I opened my mouth and closed it again.

'Look, 'Lawrence was saying. 'Don't the other twenty-odd kids in the class deserve to be taught properly? Sometimes you have to make hard decisions: the well-being of the majority against the needs of one individual.'

Of course, Sami never received the help she needed. Lawrence said he would follow up my concerns, which he did, in a sense, but it wasn't what I was expecting. I had to admit I'd seen her on school premises on an evening when she hadn't been in school. It turned out she had been excluded that day for...I forget what crime against Hillmore High School. Anyway, a few nights later Lawrence hung about outside the side entrance and caught her. He had a fellow member of staff with him, and they found a lump of cannabis resin stowed in the lining of her tie. The school had a strict policy on drugs – it had a strict policy on everything – and so there were no second chances for Sami. She was out, permanently excluded. I used to see her sometimes, hanging around outside, waiting for the others to come out. I thought she was lonely. Lawrence said she was looking for an opportunity to sell drugs.

Now I was worried that Lizzie might also be involved. Should I have told someone – and risk the same thing happening to her? Of course, I didn't tell anyone. I wanted to protect her, my precious girl.

As weeks became months and months became terms, I began to feel I was making a little cautious progress in my attempts to win Lizzie over. The child had been more withdrawn than ever after the permanent exclusion of her

Jenny 2

only friend, and I felt torn about the whole thing: on the one hand I was relieved that the bad influence of the other girl was no longer around, but on the other I wondered who would be looking out for Sami now that the school had washed its hands of her.

By the end of Year 9, however, Lizzie would occasionally speak to me and sometimes even let me discuss her work with her. I was cautious about making too much of the spelling problems and held back from suggesting possible dyslexic tendencies until the girl's parents came in for the annual parents' evening just prior to the SATs tests. Although the school's policy was that students should accompany their parents to these events and hear what was being said about them, Lizzie was not with them as they took their seats on the plastic chairs arranged opposite my table in the school hall.

I had my mark book and copies of the set texts ranged in front of me, every inch the professional. Like the other subject staff, I had arranged three chairs in front of the table; most of the parents chose to sit with their offspring between them, although one or two preferred to sit together and place the child at the end of the line. Lizzie's parents, however, chose to sit on the outer chairs, with Lizzie's empty chair between them. I sensed tension in the air.

'Well now,' I began, encouragingly, 'I would say that Lizzie has become more engaged with lessons this term. I would even go so far as to say she has enjoyed some of the things we've done...'

'Yes, fine, but...' Her father leaned forward, earnestly. 'What is her predicted level in English? You must have noticed her writing's pretty atrocious.'

The mother placed a restraining hand on his arm. There was something vaguely familiar about her.

'Sh! We agreed we'd try to be positive this evening.' She smiled wanly at me. 'You probably know about the... the trouble she's been in, truanting and so on....'

Jenny 2

'She doesn't do herself any favours being absent from school, that's true, but she has quite a way with words....'

'Especially if they begin with F...' interjected the father.

I was surprised. 'So you have some...difficult behaviour from her at home?'

For some reason I had imagined that it was just school she was rebelling against.

'Where do we start?' Lizzie's mother looked at her husband, who shrugged.

'Look, as far as English is concerned...' I decided I'd better get back to the subject in hand. 'I genuinely believe there is an articulate and intelligent student in there, trying to get out, but I think she is very frustrated by her difficulties in communicating on paper. Have you ever thought... has it ever occurred to you... that she might be dyslexic...have dyslexic tendencies anyway?'

There was a heavy silence.

'You know people with dyslexia are often very intelligent...'

It was the father who finally spoke. 'Yes, we know all about that; we've heard all that stuff before. I'm not sure we want to go down that route again, do we?' He turned to his wife, who nodded uncertainly.

'So,' he continued. 'You are basically telling us that she's going to fail her English SATs?'

'No, she won't fail, because there's no such thing as failing these tests, but we have to be realistic about the level she's likely to achieve because of her ...difficulties. As I say, we can look into getting her extra help in school, and there's a lot to be said for having her assessed before she starts on her GCSE courses...'

The queue beyond the table seemed to have grown considerably. A clearly irritated woman was waving her appointments list, and I said, with a smile I didn't feel, 'Do please take a seat at the end there. I'm afraid everyone's in the same situation.'

'Now...' I turned back to Lizzie's parents, but they were already standing.

'I don't think there's anything else to say, is there?' the father said, as he shook my outstretched hand perfunctorily and began to stride off.

The mother hung back for a moment.

'She does like your lessons, you know,' she whispered. I still couldn't place her.

By the time I got home that night, my head was throbbing. Parents are such an unrealistic lot, some of them, anyway. They seemed completely uninterested in hearing what their child was really like, as a person; they didn't want to know what animated them in the classroom, what worried them, what might help with their learning. No, the question was always: what grade, what level, what result? And if the answer wasn't to their liking – and it usually wasn't – they wanted to know what I was going to do about it, as if the child were merely a passive recipient of the teacher's input. It was no use, it seemed, telling them that little Jane or Jimmy had improved this term, that they were working as hard as they could, that what they had achieved was, for them, a very real achievement, worthy of praise. No, if it didn't measure up to the parents' own preconceptions of success, all of that counted for nothing.

I ate an omelette with little appetite – I had no energy to cook anything else - and threw myself down on the bed fully dressed. I promised myself I would go to bed properly in a minute; instead I fell into a deep sleep punctuated with dreams of Jenny in a Hillmore High School uniform, looking neat and demure as she completed extra homework and smiled up at me.

It was six in the morning when I woke with a crick in my neck, feeling cold and spaced out, the taste of the slightly

Jenny 2

overcooked omelette still in my mouth. I bustled round getting myself ready for school, and set off, still haunted by the Jenny I had seen in my dreams. I wasn't sure it was a Jenny I especially liked any longer.

Chapter Twelve

Rachel

Rachel

After the summer holidays I was asked to take on a Year 10 tutor group. I was instinctively aware that the role came with high expectations of rigid discipline: these fourteen and fifteen-year-olds would need to be drilled in the ways of working that were appropriate to young people embarking on their GCSE courses. That would no doubt include rigid adherence to all the rules of school uniform, which, as everyone knew, made *all* the difference to academic progress. I was becoming more cynical as the terms went by.

We were addressed by the Head at a staff meeting the day before term started.

'Now it's important that we all keep a firm eye on matters of school uniform...'

A *firm* eye? She was a great one for mixed metaphors.

'Things have grown very lax during the last couple of terms.'

She allowed her gaze to travel over each and every member of staff. You could tell that the old stagers had mentally switched off already, but the newer ones, like me, shifted uncomfortably.

'Year 10 form tutors have a special responsibility...' She allowed herself a dramatic pause and another beady-eyed look. 'It is your duty to ensure that the students under your care make the best possible start to their GCSEs. That is why you will inspect their uniforms at the start of the day

Jenny 2

and ensure that no student is seen about the school if they are incorrectly dressed.'

I muttered something mildly rebellious and Francine Rogers, seated just in front of me, turned her head and gave me a withering look.

The Head droned on. 'We have had some very pleasing exam results in the past couple of years, but it's vital that we don't let up one inch. We want this year's cohort to not only reach their full potential, but to exceed it.'

Sorry, what? How do you *exceed* your potential? I saw Barry Watkins, the Head of Year 10, and another teacher, give a muted high five at that. They were playing Staff Meeting Bingo; that particular phrase was a regular of the Head's, it seemed.

Barry caught me as I was making my way out. He was still in a jaunty mood.

'Did you enjoy that?' he said, grinning.

'Couldn't we just get on with teaching?'

'Oh, world-weary already, Rachel? Well, I have something here that should cheer you up.'

He handed me a stiff-backed register.

'Your Year 10 tutor group register,' he said. 'Enjoy!'

The Year 9 groups were to be mixed up to form new groups for Year 10, and so the list contained names I didn't recognise. Glancing further down, my eyes alighted on one name I certainly did know - Lizzie was to be in my tutor group. How would that work out?

Next morning, I was waiting for them. I cast a quick eye over ties, jumpers, and shoes, hissing, as I'd heard my colleagues do: 'Tuck your shirt in! Top button! Tie!' I hated it.

My eyes were now on feet, as the last stragglers came into the classroom.

Jenny 2

'Where are your proper school shoes, Adam? You know I'll have to send you to the Head of Year, don't you, if you haven't got them?

In the end I sent two tie defaulters and three trainer transgressors along to Mr. Watkins' room. I knew they would stay there all day if necessary, if their parents couldn't make it into school with the right shoes and ties to bail them out. It was ridiculous: they would miss the start of year assembly; they would also miss being given their timetables, to say nothing of the stirring pep talk I planned to give them... Rebellion was always just below the surface of my thoughts these days.

My inner mutterings were brought up short by the arrival of one last student, a leggy girl in very definitely the wrong shoes, a too short skirt, no tie, and - what? Who? For a few seconds I didn't recognise her at all. Surely that mess of pink candyfloss on her head, cut seriously short at the sides - surely that couldn't really be Lizzie? Her lovely hair! I wanted to cry out. Her golden curls! It was then I realised just how much I had invested in this girl: I wanted to be the one to brush the tangles from her hair; to soothe the knotted emotions beneath. And now look at her...

Biting back what I really wanted to say, although goodness knows what was showing on my face, I beckoned her to my desk, while instructing the others to take a seat and wait for the bell for assembly.

'OK, Lizzie. Let's see what we can do here. Do you have your tie with you? School shoes? What about your skirt: is the waistband rolled up? Maybe you can pull it down a bit? No? OK.'

I knew I said OK a lot when I needed thinking time. I wanted to protect Lizzie from the wrath of Mr Watkins, who was not known for his gentle approach, but there was nothing I could do. I congratulated myself on not asking what on earth she had done to her beautiful hair and I didn't ask why she'd done it. I guessed she'd already had plenty of that from her mother. The father would be more forthright, from my impression of him on parents' evening. In the meantime, there was a greater problem. Pink hair was very definitely not regulation school uniform.

It fell to me, as Lizzie's form tutor, to contact home, firstly to explain the nature of Lizzie's crimes, and secondly to explain the sentence handed down. Lizzie would be kept in the isolation unit until she appeared in school correctly dressed and with an appropriate hairstyle. So, for several months, then, if by that they meant she had to wait for the pink dye to grow out!

I caught myself muttering 'isolation,' as I made my way with my new tutor group to the school hall for what would be no doubt an unbearably hectoring assembly. Isolation! Makes it sound as though they're afraid the others will catch something from her.

In Learning Support, the official name for the isolation unit, a row of desks faced a blank wall, each one partitioned off from its neighbour. Students were stationed there after school each day for detention, if their behavioural failings were serious enough to warrant it, but the new crackdown on school uniform was producing so many defaulters that the overspill now had to be corralled in the smaller school hall.

During the day, the isolation unit was used to support some of the students with special needs who, for whatever reason, were unable to work in the classroom. It was also used for students on internal exclusion; in management's eyes a mixed blessing, since it meant that they could be set work by their subject teachers each day, and forced to complete it under strict supervision, while the downside was that they were still on school premises, and potentially a bad influence on those around them. To

Jenny 2

overcome this, they had decreed that break and lunch-times for those on learning support - most of the staff still rebelliously called it 'isolation', while a few used the words 'banged up' - should not coincide with those of the rest of the school, and that they should be detained until thirty minutes after the rest of the school had left. This was not a popular arrangement with those detailed for supervision duties.

I was required to set work for Lizzie from day one, which was difficult, because the girl had not yet attended any of the lessons on which to base it. Furthermore, as the days went on, she was missing more and more of the new syllabus. I debated whether I should give her the set texts to read? Lizzie tended to read slowly, and without enthusiasm. While I was sure I could bring them alive for her in the classroom, I could not see how to help her without context and any sort of stimulus. Besides, she would have maths and science and history and all sorts of things thrown at her, as she sat at her little desk between the partitions. I was close to tears of frustration, when I hit on a partial solution.

Over the following weeks, I spent my lunchtimes and long stretches of time after school most days seated beside Lizzie in the Learning Support unit. It pretty much amounted to private tuition. I remember that first session with Lizzie with painful clarity. At a bit of a loss, I gave her an open-ended task at the beginning of the day.

'Just write about anything you like,' I said briskly, placing a couple of sheets of A4 in front of her. 'School, friends, my favourite songs, anything…'

Lizzie looked listlessly at the paper, and said nothing to indicate she had even heard.

'Right, I'll leave you now. I need to get the rest of the class to assembly.' Those that haven't been sent away to remedy the defects in their school uniform, I thought.

Jenny 2

When I returned after the last bell, Lizzie was sitting in exactly the same position as I'd left her, slightly hunched, eyes elsewhere.

'Hello, Lizzie,' I said, as brightly as I could muster. 'How're you getting on?'

The girl grunted, and shifted slightly in her seat.

I tried to sound positive.

'Let's see what you've been doing.'

There were papers scattered all over her desk, and some screwed up on the floor. I tried to create some sort of order. There was a maths worksheet, with a half-hearted attempt at completion; a map of Europe with some ink marks on it, and an empty crisp packet. The rules expressly forbade the consumption of any sort of food or drink in the Learning Support Centre; of course they did! No luxuries in prison.

I looked around for the work I had set Lizzie at the start of the day. The sheets of A4 eventually turned up on the desk next to hers, still immaculate.

'Oh, Lizzie, I was looking forward to reading something you'd written.' I tried to make my disappointment sound like encouragement.

Lizzie muttered something.

I tried again. 'Come on, let's look at it together. Perhaps I should have given you something specific to write about? Sometimes it's hard to make decisions about what to do if you have too much choice, isn't it? What about: My First Day at School?' Even as I said it, I winced. What an unforgivable old chestnut.

Lizzie looked at me with an expression somewhere between scorn and disbelief.

'What?'

'If you can't remember your first ever day at school, what about your first day at Hillmore High School?'

'You *are* joking!'

'No. Can you remember your first day?'

Jenny 2

'Can you remember yours?'

'At Hillmore High School? Yes, I can as a matter of fact. I had to teach a difficult Year 9 class, and there was an interesting student with a lot of blond hair and plenty of attitude. She was clearly bright, but lacked confidence...'

The corner of Lizzie's mouth quivered.

'What? I thought you hadn't noticed me at all...All the other teachers used to come in and start on me right away: sit down properly! Sit up straight! Where's your homework? Look at me when I'm talking to you! You - you just carried on teaching the lesson, talking to everyone else as though I wasn't there. It was kind of...funny!'

'Oh, I noticed you all right! But I didn't think you needed me telling you off as soon as I walked through the door.'

There was a pause. Lizzie was evidently thinking about this. I followed up my advantage with another question.

'So, what about *your* first day? You must have started in Year 7 with everyone else, I suppose?' Lizzie's face seemed to crumple, as though she was fighting back tears. Or did I imagine that? When she had regained control of her features, she responded obliquely.

'What do you think of the uniform they make us wear? Really? '

'Well....' I wasn't sure how truthfully I should answer.

'I mean, would you like to wear it?'

'I'm not sure that's the point.'

'I don't see why we should be made to wear something ugly and uncomfortable and that makes us all look the same.'

I opened my mouth to make some non-committal reply, but Lizzie continued,

'And a tie! I mean, why make the girls wear a tie? It's not as though we'll have to get used to wearing them

Jenny 2

when we leave school, is it? I know they say that's why the boys have to wear them, but why the girls?'

'I suppose you might have to wear one if you joined the army. Or the police force.' I realised how lame this sounded, even as I said it. Before I knew it my face had cracked, at the idea of pink candy-floss Lizzie in uniform on the parade ground.

Lizzie seemed to catch my mood.

'Can you see me in the army, Miss? Or the Police Force?'

'In any case, Lizzie, when did you last actually *wear* your tie?'

I persuaded her to start writing down her arguments against school uniform. She had a sharp mind, and just needed a bit of help organising her thoughts. I was already only too well aware that she could argue her point of view on most subjects, verbally, but shied away from writing because she knew her writing and her spelling made her look less intelligent than she really was.

That night I re-ran the scene in my mind. I thought there must be a lot of pressure from home; they were an academic lot, and her brothers were always referred to in school as 'having a great future.' The parents' evening conversation suggested they were disappointed in her, and the father in particular lacked patience. I also sensed, from her manner, that she'd been bullied at times, although I struggled to get her to talk about that...

As I sat at my table, a pile of unmarked books in front of me, I suddenly found myself sobbing. Poor Lizzie: how could they... how could anyone...so little, so vulnerable.... How could they hurt you, my baby? How could they do that to you? They took you away from me, wrapped you up, put you in a box, or an incinerator, or the rubbish heap for all I know... Oh, Jenny, Jenny, my Jenny...'

Jenny 2

A memory came back to me: there had been an evening when Dave told me I shouldn't get too attached to the children in my care. I had been so angry with him at the time, but now I knew that he had simply wanted to protect me, and I was too stubborn to see it.

All the time Lizzie was in isolation I was gradually coaxing her to express herself. The plan was to progress from there to writing it down, perhaps keeping a kind of diary, but after a while that took a back seat. Sometimes listening to what she had to say was uncomfortable; Lizzie felt that the school, the system, the world at large, was out to get her. She couldn't get anything right; everything she did at home was wrong, and now everything she did at school was too. I pointed out gently that dyeing her hair and contravening all the school uniform rules at once probably wasn't helping her much, but she brushed that aside.

The odd thing was, underneath all this, I had a feeling that what Lizzie really wanted was to fit in, to blend in with the others, to stop feeling different. Just what school uniform was intended for, some would say.

One afternoon, when Lizzie had set off home after a half-promise that she might try to read a chapter of *Of Mice and Men* I picked up the telephone in the Year 10 office. The rest of the students and my colleagues were long gone, and my voice sounded strange to me in the unaccustomed silence. Consulting my tutor group record I dialled the number and waited. Lizzie's mother replied, and then her voice became very tense when she heard who it was.

'No, there's nothing wrong, at least, nothing new.' The parents had been kept informed of what was going on with Lizzie and Learning Support.

'I've been thinking, though. Lizzie is missing so much of her schooling while she's out of the classroom. Would it be possible, do you think, to persuade her to dye her hair back to something like her natural colour, and then

Jenny 2

perhaps have a, you know, sort of standard cut? I'm sure we could get her back into lessons if she would do that.'

There was a long silence on the other end of the line. 'Have you ever tried to get that girl to do anything she doesn't want to?'

'Well, as a teacher I spend most of my working life trying to get young people to do things they don't want to! Is there any way you could make her *want* to do it?'

'Well, it's no good telling her how awful she looks; I've tried that already…'

I'll bet that went down well.

'What about a reward? Is there anything she really wants, something she'd be willing to compromise for?'

'That sounds like bribery!' Lizzie's mother's sounded shocked.

'Yes, that's a good idea. Do you think you could make it work?'

There was a sigh and then, gratifyingly, a small chuckle at the other end of the line.

'I'd better not tell her father then!' Another pause. 'All right. Leave it with me.'

I never found out what Lizzie's mother did to persuade her to modify her appearance, but it worked. I had to work quite hard myself on the Head of Year to get her a reprieve, but once her hair looked more normal, and she'd put a tie round her neck, he agreed, grudgingly, to let her back amongst the general population. She even started to make friends, of sorts. I think some of the more disaffected kids saw her as a kind of champion, which wasn't ideal, but at least she wasn't so isolated any more.

'Mrs. Brown? Do come through to the office.'

Barry Watkin's office was available, as he was away on some jaunt, and I was wearing my best professional look, calm, poised, and sympathetic towards the mother of a

Jenny 2

student who was having a difficult time. That's what I told myself I was doing.

'Do please take a seat.' My voice had come out rather breathy. I'd have to do better than this. I made an effort to lower it, and asked, 'How was the readmission interview?'

Mrs. Brown grimaced.

'That good, eh?' I managed to smile and the tension was broken.

It was Mrs. Brown who had requested the meeting. Little headway had been made with the Head of Year, and she admitted that she and her husband had gone home in a state of bemusement, with no idea of what should or could happen next.

I took a steadying breath. 'Look, as her form tutor, I want to see what I can do to try and help her settle back into school.' I wondered whether the mother had any idea of how it was for Lizzie.

'What does she say to you about school?'

'I'm not sure it's repeatable.'

'She's a bright girl. She could do really well if she chose.'

'But she doesn't choose, does she?'

'It sounds a bit as though you've given up on her.'

'There are times, believe me, when I'd like to.'

I probably looked as shocked as I felt.

Mrs. Brown bristled.

'Are you judging me?'

I spluttered a protest, although she was right. Of course I was judging her. The file of papers in my hands felt suddenly damp, and when I glanced down I saw that the ink was coming off on my skin.

Mrs. Brown leaned forward: she was already sitting on the edge of her chair, and now there were only a few inches between us.

Jenny 2

'Since the moment she was born, well, even before actually, she's given us nothing but worry. I had a difficult pregnancy -- '

I gave an involuntary shudder and leaned back a little, away from that angry face and the memories it provoked, but the words continued.

'...a difficult birth,' she was saying. 'We nearly lost her when she was born. As a small child she was always awkward and clumsy; she broke everything, she tripped over everything...'

I dutifully made soothing noises I did not feel: I had never seen Lizzie drop or break anything in school – at least not accidentally.

'We tried everything: sanctions, rewards, taking her out of school, sending her back to school... I'm tired of it all, I really am.' She was silent for a moment, her body tensed. 'There's nothing like this anywhere else in the family...'

'Nothing like what?'

'This.... this *behaviour*! The way she looks! The way she dresses!'

'She's an individual, and...' I realised I was beginning to lose my professional distance, and didn't complete the sentence.

'Look,' I said, making an effort to be Mrs. Daniels the form tutor again, 'We'll continue with the daily monitoring. I'll be checking with all of her subject teachers...'

'Yes, yes, I know the drill. We've been here before ... I've lost count of the number of monitorings and detentions and special meetings, exclusions, more meetings...and where does it get us?'

I wanted to say that it sounded as though she was blaming the school, but I held back. I even felt the teeniest twinge of sympathy; she did sound very weary.

Of course, I decided not to tell her about the forged note I had received from Lizzie only that morning, excusing her lack of homework and saying it was 'alright becos I no

Jenny 2

about it' and signed, improbably, by both parents, in a childish imitation of adult handwriting.

Chapter Thirteen

Lizzie - Hannah

Lizzie

It was the end of August, and I'd had a long, hot summer. While the other girls pranced around in spaghetti straps and shorts that left little to the imagination, I was covered up. It was yet another thing that alienated me.

'You're weird, you are.' That was Gina, always up for a row. 'Why don't you take that stupid sweat shirt off? You must be boiling!'

'Just because I don't want to go around showing everything I've got - like some people...'

I shouldn't have done that! These were the closest thing I had to friends, so it probably wasn't a good idea to piss them off. I wish I knew how to make friends. The other girls make it seem dead easy, but that's just one more thing that doesn't come easily to me. I'm not sure this lot think of themselves as my friends, exactly, but they all show up at the rec at the same time most days, and so I hang about with them, and they don't stop me. I'd asked Sami to go with me, but she was always busy after she was kicked out of Hillmore, though I couldn't for the life of me work out what with. None of her other schools lasted long.

'I don't think school's for me!' she'd said, one of the last times I'd seen her. We'd been mooching about the shopping centre one afternoon, when I should have been in double PE.

'That's what my Mum and Dad thought about me, for a while. Decided to home educate me, and then changed their minds. They'd had enough of me under their feet at home, I guess.'

Jenny 2

'Well, you're clever, aren't you? Not like me. And your Mum and Dad know about things; they can help you. I'll bet you could go to Uni if you wanted to.'

That made me laugh, although it wasn't funny in the slightest.

'Oh, I opted out of that competition years ago.'

'You what?'

'Are you kidding? My Dad? My brothers? I'm nothing in comparison with them.'

There was a mutual silence for a while, until Sami decided to cheer me up.

'So do you want that new mascara or what?'

We'd already spent some time in front of the make-up counter at Supergirl, drooling over the cosmetics. They weren't half expensive. I had no money: Mum and Dad's latest technique for reining me in was to withhold actual cash, although if I asked them to buy me something specific they didn't hesitate. I'd been cadging cigarettes off Sami for weeks and felt bad about it. I hardly dared to think what they would say if they'd known I was planning to sell my expensive digital camera to get the money for a tattoo.

'Nah – no money.'

'Who needs money?' I was a bit uncomfortable at this. I knew there was never cash to spare in Sami's house, except when there was, and then there would suddenly be a lot all at once, that disappeared just as quickly. I didn't like to ask where it came from: I probably wouldn't like the answer.

'Come on!' Sami was urging me back into the store. As we reached the make-up counter, she suddenly gave me a massive push that sent me careering into a stand piled high with special promotions. The stand and I clattered to the floor, and I heard an assistant call for her manager, while a couple of nice, elderly ladies asked if I was 'All right, dear?'

Somehow I scrambled to my feet and said I was sorry, that I'd tripped, I was fine, then I got out of the shop

Jenny 2

as quickly as I could. Sami seemed to have disappeared. I wasn't sure for the moment what to do, so I began walking slowly past the arcade of shops. Halfway along Sami sprang out of a doorway and linked arms with me. I shook her off, annoyed.

'What was that all about?'

'Sorry about that! Should have seen your face! C'mon!' She pulled me into the nearest shop and headed for the Ladies' toilets. 'It's called causing a diversion. Wouldn't work if you'd known what was coming.'

Before I knew it, we were in one of the changing cubicles and Sami was peeling off her top.

'Sami, what on earth...?

'Shh! Don't say anything...'

I felt embarrassed for her. Her bra was rather grubby, and there was a stale smell as she raised her arms. Didn't seem to bother her, though. I could see now that she had a number of items tucked into her bra, and one of them was the mascara we'd been looking at. She handed it to me, putting a finger to her lips at the same time.

'Happy birthday!'

'But it's not my....'

'Shh!' Again, the finger to the lips.

'Oh! OK, er... thank you.'

I took it, not sure what else to do, and tucked it into the bottom of my bag, beneath the sandwiches Mum had, for some reason, insisted on making before I left the house.

'You don't look very happy with what I got for you.'

We were trudging back out of town towards the estate where Sami lived.

'I thought you said you liked that one?'

'I do, but...'

'Oh, come on. Everyone shoplifts a bit, don't they? It's not really stealing, not like taking something from an old granny...'

'I don't know.....it's still....it feels wrong.'

Jenny 2

'These shops, they've got masses of money, and they pay the staff slave wages. It's only taking back what they owe us.'

I was struggling to make sense of her logic. Instead, I said, 'I've got to go, now. See you tomorrow?'

'Dunno. Might be busy tomorrow.'

Sami disappeared into the maze of alleyways that made up the Rivers estate.

The estate was so-called because the streets were all named after rivers, and I'd noticed before that the planning people must have had a woeful grasp of geography. Avon Street ran into Forth Road, while Mersey Street and Severn Street merged with Humber Street, which then became Orwell Place. It reminded me of the fun I'd had with Mum, years ago, before Hillmore High School; we used to go on spontaneous outings around town, looking for interesting things like blue plaques that showed where famous people had lived, or spotting the different styles of houses. Mum knew quite a lot about architecture, and could tell when they had been built, just by looking at the style. The memory made me feel very sad. On the way back home, quite a distance from Sami's, I stopped near a large litter bin. It had a notice saying: *Keep your town clean and green*. I took a quick look round to make sure no-one was about, and then upended the bag, sandwiches and all, and walked briskly away.

So after that, during the school holidays, I had to find ways to occupy my time. I was always on the fringes of the crowd down at the rec. One of them befriended me for a while. He was in Year 11, at our school, although he wasn't actually on the premises much. There was this day when he pulled off his leather jacket; he was only wearing a Tee shirt underneath, but to begin with I was confused.

'Well, what do you think?'

Jenny 2

It took a while for the penny to drop. Those weren't patterned sleeves down to his wrists: that was his skin. I didn't know what to say, so I prevaricated.

'Gosh! Where did you get it done, Deggsy?'

Maybe he took that as a sign I was keen to have one done myself? Suddenly everyone in the group was interested in me. I couldn't back down now, and anyway, I could see it would give me some sort of status. Deggsy actually took me to the Tattoo parlour himself. It was gloomy inside, with spotlights trained on a chair that looked rather like a dentist's chair. There was a box of latex gloves on a small table, alongside a number of pattern books. I flicked through them half-heartedly.

'How much?'

I was shocked to learn the price of putting ink under people's skin with the vicious-looking needles. 'I'll have to...to see if I can get it...'

The tattooist, to give him his due, was charming, and gave me as much time as I wanted to look through the pattern books. He even let me watch another client lying still and apparently unconcerned while he drilled into the delicate skin of her back. I started to feel sick, but the sweet little rosebuds in the pattern book were very pretty, and I said I would have the same, when I could afford it.

Parting with the camera I'd been given as a special birthday present was a wrench, but the others kept asking when I was having it done, so on the day of the appointment my head was all over the place. Somehow I allowed myself to switch from a rosebud to something very different and far more provocative. It didn't even feel like my choice, to be honest, but I was on a high when I unveiled it to the crowd at the rec the following week, when it was starting to heal and I'd been able to take off the protecting cling film. I'd never smoked, never even seen, a cannabis leaf in real life at that time, although there were colourful images sprayed on the walls and the lock-up garages round Sami's house.

Jenny 2

I'd known about Sami, of course. That was how she had got kicked out of school, the idiot. I had seen her a few times, pupils dilated, expression totally spaced out, but I'd never been tempted to try it myself. The tattoo, though! That seemed to open the way for a new, more daring Lizzie. First of all, though, I had to work out how to come clean about the tattoo.

On the day I decided to tell her, Mum seemed to be in an unusually good mood.

'Hello, Love. Had a good day?'

'Not bad.' I was trying to think how best to phrase it. 'Er... Mum?'

Then it all came out: my new 'friends', the fact that I was still sometimes seeing Sami, the visit to the tattoo parlour, the sale of the precious camera, and finally...

Mum clapped her hand to her mouth and her eyes nearly burst out of their sockets. If it hadn't taken her breath away I swear she would have been screaming loud enough for the whole street to hear.

There was a silence, broken only by my poor brother. Miles strolled in, fresh from a game of tennis, to an atmosphere taut as his racquet strings.

'What?' he said, looking from me to Mum and back again.

'Did you know about this?'

'Er...' Miles clearly wasn't too sure what the right answer would be. I had, of course, sworn him to secrecy.

'Don't start on him, Mum.' I didn't see why he should get into trouble for my actions. 'It was my decision. Just relax. It's cool.'

Cool was not how Dad saw it when he finally returned from work that evening. Miles had retreated to the safety of his own room, but I bet even there he could feel the vibes coming from downstairs.

Jenny 2

'This is it. The final straw! Where does it go next? Don't think you are leaving this house again young lady....ever! And you will be in school on Monday, in your correct uniform, if I have to march you there and march you back again.'

I wanted to laugh at the inconsistency of being given two mutually exclusive orders, as I sat and let the tide wash over me. It was not as if it was the first time I'd incurred the wrath of my parents. I wondered what they would they come up with this time?

What they came up with was yet another attempt to change a parenting style that clearly wasn't working. They decided that, if they could keep me at home and with them, then there was less chance I would be influenced by the undesirable types I was spending the summer with.

So, hilariously, I was offered my favourite food – so long as I ate it in their company; new clothes, which I was at liberty to choose myself, so long as they were bought in the company of one or other of my parents; and, really, anything else I wanted, so long as it didn't involve leaving the house.

There was a day we were all sitting, sighing and pretending we were just being a family, while I was screaming inside, so I just asked. I don't think they were expecting it.

'What I really want, more than anything, is a pet, something small and furry that could live in my room.'

I watched as Mum swallowed hard. She has such an expressive face.

'You know,' she said, after several more swallows, 'I've often wondered about that.'

I could see what she was thinking: having a pet in my room might be a way of keeping me there.

Jenny 2

'Do you remember, when you were little, you know, when you were being home educated, and we used to go to the petting zoo...'

For a millisecond I was back there with a happy memory. Then it was gone. This being pandered to was worse than always being in the wrong.

Mum sighed and Dad took up the baton.

'How would you like it if we had a trip to the pet shop tomorrow?'

The next day was a Saturday, so he couldn't use work as an excuse, not that that always stopped him from working at home.

Hannah

Of course, we should have realised much sooner. The problems were serious and we were trying to either ignore them or paper over the cracks. I know now that she was unhappy, so unhappy. And we were just, kind of, caught up in our own problems: Jono's work, mine, the boys.... But we should have seen it, all the same. That awful business with the teaching assistant, taping her to the chair, and then we thought we'd solved the problem by taking her out of school, but really all we did was shelve it, store up trouble for the future.

And then, after she'd been at the senior school for a while, she started to change. She was still quiet, but she became almost secretive. I blamed her little friend, Samantha – Sami - but it was at least as much my fault.

Jono didn't seem to feel the same level of responsibility at the time. Of course, he was so wrapped up in work – things went well, and then they didn't. He became rather withdrawn when they lost a big order, and he suspected some underhand dealings amongst his competitors. All the time I just felt I was left to cope on my own, and I was inadequate for the task.

Jenny 2

Elizabeth had been my baby, so pretty, with her big blue eyes and blond curls; by the time she was fifteen her hair had been every colour imaginable, so long as it wasn't natural. Shaved up the sides: awful. I was ashamed to be seen with her.

And the piercings. Of course, Jono blamed me for letting her have her ears pierced in the first place, but I just thought she would feel better if she could be more like the others. She had always said she felt different. She'd be eleven or twelve, maybe. But then, within a few years she had piercings all round her ears, her nose - even her tongue! It made me shudder every time she opened her mouth.

Someone said she was experimenting, trying to find out who she was, but I thought she was trying to show who she wasn't: that she wasn't part of our family, that she didn't belong, didn't see herself as our daughter...

We didn't understand her, that's for sure, not even when she was six years old. She must have been so unhappy, and we did nothing to help her. We thought we were doing the right thing by removing her from the school where she was so miserable, but then we nearly drove ourselves mad trying to educate her at home. And after all that we sent her to another school where she was twice as unhappy.

She hated that school. She hated the system: why did she have to wear a tie like a boy? What did it matter if her socks were the wrong colour? She couldn't understand the need for rules, yet at the same time I think, paradoxically, that she was trying to conform, to be the good girl.

Then one day, it seemed, just like that, she became someone different. It was as though she gave up trying - or maybe she decided it was time to fight against the system. From then on she was always in trouble over the piercings and the hair colour...always being excluded for days at a time.

Jenny 2

I used to dread the ringing of the telephone during the school day. If I went out I came home to the little flashing light. I knew who the message would be from.

'Mrs. Brown? I'm afraid we've had another incident in school today. Elizabeth is in isolation. Would you please come and collect her? I think we should make an appointment for another meeting.'

Of course Elizabeth's view of her misdemeanours was always the same.

'I wasn't being rude to Miss Briggs, but if you don't stand up for yourself in this world you just get trampled on.'

'Elizabeth, Miss Briggs is your teacher. She has a perfect right to reprimand you for your behaviour in her classroom.' I was trying to make my voice sound calm.

'She has no right to belittle me and make me feel stupid…'

'No, but that doesn't give you the right to be rude to her.'

It was always someone else's fault, according to Elizabeth, and maybe she had a point, sometimes.

At the time I felt sure the incident with the test tubes was down to a teacher being unclear in her instructions. Jono and I had both been out of town, and when we got back, there was Elizabeth with her feet up and her arm bandaged.

'Seven stitches!' She sounded almost triumphant. 'The Doctor in A & E said it was a very nasty cut - he'd never seen anything like it.'

Of course, when I went steaming up to the school, it appeared that their version of events didn't quite match Elizabeth's. At the time I wasn't sure who to believe.

Theo was in the Sixth Form by then. He alternated between defending Elizabeth against our so-called 'unreasonable expectations' and feeling exasperated by her

Jenny 2

himself. He'd even been against her attending the same school as him in the beginning. It would be embarrassing for him to have her in the same school. Couldn't we send her somewhere else? Please?

I became impatient with him at that point.

'Theo, please...you've got to understand...poor Elizabeth...'

'For goodness' sake, Mum, stop waving your arms about like a helpless beetle! Try to hear it from my point of view for once.'

Then he stormed off up to his room without giving me a chance. Elizabeth and her problems were unsettling the whole family.

As a school prefect, though, he did keep a discreet eye on her, but said she really didn't help herself. What she saw as interesting modifications to her uniform made her stand out from the crowd - and not in a good way. They also brought her into ever-increasing conflict with authority. It was a school which set a lot of store by rules and regulations, and we had thought it would be a good thing for Elizabeth, but he disagreed: this was another reason why it was completely unsuitable for Elizabeth.

We came round to his way of thinking after a bit, when it was too late. I think he knew about the tattoo before we did, but he never let on.

Jono and I had endless 'what shall we do about Elizabeth - sorry Lizzie' - conversations.

'You know, I sometimes wonder if we've been too hard on her,' Jono was already reaching for the wine bottle and looked a bit taken aback to find it was already empty.

'I'll get another one.'

I trod the well-worn path to the temperature-controlled wine cabinet.

'I can't believe you've just said that, you know,' I called, as I struggled with the cork.

Jenny 2

'Said what?'

He appeared at my shoulder and took over the corkscrew. The cork slid out with a satisfying retort.

'That we're not soft enough!'

'Well, you have to admit,' he said, tilting the bottle expertly to refill our glasses, 'All the sanctions and rules and talkings-to aren't exactly having an effect, are they? Don't you remember what Dr. What's-her-name said?'

He sank into the new plush sofa and contemplated the colour of the wine as it swirled around the glass. 'You know...that psychologist woman we took her to see?'

I laughed at that, although there was nothing funny about it.

'Which one? There were so many!'

'Oh, one of the early ones. Maybe even the first one. You know, she had a separate annexe where she saw clients.'

'Not sure. What did she say, anyway?'

'That she thought Elizabeth - Lizzie - didn't feel loved within the family.'

'As opposed to the other one, who said what she needed was firm handling and a strong sense of boundaries?'

There was silence for a while. I thought that maybe it was true. Maybe she didn't know we loved her. I said aloud,

'I haven't always been very loving, have I?'

'Well, it's hard for you, isn't it? You're the one who has to get them all organised and keep them in order, as well as all the practical things involved in running the home...'

I was staring at him. That must have been the first time he'd acknowledged how difficult I found it.

'I do realise, Love. Not that it's any picnic for me either, of course, going into that place day after day.'

Jenny 2

He had been very crushed by seeing his hopes of early success dashed, and couldn't fathom the attitude of some of his management colleagues, people he had appointed and promoted, yet who seemed dismissive of him. I could see how it must have felt for him to leave all that behind at the end of the day, and then walk into some sort of war scenario the moment he put his key in the lock, but I wondered how far he really saw it from my point of view.

'And just at the moment when I've had it up to here with them - well, let's face it, usually with Elizabeth - I am desperate for you to get home and give me some support…You get home later and later…' I didn't use the phrase 'letting me down' but I expect my face said it anyway.

The 'what shall we do about Elizabeth - sorry Lizzie' conversations had a habit of turning up other areas of dissatisfaction in our family life.

Chapter Fourteen

Lizzie – Hannah

Lizzie

The first time I ran away I didn't get very far. I hadn't really planned it, so I only had a few things with me, and they were the wrong things. I took my leather jacket 'cos I loved it. It was really special. Dad had bought it for me one day when they said they were pleased with me; pleased with me for trying to be like them, to conform. I'd been trying to do that my whole life - didn't they know? Just, somehow, I'd never managed it. It was like I was made differently from the rest of the family. Sometimes I wondered if there was a big secret they hadn't told me. Was I really adopted? When I was younger I used to daydream a lot. My favourite one was that they found me, a tiny bundle on their doorstep, and that one day I'd be restored to my real family, where I'd be loved just as I was, just for being me. I grew out of that one pretty quickly.

Anyway, the jacket soon got scratched and stained, 'cos I didn't have anything else to lie on, and then it got nicked, so that was that. I didn't have the right shoes, either. They hurt my feet, but I had to keep walking because what else do you do all day when you've nowhere to go? I had some biscuits and crisps – grabbed them out the cupboard as I left. The biscuits didn't last long, and then I felt sick, and the crisps were in my pocket, so they went when the jacket went. What I really wanted was some of Mum's homemade soup – thick and wholesome. When I finally dropped off for a few minutes at a time I dreamed about the soup. I could even smell it.

It was scary, too, after dark. Everyone looked menacing and bigger than they do during the day. The

Jenny 2

second night some people started yelling at me, and I was scared, so I ran off, and then I hid round the back of Sainsbury's, where the big bins are. That was all right until they closed, and the staff came and tipped stuff into the bins, and then the whole area came alive – swarming with all sorts, scrabbling about in the bins, climbing in there, some of them. They were like human rats.

There was this one guy, I'd say he was about twenty-something. He wasn't grabbing stuff and pushing it in his mouth like some of them. No, he was kind of methodical, reading the labels and then putting the food he liked the look of into bags he'd brought with him. It was like he was going shopping, only he wasn't paying at the checkout. He came across to talk to me.

'It's terrible the way these big supermarkets waste food, don't you agree?' he said, as though we'd met at a party or something. I didn't say anything, so he went on. 'Look at all this – tomorrow is the best before date, but it's all perfectly good to eat. The sandwiches aren't even stale, and these tomatoes – they're a bit wrinkled, maybe, but someone could cook with them.' He carried on going through the bin nearest me. I suddenly remembered that I was starving hungry. Mum shops at Sainsbury's. It made me feel homesick as well as hungry.

'Here, you look hungry,' he said, holding out a packet of sandwiches. It was as though he could read my mind. 'Go on – they're perfectly safe.'

'What're you going to do with the rest?' I asked, between mouthfuls. It was cheese and tomato. Fabulous!

'There's a homeless persons' shelter down the road. We recycle what the supermarkets don't want.... there's usually enough for an evening meal. Look at that!'

He broke off as he uncovered a packet of sausages and what looked like a whole stack of ready meals. My stomach rumbled.

Jenny 2

'Who goes to this shelter?'

'Anyone who doesn't have a bed for the night - while we have beds available, of course. There isn't room for everyone. But we can feed all the people who come to us. There'll be hot soup tonight....'

'Which way did you say it is?'

He smiled, a really nice, warm smile. He didn't even seem to notice that I was all grimy and my hair in knots. 'It's this way. Come on, I'll show you; I've got as much as I can carry for the moment.'

I had a sudden thought. 'Isn't it stealing?' I remembered Sami and the mascara, and how bad I'd felt.

'Well, they've thrown it away - we didn't take it out of the shop, did we? Anyway, if you ask me, some of these big corporations with their obscene profits – they're the ones who are stealing, stealing from the poor.'

I was jogging along, trying to keep up with him. The sandwich I'd eaten was forming hard little knots in my stomach, and I felt desperate for a drink - tea, coffee, water, anything. I tried to remember my last cup of tea, and I thought it was probably the one just before the massive row, just before I stormed out with nothing but my clothes and some biscuits and crisps – oh, and my copy of Henry V. That's a laugh. I'll bet Mrs. Daniels would be dead impressed.

We stopped outside a dowdy little redbrick building. It looked like some sort of warehouse. I'd have been scared to go in there on my own, but Gary – he'd told me that was his name at some point – ushered me in. We went through a sort of lobby, with a reception desk, only not like they have in the posh hotels Mum and Dad used to take us to. This was a sort of scruffy office, with a sliding glass window.

'All right, Gary?' the man behind the window called. 'You got a good haul tonight?'

Gary lifted the bags up a bit so the man could see.

'And who's this young lady?'

Jenny 2

'Oh she hasn't told me her name yet, but I expect she will when she's got some food inside her.' He smiled at me again. They were so smiley, these people. Perhaps it was all that doing good they went around doing.

A woman came round the corner. She was on the plump side, comfortable looking, and yes, she smiled at me too. 'You're in luck, we've one bed left for tonight. You come with me, dear, and tell me your troubles.'

She drew me along a corridor and up some stairs. It was dingy, but someone had tried to cheer it up with some posters, and there were children's drawings on some of the doors. We stopped at one of the doors on the upper floor.

'Now, dear, would you like a nice warm shower?'

For some reason I was nearly crying when she said that. Then I remembered something else I should have brought with me, besides Henry V.

'I don't have any shower gel, or a towel or anything...'

She smiled yet again. 'That's all right sweetheart. We've got all those things here for you. Don't worry,' she added, mistaking my expression. 'The towel's perfectly clean.'

That night I slept better than I usually sleep at home. I drowned myself in sleep, and when I surfaced I had trouble working out where I was. Then I remembered, and I wondered what my Mum and Dad were doing, and whether Theo and Miles were getting it in the neck instead of me, and then I decided that probably wasn't going to happen.

I went downstairs - I'd slept in my clothes 'cos I didn't have anything else to put on, and nothing to brush my hair with, beyond my fingers, so it didn't exactly take me long. I hoped they were going to offer me breakfast, but when I got to the room where we'd eaten the night before, the smiling lady - Jan, she was called - looked a bit less smiley, more sort of regretful. She put an arm round my shoulders.

Jenny 2

'Just come with me a minute, sweetheart,' she said, and led me towards the office near the front door. There was a big policeman standing there, in uniform, looking very official.

'It's all right, you're not in any sort of trouble,' Jan said, but I couldn't help feeling that I was. 'I'll tell you what, let's go into my office - round here, Officer. Now then…'

I think I sat down on the chair I was offered, and Jan and the policeman sat opposite me.

'My name is PC Meadows,' the policeman said, in a surprisingly gentle voice. 'Would you like to tell me your name?'

'Lizzie.'

'Is that short for Elizabeth?'

'Yes.' I was mostly looking at the floor by now, so I couldn't see if he was smiling or not.

'We've had a missing person report - an Elizabeth Brown. She fits your description.'

'What, they bothered to tell you I'm missing? I thought they'd be glad to be rid of me.'

'Let me tell you: your Mum and Dad are in a dreadful state. They've been all over the place looking for you, and when you didn't come home on Tuesday night, they rang us. As you are a minor, we didn't have to wait for you to be gone twenty-four hours before starting to look for you.'

There was a bit of a pause while I tried to take it in.

'I've got a police car waiting outside. Would you like a ride in it and I'll run you back home?'

I started crying then, although I wasn't sure why.

Hannah

Jono was pacing backwards and forwards, in a sort of agitated figure of eight shape, listening to whoever was on the other end of the phone. Miles was staring at the carpet,

Jenny 2

as though he expected to see a groove appear any minute. I was just sitting in a heap at the other side of the room, sniffing and tying my fingers in knots.

'Yes! Yes, it is,' Jono said at last. Evidently he had finally got through to someone at the police station who was willing to talk to him. 'Yes, I understand. Yes....What? They have? When?'

There was more pacing. 'Hello, yes, I'm still here. Yes. Now? Yes, we're at the house – we're not going anywhere. You will? Right. Thank you.'

'So?'

'They've got her. They're bringing her home.'

'Oh, Jono...I never want to go through that again....How is she? Where was she? Is she all right?'

He raised both hands to fend off the questions he couldn't answer. 'I don't know. They didn't say. Just that they've got her safe and they'll be here with her soon.'

'Are you sure she didn't say anything to you, Miles, anything at all?'

I shouldn't have interrogated Miles like that; I imagine he knew, or at least suspected, a great deal more about his sister than we did, but didn't consider it prudent to say anything.

'Leave it.'

Jono had stopped pacing, all his nervous energy suddenly dissipated. He sank into a chair.

'D'you know what I keep thinking about? I keep remembering that night when she was born and almost died.' He gave a cry, almost a howl, burying his face in his hands. 'Her whole life so far has been a constant repetition of that time: anxiety, followed by relief, followed by further anxiety. I am so weary of it. Will it never end?'

Chapter Fifteen

Rachel - Hannah – Lizzie

Rachel

I considered that the professional manner I'd cultivated at work meant I remained calm in most circumstances, but that day it deserted me. Eyes flashing, I stalked the length of the corridor from my classroom to the Head of Year's office, opening the door without knocking and almost fell into the room. Barry was at his desk, calmly staring at his computer screen.

'Do you mind telling me…' I began, but Barry raised his hand to silence me.

'One moment.'

He continued to attend to something on his screen. I could have sworn he was doing it to annoy me.

'Now,' he said at last, an insincere smile adorning his smarmy features. 'What can I do for you Rachel?'

'Why has Lizzie Brown been put in Headteacher's detention?'

He opened his mouth to speak, but I couldn't wait for whatever garbage was going to come out.

'You knew I had a plan! You knew I'd been working on it with her parents! We agreed - you agreed - that a co-ordinated plan, after school, helping her to catch up, boosting her self-esteem, keeping her out of harm's way…' Then I ran out of words and just flapped my hands, helplessly. 'It was agreed.'

He sat there looking at me, so I took a breath and added, 'Instead of endless punishments, she would be given the chance to make good…'

He waited a bit longer to make sure I'd really stopped, and then said, 'I think, Rachel, if you're honest, you'll find that the agreeing was all on your side.' He swivelled round in his chair and leaned forward to face me full on.

'Anyway, what happened today really wasn't something we could turn a blind eye to.'

Of course, I knew there were things Lizzie got up to that should have been reported, that would have been reported were it any other student, but I could also see, as clearly as daylight, that endless punishment only had a negative effect on her. I waited. What had she done now that was so terrible?

'Did you know about the rat?' There was no attempt to smile now, sincerely or otherwise.

'The, er, rat?'

I had known about the pet rat, of course. Lizzie had told me excitedly about the family trip to the pet shop, during one of their phases of attempting to draw her back into the fold of the family. I had heard how she looked listlessly at the scampering gerbils, the white mice, the fluffy rabbits, and declared herself uninterested in any of them. The one creature that attracted her attention was a solitary rat, in a cage which looked far too small. I guessed she had developed a sort of fellow-feeling for it, and so she asked tentatively whether she could have that. Her brothers, to be fair to them, had been quite impressed by her choice, but her mother had squealed in horror, and her father had wrinkled his nose, as if there was a bad smell in the room, which, to be fair, there probably was.

At this, Lizzie had grown stubborn, and said it was the rat or nothing. So it was nothing, and the family returned in silence from their pet shop expedition, with only feelings of dissatisfaction all round to show for their trip.

When she talked about it, Lizzie had been really down, and it weighed on my mind so much that, in my dreams of Jenny that night, my daughter appeared before me, immaculately dressed in Hillmore High School uniform and carrying a large and spectacular talking rat.

It must have been still present in my mind next morning, for I found myself setting rat-related homework all day: imagine you are one of the rats in The Pied Piper of Hamelin: describe your impressions of the Piper. Write discursively on the subject: should rats be used in laboratory experiments? I gave Year 8 a 'writing to instruct' exercise on the proper care of pet rats, and even my Sixth Form groups found themselves drawn into an exercise in descriptive writing which featured rats.

That afternoon, when Lizzie appeared at my classroom door for her regular after-school report-signing, she'd looked much brighter than I'd expected.

'What sort of a day have you had today, Lizzie?' I asked, my tone carefully neutral.

'Pretty good, Miss. I've only had three demerits, and that was only for talking when I shouldn't! Oh, and another one for forgetting to do my maths homework. Can you keep a secret, Miss?'

'It depends. You know there are some secrets I'm not allowed to keep...'

'Oh, it's nothing like that, Miss. Nothing dodgy or anything. You know I told you about how my parents took us to the pet shop and said I could have anything I wanted? And then when I found the most adorable little rat, they wouldn't let me have it? Well, one of my friends owed me some money for...well he owed me some money, and he gave it to me at school today. There's enough for the rat *and* the cage, and probably a little treadmill wheel thing as well! I'm so excited.'

'But I thought you said your parents wouldn't let you have a rat?'

'*They* wouldn't buy me a rat, no...but now I can buy it for myself!'

Jenny 2

'Don't you think they might notice if you go home with a rat in a cage?'

'They won't be home till later. I'll have plenty of time to set it all up in my room.'

'In your room?' Despite my best intentions, I did shudder at that. 'I'm not sure that will be awfully...hygienic.'

She looked disappointed. 'I didn't think you'd be prejudiced like all the others, Miss. They're really clean animals. The pet shop man said they make really good pets...'

I had to wrench myself back to what the Head of Year was saying.

'I know your intentions are good, Rachel, noble, even, although I can't help feeling you're wasting your time with that one. But even you would have to agree that bringing in a verminous creature and setting it free in double French deserves a Headteacher's detention. Her actions have to be seen to have consequences. She is absolutely on her last warning. To be honest, without you championing her, she'd have been permanently excluded long ago.'

I was still trying to work out what had happened.

'How? I mean, didn't anyone notice? A rat in a cage is hardly inconspicuous, is it?'

'That's just it. The rat wasn't in a cage. She was wearing it!'

'What?'

'It was somewhere about her rather unhygienic person - under her jumper, or lurking in all that tangled hair of hers, I shouldn't wonder.'

I wanted to smile, but supressed it as best I could. I really wasn't sure how Lizzie had managed to get away for so long with what appeared to be incipient dreadlocks, but now that I thought about it, I began to wonder how long the rat – Rory, his name was - had been accompanying my wayward student to school. It might account for the peculiar smell. I couldn't imagine, though, that she had released her pet deliberately into the midst of her unsympathetic classmates.

'It's no laughing matter, Rachel,' Barry was saying. 'It caused uproar in Miss Chappell's lesson; one girl was bitten, and two fell off their chairs and sustained serious bruising.'

'Where is the rat now?'

Barry made a face of disgust. 'In the nearest sewer, probably. That is, if the poison outside the languages block hasn't put an end to it.'

'Poor Lizzie,' I thought. 'She'll be heartbroken.'

Hannah

I was speechless when I found out. Shocked at what they said Elizabeth had done and angry at the Head of Year's judgemental stance. I was not going to take that lying down. Afterwards, I realised that my indignation was probably a bit misplaced. It was only later, also, that I realised the absurdity of telling them that I would fight for my daughter's right to stay at a school where she had made so much progress. The Head of Year said, a bit sourly,

'If you'll forgive me, Mrs. Brown, progress, in Lizzie's case, is a relative term.'

What worried me most was that I had no idea what would happen if Lizzie were to be permanently excluded, but it surely couldn't be good. I'd arrived at the school alone, just like all the other times: Jono, unfortunately, had to be elsewhere that day. Mrs. Lucas, the year 11 office administrator, ushered me tersely into Mr. Watkin's office, and a few minutes later Mrs. Daniels joined me, leading Elizabeth, who looked even less pleased to be there than I was. Mrs. Daniels came and sat beside me, exuding

Jenny 2

reassurance and sympathy, or what passed for it. Elizabeth chose the seat farthest away from both of us. Mr. Watkins arrived a few moments later, and the meeting began.

'I'm sorry we have to meet again so soon after the previous incident,' he said as he shook my hand. 'I'll come straight to the point, Mrs. Brown. 'Young Lizzie here is on borrowed time as far as Hillmore High School is concerned. If it were not for Mrs. Daniels here, her form tutor, I think she would have been out on her ear long ago. I'm sorry to be so blunt, but there it is.'

There was an awkward silence. There didn't seem much to say after that.

Mrs. Daniels leapt in to fill the gap.

'Lizzie made a good start here, I believe. That was before I came, of course. When I started teaching her, she seemed interested in English, and so I tried to encourage her as much as possible. Then, when she came into my tutor group, and I had pastoral responsibility for her, I began to understand how unhappy she has been throughout her school experience.'

Lizzie was staring fixedly at the floor, her mouth twitching a little as her teacher spoke.

'After a little while problems began to emerge. I don't think Lizzie likes school uniform very much.' This was said with a smile, but if she expected the rest of us to join in, she was disappointed. 'That has been one problem area. Lizzie has been excluded from class whenever she has been incorrectly dressed - as indeed are any students in the same situation. This has meant that she finds it difficult to keep up with her homework.'

The woman paused, long enough for Mr. Watkins to have his say.

'Lizzie doesn't like school uniform, as Mrs. Daniels so rightly says. She also doesn't like school rules very much. In fact, she doesn't like *being* in school very much.'

Jenny 2

He glanced in Lizzie's direction, and she let out a sigh. She managed to make it sound insolent.

'We never encouraged her truanting.' Why did I say that? It made me sound weak and pathetic. If only Jono had been here to fight back on our behalf. He's so much better at this sort of thing than I am.

'And she has been punished, both by the school and at home, on every occasion.'

That probably made it sound even worse.

'And at every readmission interview she has been warned that she cannot continue like this indefinitely,' the Head of Year intoned, giving the impression of an infinitely patient man who was about to lose his patience. 'If it weren't for the efforts of Mrs. Daniels here...

He left the rest unsaid. Was I supposed to be grateful to her?

Then he turned towards Lizzie.

'Well? What do you have to say for yourself?'

After hesitating for a few moments', Elizabeth – Lizzie - raised her eyes from the carpet. I think we could all see the tears; then they were gone. She tilted her chin.

'I'm not sure you're really interested in knowing what I think, but here it is anyway. I think school uniform is stupid; I think most of the rules in this school are only there to humiliate the students; I think I would learn more if some of the teachers spent more time teaching and less time worrying about my hairstyle and my indoor shoes.'

Then she glanced at Mrs. Daniels and muttered, 'Not you, Miss.'

'Lizzie, even you are not so stupid that you think bringing a rat into school is acceptable?' Mr. Watkins was clearly losing all patience now.

'Is there a rule against it then? Do tell me! There's a rule against everything else.'

'Lizzie, you're not helping yourself...' Mrs. Daniels began, but Lizzie rose from her chair in a rush so that it tilted,

145

Jenny 2

and I watched as it hovered on one leg for a long moment before crashing to the ground. By the time order had been restored, Lizzie was gone, and I was desperately holding back the tears.

'Another temporary exclusion, I'm afraid, Mrs. Brown, while we decide on the best long-term plan for Lizzie. Now do excuse me,' Mr. Watkins added, looking at his watch. 'I have a Year Assembly to take,' and with that he was gone, leaving Mrs. Daniels and me looking at each other, stunned.

'Come on,' she muttered. 'I'll take you to the staff room and make us some coffee.'

Lizzie

The second time I ran away I managed to stay away for a bit longer. Sami hid me in her house. It didn't take much hiding, to be honest. Her Mum never knew what time of day it was, she was usually so far gone, and there were people in and out of that house all the time.

To be honest, I didn't like it much. It wasn't very clean, and some of the people who hung around were pretty scary. But still, it was better than being in my spotless house with the fitted kitchen and massive fridge that dispensed ice cubes, and the poisonous atmosphere that crushed me and kept reminding me what a failure I was.

There was a point, somewhere between Year 9 and Year 10 when I just gave up. I gave up trying to be the perfect child they wanted. I gave up trying to please everyone. I gave up caring that I was clumsy and awkward. I decided just to be myself. By the time I was in my last year at school I didn't care who knew it, either.

Of course, the problem was even I didn't know who I was, not really. So I tried being like Sami. She was great: no-one could put her down. She stood up for herself, and

Jenny 2

she stood up for me as well, until I started to do it for myself. Even after she was excluded from school, she was there for me. I didn't tell my parents I was still seeing her; they wouldn't have approved. I used to go round there when they thought I was at some after-school club or something, and sometimes I went round when I should have been at school. She was cool with me staying that time, but then we had a row about something or other – I can't remember now, and I went home. I actually went home of my own accord.

The weird thing was, they hardly batted an eyelid. They acted as though I'd just been out to the shops or something. My place was laid at the table, and I just sort of slotted back in, sat down, ate the meal, said thank you out of habit, and went up to my room. It was good to get out of the clothes I'd been wearing more or less non-stop for a couple of weeks; good - better than good – to soak in a bath so full of hot water that it overflowed, and I got into trouble afterwards for making the bathroom all wet. It almost felt good, being told off for making a mess; it was a familiar pattern; I knew where I was with that.

I was even glad to be going back to school, believe it or not. I'd missed Mrs. Daniels. I liked her lessons, and besides, she was the only one who ever stuck up for me. She treated me with respect, if that doesn't sound too odd. I know we were supposed to be respectful towards them, even if they treated us like dirt - and some of them did, or was that only me? I felt they should have to earn our respect, but that idea didn't go down too well.

Mrs. Daniels was different, though. It was as if she could see something, or somebody, in me that I couldn't see myself. I didn't need to challenge her all the time, like I did with the others. She even listened to me...

But, somehow, by the time I got to Year 11, I knew I'd missed the boat. I was never going to get the GCSEs, not at a level that would have satisfied my Mum and Dad, anyway. I'd missed too much. It was too late... Sometimes I really wished I could go back to the beginning and start all over again...

I was angry all the time, too, especially after I lost Rory. I kept thinking about him out there, lost and frightened. It was all right for Mr. Watkins to say he'd probably end up in the sewer, but he was a pet rat; he wouldn't have any idea of how to survive without me. He would be all alone and frightened, and I'll bet the others, the wild rats, would pick on him.

He was quite a nervous little thing; sometimes, when I held him, I could feel him trembling, and he would burrow under my hair until he was against my shoulder or my neck. It felt so warm and...sort of safe, as though he was looking after me. After a bit it got so I could walk around, and he would just hold on. Half the time I forgot that he was there. I think that was partly what happened that day, that, and wanting to have him with me, to make me feel safe and kind of - it sounds daft – but loved. I think he did love me, in his little ratty way. And then I let him down. He was really frightened in school, and I did nothing to protect him. He only bit those silly squealing girls because he was frightened of them, but I didn't go after him when he ran away. I let my baby go...

That's when I knew I couldn't take any more of it: the being on report, the exclusions and readmission interviews, my parents and their eternal disappointment. And then the whole thing escalated. Suddenly I wasn't just a problem at school, and at home, but I was a threat to society at large. They called in the social workers!

It broke my heart, what happened to Rory. I'd found him so easy to talk to, easier than any other member of my family. I used to tell him that as I refilled his water bottle every evening. Mum and Dad didn't suspect a thing, and I knew Mum wouldn't come into my room: she called it a 'no-go' zone. My brothers had started to be a bit kinder, and when Theo found out what the squeaking and scratching

Jenny 2

noises were that were coming from my bedroom at night, he agreed to keep it secret, and things would have stayed like that if it hadn't been for the phone call from Mr. Watkins that evening. There was going to be yet another meeting the following morning.

I refused to come out of my room; I wasn't hungry, and I certainly didn't want to talk to anyone. Mum said she wanted to talk to me, but I'd pushed the chest of drawers against the door, so no chance.

I just sat there all night, facing an empty cage. I thought my heart would break.

Chapter Sixteen

Lizzie – Jonathan - Rachel - Hannah

Lizzie

The case conference took place the following Thursday. They were all there: Mr. Watkins, looking moody; Mrs. Daniels, looking as though she didn't want any part of it; the Education Welfare Officer, who had never so far shown any interest in either my education or my welfare; the man from the local authority education department; two social workers, a fat one and a skinny one; and *both* my parents. That's when I knew it was really serious: my Dad had taken a day off work.

Jonathan Brown

I pushed open the door of the room I'd been directed to, knowing I was already late. They all looked up as I entered and gave my apologies. I'd been sitting in my office for an hour, the papers on my desk unread, images of Lizzie crowding in. She'd been little Elizabeth once, my longed-for daughter, and I ached to have back that time when I'd held her in my arms, all warm and safe, her blue eyes gazing trustingly up at me.

    The labour had been long and difficult and yet I had remained calm at a time when men are generally held to be useless. Even during that terrible time immediately after the birth, when it had been far more touch and go than I'd

Jenny 2

admitted to Hannah, I was calm, but then I covered myself with embarrassment by fainting when the worst was over. I realise now that I've been steadily letting Hannah down more and more ever since. I wish I'd been able to be the strong and supportive partner she deserved.

My failures were all around me: my career, which might have looked fine from the outside, but I knew I would never now reach the status of a captain of industry I'd aspired to; my image of myself as the father of sons who would see the wisdom of my advice rather than casually disregarding it... Today I realised I could no longer use work as an excuse to avoid facing up to my own uselessness.

I could see Hannah, the teachers from the school, various other professionals: but where was Lizzie? At the far end of a long table a cropped-headed figure slowly looked up and met my gaze. She looked so tiny. And what had happened to her hair? I only knew who it was because she was seated next to Hannah. Feeling self-conscious I took the vacant seat on the other side of her. The man from the Local Authority immediately introduced himself and explained the purpose of the meeting, and then it proceeded. I hadn't really known what to expect; truth to tell I was still feeling stunned that my family – my family! – had become clients of social services. The social workers for their part also seemed a little surprised that they were being asked to take on a teenager who had two married parents living at the same address.

The Local Authority man explained that this was not a tribunal, they were not looking for anyone to blame for anything, and that the aim was to find the best way forward to help Elizabeth. He glanced at his notes and addressed her directly.

'You prefer to be called Lizzie, I believe? Well what we want to do, Lizzie, is to help you find your way back to your family and your education.'

Jenny 2

Each of the professionals around the table spoke in turn about the problem as they saw it, the male teacher, the Head of Year, barely concealing his dislike of her. The social workers were fairly neutral in their comments, and her form tutor, the rather crazy Mrs. Daniels, spoke up for her quite forcefully. She gave the impression of really caring about her.

Throughout it all Lizzie sat with her head in her hands. I was glad to see the dreadlocks gone, but wished she hadn't cropped her hair quite so short. Hannah sat on the other side, tense and upright, and when asked what she saw as the problem, spoke in broken sentences with long pauses, quite unlike her. My heart ached as I realised how much I had left her to bear alone. I wanted to reach out, squeeze her hand, whisper that I would be there for her from now on, but Lizzie was between us, and I couldn't.

At the end of the meeting the Local Authority man summed up briefly and promised a report within the next ten days.

Rachel

I'm not really sure I did the right thing. I asked if I could take Lizzie back to school with me, and I whisked her away from her parents. I should have left her with them, shouldn't I? Then they might have talked, properly. Everything was out in the open now – the drug use, the seedy people she was involved with, the petty theft... Lizzie no longer had anything to hide. She could have talked to her parents properly. It was obvious - or it's obvious to me now, looking back - that they really cared about her. They loved her. Just like I loved Jenny; only Jenny was starting to fade a bit: Lizzie was taking her place. Or perhaps they were just melting into one.

After school I went round to the house. It was a beautiful house in a 'desirable' part of town, set well back from the road. It matched my preconceptions of them.

Jenny 2

Walking up the drive I took some deep, slow breaths, like the breathing exercises we'd done on the voice care section of the teacher training course. I didn't want my voice to wobble when –

'Yes?'

It was Mrs. Brown who opened the door, even before I'd rung the bell. She must have been watching the front gate.

'Oh, it's you. Where's Lizzie?'

'Didn't she come home? After the bell went?'

'Obviously not.' The voice was cold. 'You'd better come in.'

I followed her along the hall – 'spacious' my obnoxious estate agent would have called it – and heard my own footsteps ringing on the expensive stone tiles. Apart from that, the house was silent.

I sat awkwardly in her kitchen while she made coffee. Neither of us spoke for a while. It was a vastly superior kitchen to mine, with the makings of a real family kitchen, only a bit too pristine, a bit too... unused. I thought of the life Jenny could have had in a home like that. If Dave and I hadn't split up, we might have had a house like theirs. I was drowning in a sense of what might have been, if only...

Of course, Jenny would have had all the advantages. I looked around, and I could see her, letting herself in through the front door, or maybe coming in through the back, straight into the kitchen, all warm and smelling of fresh baking.

'Mmm! Something smells good!' At sixteen she was slender, pretty, even in her school uniform. She dropped a kiss on my head, her silky hair slipping forward to embrace us both. Then with a laugh and a shake of the head, she

Jenny 2

seated herself at the breakfast bar, pulling out a pile of books.

Guess what?' She opened an exercise book, and, pointing to the bottom of the page, slid it across for me to see. 'Excellent work. Continue like this and there is no doubt about that A*. You would be well advised to continue to A Level, where I believe you will excel.'

Mrs. Brown seemed lost in her own thoughts too. Her movements were slow, and she spilt some of the coffee grounds as she scooped them into the cafetiere. While the coffee brewed, I asked her what she wanted to do about the fact that Lizzie hadn't come home after school. She was strangely offhand.

'Oh, that's nothing unusual. She usually turns up sooner or later.' I found myself thinking she could do with some breathing exercises too, to stop her voice being so croaky.

'Except when she doesn't,' she added, giving me a tight little smile.

She told me all about the times Jenny had run away from home. I could hardly bear to listen. I just kept wondering what they had done to drive her away. She was such a lovely girl, she had so much potential. *She* didn't say Jenny, of course – that was my mind going off on its own unhealthy course…

'I have been aware for some time of how unhappy she is.' My voice had reached something akin to a professional register by this time. 'And of course, as her form tutor, I have been able to give her lots of nurturing.'

Did I really say that? How pompous that sounds now.

'I've been able to take her under my wing, first of all during the Isolation sessions, and then later, when we put interventions in place.'

Jenny 2

The mother gave a stiff nod; she knew about that, of course. She'd been into school when we discussed her Plan, but somehow it seemed to have escaped her that I was so involved.

'It seems she's spent far more time with you over the past couple of years than she has with her own family – with her own mother anyway. No wonder she didn't want to come home when she was getting so much undivided attention from you.'

It was impossible to miss the bitterness in her tone, but I said the right things, I think, trying to speak as gently as I could.

'It's often easier for an outsider to relate to an adolescent than their own family. I've seen it time and time again.' Under my words, though, I could feel my own resentment bubbling up. I had given so much to Lizzie. I understood her: she had come between me and my sleep.

'I suppose it's easier for you,' she said. 'You can take an objective view - and walk away from it at the end of the day.'

Did she not know anything about how hard teachers work?

'I'm not sure it's quite like that. We spend a lot of time planning lessons, preparing material to suit all of our students... recognising that they have individual learning styles...I find I even dream about the students sometimes...especially the troubled ones.'

Suddenly her whole manner changed and she sort of crumpled. 'I had such hopes when Elizabeth - Lizzie, as she calls herself now - when she was born.'

She was looking in my direction, but she wasn't seeing me.

'We had the two boys already, and it seemed a dream when we had a little girl to complete the family. Family life is so busy - I really don't think teachers appreciate how hard it is to fit everything in.'

Jenny 2

I bristled at that.'

'My middle child, Miles, showed real promise in sports from very early on, and that meant a lot of ferrying him around, picking him up from practices, shopping for specialist equipment. And then he would need physio for some strain or pulled muscle...'

She locked eyes with me then, as if trying to be certain that I'd understood her difficulties. Then she went on in the same, strained vocal tones.

'Theo, the eldest, he was a dream child: model student, tidy by nature, loved school.'

She gave a wry little smile then.

'I think he found it a bit of an embarrassment when Elizabeth - Lizzie - started at Hillmore High School. Jonathan, my husband, was so proud of him. He'd been very academically successful before setting up the business – well, you probably know that. He thought - he assumed - that Theo would want to follow him, do a business degree, an MBA; but then he absolutely refused to take any advice....'

Her whole body sagged, and she looked weary beyond imagining. I did feel sorry for her, sort of. I risked placing a hand on her arm.

'Come on, we can look at this together. I'm here now. I'm on your side.' Even as I said it, though, I knew in my heart that what I really wanted to say was that I was on Lizzie's side.

Mrs. Brown moved jerkily away to pour the coffee.

'Milk? Sugar? No sugar?'

The ordinariness of it appeared to pull her back from the brink of total collapse. She placed the mug in front of me and sat down again, cradling her hands around her own. There was another silence.

'What will happen if they send her away to that, what was it? Referral unit? The social worker kept mentioning it...'

Jenny 2

'We must see that doesn't happen. I'm going to speak to the Head tomorrow morning. I will take personal responsibility...'

In a sudden burst of energy that seemed to come out of nowhere, she said,

'I sometimes think it's time *she* was the one taking responsibility. Or us, her parents...' She gave me a cold look. 'Not her teacher.'

'Well, yes, but of course you don't see her, how she is, in school.'

'The Unit might be better for her. They said it would be smaller, and without all the rules and pressures.'

'No, that's wrong. She's much better off where she is, in school, where I can keep an eye on her...'

She shook her head, slowly.

'She's never liked school, you know, not from the beginning. She had a tough time even as a five-year-old, and it just kept on getting worse, until we took her out of school altogether.'

'You took her out of school?'

'Yes, she was home-educated for a few years. At the time it seemed like the only solution, even though I had to give up work to be with her.'

I tried to imagine what it would be like to spend the days at home with my own child, instead of working with other people's in a classroom. I let out a sigh, but Mrs. Brown seemed to have forgotten I was there.

'She had a truly awful experience. There was a Teaching Assistant at the school, seemed to have it in for her. We only found out afterwards how much of a bully the woman was. People like her shouldn't be allowed...Anyway, there was an incident when this woman taped up her mouth because she said she was talking too much, and taped her to the chair to keep her still.'

I sat there, rigid. Surely this couldn't be happening? Surely she wasn't telling me that the wayward Lizzie and my

Jenny 2

little golden angel, my second Jenny, were one and the same? Now I was the one struggling for breath.

I left soon after that.

Lizzie

Down at the rec the others were listlessly kicking their legs against the broken slats of the seats. Sami was there for once, perched on one of the toddler swings, concentrating hard on rolling something in a large Rizla. A long thin boy - I didn't know his name, but he was all wrists and knee joints - was demonstrating his skills at keepy-uppy, while Deggsy was trying to get the ball off him.

'Clear off, Degs!' the boy yelped, batting at him ineffectually with one thin arm. I thought it was going to turn into a fight, but they stopped when they saw me. I must have been quite a sight, still in school uniform, all dishevelled, running, panting, crying.

'What the fuck's happened to you?' asked Deggsy. I think he was more curious than sympathetic. Deggsy and his sort don't do sympathy.

Sami called out without moving from her perch on the swing, 'Don't tell me - you've decided to join the drop-out no-hopers at last!'

I was completely out of breath and exhausted by everything that had happened that day. I dropped to the ground. Sami passed her spliff to another girl to hold, and came across to where I was still stretched out on the scrawny grass.

'Here, what's up?' She sounded a bit more sympathetic than Deggsy.

'Parents. I've had it with them.'

'Tell me about it!'

'And school. They're all out to get you.'

'Yeah, can't argue with that.'

Jenny 2

'What I don't get,' said Deggsy, coming across and squatting on the grass beside us, 'is that you've got two parents, and they both live together, in the same house. How posh is that? And they've got money!'

He didn't understand a thing. 'Money isn't everything. I'd sooner they loved me.'

Now I couldn't stop the tears. I watched as they fell on to the grass in front of me and slithered down the blades into the dark earth.

'Well, you know what? I've had it with them. They're not going to push me around any more. I'm not the daughter they want and I'm...I'm...' I had to stop then, looking for the right kind of language to express the rage I felt. This lot were so streetwise and I wanted suddenly to sound like one of them. 'I'm fucking well not going to try to be her.'

A cheer went up at that; I had obviously brightened up a very dull afternoon for them. Sami gestured to the girl she'd given her spliff to.

'Here y'are, Lizzie. Here's what'll make you feel better.'

Rachel

Once I'd got myself together again after the shock of discovering who Mrs. Brown was, I decided I'd better arrange to see her again, in a professional setting this time. Before I had time to do anything about it, though, I had a formal note from my Head of Year, saying that Lizzie Brown would be absent from school for the foreseeable future. I stormed off to his office, of course, assuming that she had been permanently excluded, or packed off to the Unit without anyone consulting me. That's when he told me. The parents had phoned to say that she had absented herself from home, and that it was clearly permanent.

Jenny 2

Hannah

I had been rather taken aback by that unexpected visit from Lizzie's form tutor. I didn't know teachers did things like that. I asked her in, made some coffee, tried to be polite. I knew what my failings were as a parent; I didn't really need her there rubbing them in. She seemed very involved with Lizzie, and my defences were down. I told her about some of the things that had happened with Lizzie in the past. I began to feel as though she had taken over from me, as though she thought she was in charge of her, and not just during school hours, either. I'm not sure what happened at the end, but she left abruptly...

Later that evening, as we talked over what had happened, Jono uncorked another bottle of wine: we seemed to be going through them at quite a rate: another consequence of Lizzie's behaviour. I think we both knew this was some sort of turning point: we couldn't go on pretending that things would work themselves out. At least we slept well: too well as it turned out.

Miles said he'd vaguely heard Lizzie creep in after everyone was in bed, and she seemed to be moving around a bit in her bedroom. Then he must have dozed off, because the next thing he knew was Lizzie at the side of his bed, whispering and begging him to be quiet. She had Theo with her, and she said she wanted to talk to them both. She told them she was sorry she'd caused them so much trouble, and promised that there would be no more. They would be able to get on with their own lives from now on, and she... she told them that we would be happier too.

The boys thought she had been shocked into some sort of life change because of the case conference. They probably thought she had only just realised the gravity of her situation. She went back to her room, and it was only next

Jenny 2

morning, when we came downstairs and saw the letter, that we realised she had gone...

She was gone. My exasperating, anxiety-provoking, maddening daughter was gone without trace. I had to accept it, although everything in me cried out against such acceptance. That first night, when sleep was unthinkable, I wandered into her room. I registered the pathetic attempt she had made to please me, contrary to the last, the floor cleared of the usual scatter of clothes and coffee mugs, the doors and drawers all shut, the curtains neatly drawn apart. She had even stripped the bed and folded the sheets ready for laundering. But her duvet and pillow were gone. My womb ached for my child, my baby. I had not known just how much I loved her until that moment.

Exhausted, I lay on the bare mattress, but knew that sleep would not come. When I closed my eyes I was back in that hospital bed at the beginning of her life, when her living was still an uncertain thing. Suddenly, the other woman was there, the one whose loss had delayed our first meeting as mother and daughter. Was that the start of it all? Her new life blighted by the death of another whose life had never begun? And the mother? My eyes opened wide, but I could still see her. I thought she would haunt me forever, for I now knew with certainty how she had felt. Her loss was as real as mine. It had taken this to awaken compassion within me.

Other scenes passed before me: the waiting room at the hospital where I had recognised her, sitting apart with her husband, childless amongst the women with babies. I had resisted the urge to speak to her; my cowardice in not knowing what to say had prevented me. I had turned away, recalling our conversations in the ante-natal ward, snatched when we could as we waited for our babies to be born. How I longed to return to that time when we were innocent of the outcome. I wonder what became of that woman. I don't

Jenny 2

suppose I'll ever see her again, and I wouldn't recognise her if I did.

But her howl of anguish, the terrible cry of someone who has experienced the worst of loss. I heard it again, on and on it went...only now it was coming from me.

Jono came rushing to my side, the boys following sleepily. Dimly, I heard him tell them to go back to bed. He held me, shushed me, and soothed me, and that was when I realised that he too had lost his child.

Chapter Seventeen

Rachel - Hannah

Rachel

There was a police car parked outside the Browns' house when I arrived. As I walked up the drive the front door opened and an unsmiling officer approached me.

'Not a good time for visitors, Miss,' she said.

'But I'm Lizzie's teacher.'

'I'm not sure you're really needed at the moment. As I said, this is not a good time to visit.'

'But...'

There was a police car parked outside the Browns' house when I arrived. As I walked up the drive the front door opened and an unsmiling officer approached me.

'Not a good time for visitors, Miss,' she said.

'But I'm Lizzie's teacher.'

'I'm not sure you're really needed at the moment. As I said, this is not a good time to visit.'

'But...'

'Come on, use your common sense, Miss. The family need privacy just now. If we need to speak to you we'll be contacting the school in due course.'

'Does that mean...? What's happened? Please tell me what's happened?'

'Now you know I'm not at liberty to do that, and I would advise you - '

Whatever she was about to say was interrupted by a shout from the front door, where another police officer was calling.

'Right, got to go,' and with a nod she turned on her heel and I heard her say, 'Yes, Sergeant,' before the door closed with a click.

Jenny 2

I went for a walk around the block and realised that I was trembling. In the brief after-school staff meeting the Head had explained that Elizabeth Brown had gone missing, and, because there was likely to be speculation in the press, the parents had told her that Lizzie had left a note. She cautioned against jumping to conclusions, instructed us on no account to respond to questions from journalists, and dismissed us.

There was a small park nearby, with a scruffy playground in one corner. I found a bench to sit on, and that's when I let the tears fall. Loss was something I knew about, and I wondered how Mrs. Brown and her family would cope with it. She was already anxious, but she had other children she needed to be strong for. And those boys: what would it be like for them, losing their sister? I found myself thinking anxiously of Laura, wondering how I would cope if anything happened to her. We hadn't been especially close as children, but she had done her best to support me as an adult. I wanted to go and offer the Browns comfort of some sort, but perhaps the police officer was right: this wasn't the time for it.

My mind turned to the following day; the students in Lizzie's class were bound to be restless, curious perhaps, and also judgemental. I tried to prepare myself for the questions they might ask, and the need to parry them without saying anything beyond the official line. Then I needed to get them to focus on the syllabus. It wasn't that far from their exams.

When I got home I sat down at my dining table and planned, more meticulously than usual, the next day's lessons. It was only when I turned out the light that I realised I hadn't once thought about Jenny, all day.

Jenny 2

Hannah

The police took us seriously at first, perhaps because of Elizabeth's previous attempts to run away. They also took away the note she had left. Coupled with what she'd said to Miles about believing we would be happier without her, and the typical ambiguity of the wording, we began to fear that the note she had left was actually a suicide note.

I had thought that the minutes after her birth were the worst of my life, but now I realised that there was worse. We had nearly lost her then; what if we had really lost her now?

Her English teacher came round again. I was glad Jono wasn't there. I think he might have shut the door in her face, if not physically thrown her off the premises. She stood there on the doorstep, looking all droopy and pathetic, as if it were *her* child that had gone missing. That's what angered me most: it was as if she'd tried to take her over, own her, mother her. At times it had felt as if we were in some sort of competition. She had made it clear multiple times that she understood Elizabeth better than we did. What scared me most was that I found myself wondering whether she might be right.

I was in a state of nerves when I opened the door.

'What do you want?'

'I've come to see how...' She hesitated, tried a smile and found it didn't quite work. 'Look, I'm so sorry, I just wanted to see how you are.' She was so lame.

'How do you think?' I snarled.

She was silent then and I realised how weary I was. I asked her in.

Jenny 2

Rachel

There was no coffee this time, and I didn't expect any. She asked me what the school had been told and I explained that we'd simply been informed that she wouldn't be coming back to school and that this was permanent.

'No reason?'

'No. Just parental decision – or at least that was the implication.'

'But you know, don't you? You know something?'

I sighed, and admitted that I'd been round the previous day, and spoken to the police. She was shocked at that, and I had to reassure her that they hadn't told me anything, other than that the family needed privacy; their manner suggested something serious had happened.

'They wouldn't let me see you,' I finished, lamely.

She didn't respond directly to what I'd said, but started asking me questions: did Elizabeth ever talk about her home life? What did she say about her brothers? Had she mentioned running away?

'Is that what's happened? Has she run away?'

She ignored that. I noticed she didn't ask what Lizzie said about her parents. The truth was, now that I thought about it, she never did speak about them at all, not as people. The mother turned to me, her eyes hard, and I noticed that the usually immaculate make-up was absent, apart from a smear of mascara below one eye.

'Did she ever hint that she might take her own life?'

'What? No! Is that what you…?'

I didn't know what to say.

Hannah

There was a long silence. Then she said,

'You obviously don't recognise me, but I worked as a TA at Wood Road. I remember how unhappy Elizabeth was then. The incident you told me about – I was there, I saw that awful woman, with the tape...'

She faltered into silence, and it was quite some time before I was able to speak. I revisited the awful images in my mind and managed to fit her into the woman at the school who had always made me feel inadequate, even then. She was doing it to me again now, had been doing it ever since she arrived at Hillmore and started teaching Elizabeth.

'I know how unhappy she was, long before that. She knew she wasn't as bright as her brothers – at least that's what she felt. She thought she was stupid, but I thought she was dyslexic. She didn't stay at the school long enough to be assessed... We could have done so much for her...'

'You've always thought that, always thought you could do better than her own parents. You've known all this time who we were...'

'No, only since you told me about the home schooling the other day. I couldn't possibly have connected Lizzie as she is now with that little girl...'

'Even though she has the same name?'

'What?' She looked taken aback.

'Elizabeth *Brown!*' I screamed at her. 'What are you anyway – a stalker? Have you been stalking us?'

She was angry now. 'Don't be ridiculous! That's you all over. What makes you think you're so special? She was Lizzie B.

Rachel

I don't think I ever knew her surname at Wood Road, but even if I did, even if I'd thought about it, Brown's such a common name I would never have made the connection. Lizzie B bears no resemblance to the child I knew then. And as for the Brown family, all you cared for was appearances: *your* child must never be seen to be falling behind, *your* child mustn't be allowed to get in the way of your important job, your busy life; your perfect life!'

'My perfect life! Perfect? You think *this* is perfect?' I thought about the rows, the disappearances, the suspicions I had about drugs; I recalled with a shudder the tattoo she had only recently unveiled with a flourish, the foul language she used, the endless complaints about her from the school. And the rat, the ridiculous business of the rat. I couldn't find any way to put it into words. Instead, I said, as calmly as I could,

'You were at the case conference. You saw how it really is.'

'Yes, and I did my best to support her – which is more than you and her father were doing!'

I stood so quickly that my stool toppled over with an appalling crash. I noticed later that it had chipped the glaze on one of the floor tiles. I breathed deeply and tried to sound dignified.

'I think you'd better leave,' but she was already on her way out.

I was still shaking when Jono got home. It gave me a shock because he was earlier than usual. A bit late for that: Jono was great on stable doors.

He came in and put the kettle on.

'Cup of tea?'

I nodded: I didn't trust my voice. I'd already decided not to tell him about the teacher's visit because I knew what he would be like. He was already angry and irritable all the time, and I could imagine the scene if I told him about Mrs. Daniels – he'd already expressed his view of her after that first parents' evening. The boys had given up even trying to talk to him, and he'd been spending more and more time at work. That was his way of dealing with it. Mine had been to bury my head in the sand.

Jenny 2

We drank our tea in silence. I knew that my way of dealing with it was worse: I had become withdrawn, given up, turned my anger inwards. Mrs. Daniels shouldn't have said some of those things, but I also knew there was some truth in them. That first time she came round, I saw how she looked at the kitchen: to her it must have looked so perfect. We'd spent a fortune on that kitchen when we first moved in, but no amount of expensive fittings could create harmony at mealtimes, or bring Jono home in time to eat with us, or bath the children…

PART THREE

Chapter Eighteen

2000

Rachel

Rachel

The house was set well back from the road. You wouldn't have picked it out from the rest of the row unless you'd looked carefully at the discreet brass plate beside the front door: *Cara Solomons, Psychotherapist, BSc. BACP*

There was a low stone wall at the front. I stood there, still not sure, but then, probably looking a lot more resolute than I felt, I pushed open the gate and walked the length of the path. It was one of those formal, Victorian ones, with its confident diagonal tiles and neat brick edges to the lawn on either side. If only my journey through life had been as straightforward.

The receptionist let me in as soon as my finger touched the bell; she must have seen me approaching. Her smile was warm as she led me to an upstairs waiting room, where I was offered a seat and left alone with my thoughts.

For a long time after Lizzie's disappearance, it seemed all the colour had drained from my life. Each day I went through the motions, washing, dressing, brushing my teeth... At night I alternated between lying awake for hours and sleeping the clock round. I was not in control of my own life.

Jenny 2

My sister Laura was always 'dropping in' unexpectedly, which was really code for checking up on me. By the time the second anniversary of Lizzie's disappearance was approaching even I knew I wasn't coping, and I knew that Laura knew it too. Things were getting harder at school: the kids were more difficult, management was more repressive, and my energy levels were sinking fast. Then one Saturday I just couldn't get out of bed. I was still there, unwashed and disgusted with myself, when Laura once again 'happened to be passing.' This time she made no pretence and insisted that I see the GP. I rang for an appointment on the Monday morning before school, and the receptionist must have taken pity on me when she heard the tears beneath my words, because she gave me an appointment for that same evening.

I hadn't met Dr. Gregson before. He was kind, in a brisk sort of way, but adamant that pills were not the answer, certainly not in the long term. He recommended 'talking to someone' which made me want to scream at first, especially when he admitted that there was a long waiting list for therapy on the NHS. Perhaps he saw how desperate I was, because then he said he could recommend someone who did private work, and he happened to know she had some free slots. He could see that I was still unconvinced, so he promised to see me again in four weeks' time, and if I felt there was no progress, he would definitely prescribe some medication.

'But there's no magic bullet,' he said, as I left his room.

'Mrs. Daniels?'

I was so deep in thought that I was startled when she spoke my name.

'Do come in.'

Jenny 2

The therapist gestured towards a chair and seated herself opposite me, not too close. There was a low table between the chairs, with a box of tissues on it.

'Please, take a seat. It's Rachel, isn't it?'

I gave a vague nod.

'Is it all right if I call you that?'

Another nod. I hardly trusted myself to speak.

There was something about her manner, though, that was soothing, that made me feel that perhaps, in time, I might be able to talk to her.

'I'm Cara,' she said. 'Would you like to tell me what's brought you here today, Rachel?'

I told her that I'd been to see my GP, that he wouldn't give me pills, and recommended counselling.

'What was it that made you feel you needed help from your GP?' she asked.

That was it, of course: I didn't really know, at least, not in such a way as to put it into words. I was dragging an enormous burden around with me, but it was locked on and I couldn't release the catch. Eventually I said,

'I don't know. I just felt I'd lost my way…'

It sounded feeble even to my own ears, but she picked up on it.

'What else have you lost, Rachel?'

I looked at her in amazement. How did she know? And where to start? My marriage? My home? My sense of satisfaction at work? I muttered something to that effect.

'It seems you've suffered a lot of loss over the years, Rachel. I wonder why it's only now that you've decided to ask for help?'

Well, yes, that was the big question. I'd left Dr. Gregson's room feeling let down. He wasn't going to help; all he could come up with was this idea of talking therapy. As if that could numb the pain! Then, weeks later, feeling worse than ever, I'd found the paper with Cara's number on it, screwed up in a corner of my bag, and on impulse I'd rung

Jenny 2

and made the appointment. After all, I was in a place where I had nothing to lose.

Hesitantly I explained what they'd all said - been saying for ages: that I needed to 'do something.' My sister, my colleagues, even Dave, although I'm not his responsibility any more.

'And so it's taken you some time to make the decision to come here. I wonder why you've come now, today?'

I looked at her blankly for a few moments. Why indeed? How should I know? Then I found myself telling her about Lizzie's disappearance, and her problems at home as well as at school, how she never felt good enough, that her parents expected too much. I told her about Lizzie's rebelliousness, how the more she was punished, the more she rebelled. I explained how I'd tried to support her, but then she got mixed up with Sami, and that led to more serious things...

'And then the final straw was when she took her pet rat to school and it escaped in a French lesson...'

I was babbling, now, but I couldn't stop. I rambled on about Lizzie for some time. Cara waited patiently.

'I think she was lonely, and the rat was, in a way, her only friend, especially after Sami was excluded. Then she started running away... until the last time, when she didn't come back.'

As I ran out of steam, Cara asked, 'When was this, Rachel? When did Lizzie disappear?'

'Two years ago.'

She nodded in acknowledgement. 'You have told me a great deal about Lizzie, and you are clearly very concerned about her wellbeing, but there is one thing you haven't told me: who *is* Lizzie?'

I stared at her then. Somehow, Cara, who had only met me for the first time that day, had got straight to the

Jenny 2

heart of the problem. Who was Lizzie? Who was she to me? I attempted a brief explanation, and Cara clarified:

'So, let me see if I've understood: you are a teacher – is that right? and Lizzie was your student? It sounds as though you were very close to her, very involved.'

I nodded and explained about the extra help I'd been giving her, and how vulnerable she was, and how she had disappeared, and then I couldn't say any more. I could only feel the pain of loss, deep down where it could never be healed.

After a few moments - or it could have been a lifetime - Cara said, very gently,

'So, from what you are saying, Rachel, you have been feeling low ever since this student of yours disappeared?'

'Yes.'

'You've been feeling this sense of loss for nearly two years, and it's only now that you have asked for help?'

I nodded.

'And how were things before that?'

I shook my head, willing the tears to go away. How could I find the words to tell her that things hadn't really been right for a long, long time, not since... I caught sight of a calendar on the wall behind her. Today's date: 20th April.

'Things weren't good, even before that.'

She saw me looking at the calendar.

'Is there something on there that strikes a chord?'

'Today would have been my daughter's birthday.'

'Would have been?'

'Yes.'

'Would you like to tell me your daughter's name, Rachel?

I looked at her then. Could I say it out loud? I tried.

'Jenny.' It came out in a tiny whisper.

'Do you think that has something to do with your decision to seek help, now?

Jenny 2

I shrugged, unsure where this was going.

'Would you like to tell me about Jenny?'

There was a long, long silence. I knew she was waiting for me, but I wasn't sure yet that I could launch in, strip myself bare, expose my feelings...I sat there, drenched in my own thoughts, drowning... We sat for many minutes, with me just staring at the carpet, thinking, willing her to break the silence. I began to wonder if it would be broken at all, and what she would do if we got to the end of the hour and neither of us had said anything. Would she just tell me it was time to go? Would she say I'd been wasting her time?

In the end she just said my name, very softly.

'Rachel.'

There was something about it...it was like being a child, being cared for, being safe... The tears began to fall...I thought they would go on for ever and never stop, like Alice in the rabbit hole. I thought I would drown in my own tears.

'What are the tears about, Rachel?'

'I don't know. They're...I don't know.'

'It's all right; take your time...'

More silence. It was the softness of her voice that undid me, so gentle.

'Jenny... would have been eighteen today, but she died... before she was born.'

In eighteen years It was the first time I'd said it out loud like that.

Once I finally began to tell Cara about Jenny I couldn't stop. I told her what it was like to hold my dead baby, and about all the decisions we had to make: whether to have a funeral, who to tell, where to register the birth .... the stillbirth. Horrid word! That was so hard. Dave and I went to the registrar's together, and the place was full of young parents and their babies, all smiling, glowing, happy, gone to register their

Jenny 2

baby's birth. There was an old man there too, who'd gone to register his wife's death. That was sad, yes, but I didn't think of that at the time. One of the staff came sailing out to the front office, glossy hair swept up and skirt neatly cinched at the waist. I hated her.

'Good morning! Have you come to register a birth?' Then, seeing our faces, she quickly said, 'Oh, I'm sorry. Have you come to register a death?'

But it was neither, was it? What were we registering? Not a birth, not a death, and yet both...

I told Cara about how our loss had driven a wedge between me and Dave, how I'd been unreasonable, blaming him somehow, although now I could see he must have been suffering as much as I was. I felt ashamed, selfish.

'Rachel, what is the connection between Lizzie and the death of your own child?'

I looked at her blankly. 'Connection?'

'Do you think there is a connection?'

I wasn't sure how to answer. I told her about the crazy things that had happened in my head in the years after Jenny was born, and later, when Elizabeth had taken her place at the primary school.

She listened, nodding sympathetically once in a while.

'So this child, Elizabeth, became Jenny for you, in a way?'

'Yes.'

'And Lizzie?'

I realised I hadn't explained that Lizzie was Elizabeth.

'I found out that they were the same person the day after Lizzie left.'

'Grief does strange things to us, Rachel, especially if it's unacknowledged.'

Jenny 2

'I did grieve when Jenny died, I wept and lashed out at other people and...' I found I was crying again now and Cara handed me the tissue box.

'Yet none of that really allowed you to let go, did it?'

'There's something else.'

My voice was low and I saw Cara lean forward to catch what I was saying.

'There was another one, a few years later... not a stillbirth. An ectopic pregnancy. Dave and I had got back together. We thought the new baby would be the beginning of happier times, but when we lost it – I don't know it if was a boy or girl – well, that was the end of everything. That's when we broke up for good.'

I looked up at her through puffy eyelids.

'I wasn't able to have any more children, you see.'

Cara made a soothing sound, and waited. After a few moments she said,

'And this second loss took you right back to where you'd been when you lost Jenny.'

'What can I do? How can I ever let go?'

'Well, sometimes it helps to go back to the beginning. You can't change what happened, but you can begin to see it differently.'

After the session I walked home slowly. Was Cara right? Could I find a way of seeing things differently? I had entered the counselling room with a head full of Lizzie and a heart full of Jenny, but now what? The session had been painful, and I had cried until my eyelids were almost completely swollen shut, but something had begun to shift. Back when she was my little golden angel, Elizabeth had slipped quietly into my dreams, fusing with the Jenny who was already there. Now, with Cara's help, I knew I needed once and for all to separate Jenny and Lizzie in my mind. And what was it she had said about going back to the beginning? It was

Jenny 2

something I should have done a very long time ago. Dave had said as much.

Bizarrely, since Lizzie's disappearance Mrs. Brown had also started to appear in my dreams. There she was, always standing above me, on a plinth, or a hill, or sometimes a school desk; always looking down on me, a triumphal smile on her lips. But if I was to let Lizzie go, as Dave had once urged me to let Jenny go, then I would have to see her differently too, wouldn't I? She had lost her child just as much as I had lost mine. The two losses were different, but surely the pain was as real for both of us? I think it was at that moment, that I began to acknowledge something of what she must be feeling, had probably felt all along, as the estrangement between her and her daughter increased. The triumphant woman of my dreams was my own creation, not the reality of who she was. I had begun to glimpse how I could see the past differently.

The walk up the path wasn't quite so difficult the next time.

'Come on in, Rachel. I'm glad you came back.' Cara smiled her gentle smile at me, and I sat as before, wondering how many of the tissues I might need this time.

'So last time you were here you talked about something that was deeply distressing. I wonder how the week has been for you?'

I took a deep breath.

'I've done a lot of thinking.' I gave her a little smile to show I understood the question. 'I'm exhausted!'

Cara smiled, kindly. 'It's all right, Rachel. Take your time. Tell me when you're ready.'

I took another deep breath. 'When I came here, before, I thought it was because of Lizzie's disappearance. I told you how depressed I was, how the doctor told me pills wouldn't work…'

She nodded. She was listening intently. It made me feel as though I really mattered.

Jenny 2

'I had no intention – no expectation – that I would talk about Jenny. I really didn't think Jenny was the problem. Yet that is what we talked about for most of the time.'

'Was that the first time you had talked about her – about the real Jenny?'

'The real Jenny. Yes, that's right. The real Jenny. During the week I realised how much I had avoided that.'

'Because the real Jenny died before she was born, and that was a terrible loss.'

I didn't trust myself to speak. I nodded.

'But she *was* real.'

There was a not uncomfortable silence. I liked the way she didn't jump in to fill the spaces.

She was right. I had talked about the real Jenny, the child who had died before she was born, the child I had tried to keep alive through another child.

Cara said softly, 'Yes, the important thing is that Jenny *was* real, you gave birth to her, she was your daughter. You gave her a name. Nothing can change any of that.'

After a pause, she asked. 'Are you ready to let her go?'

I was in town a few days later, mooching somewhat aimlessly round the shops, thinking over the question Cara had asked me. *Was* I ready? I knew that, thanks to the way Cara had affirmed the reality of Jenny, I was beginning to separate in my mind the loss of my child and the loss of Lizzie, or rather, I was beginning to separate the two girls. If I had done as Dave said, allowed Jenny to go at the time, I would never have allowed Lizzie to take her place. If I had mourned my loss at the right time instead of holding on to it, my grief, always just below the surface, would not have been

Jenny 2

reignited by the loss of Lizzie. Maybe I'd have been able to see Lizzie more objectively.

I began to feel shame, for the first time, for my attitude towards Mrs. Brown. How could I not have seen that she was losing her child day by day and week by week, until the final shock of Lizzie's disappearance?

I cringed as I mentally replayed some of the scenes where I had coldly judged her, remembering the even harsher thoughts I had not expressed. I was even beginning to rewrite the script in my head, the words I would now say if I could see her and tell her how sorry I was.

And what if she hadn't really lost her? If her child was not lost with the finality of my loss? I had scoured the local news since Lizzie's disappearance and seen nothing, but only Mrs. Brown could tell me the truth. If only I could see her, ask her...

Then suddenly, almost as though by thinking so much about her I had conjured her up, there she was, right in front of me. In a panic I ducked into the nearest shop before she could see me.

It was one thing to fantasise about seeing her, asking her about Lizzie, even if she had been willing to speak to me, and I'd have had to really psych myself up for it, but to bump into her in the street, to start talking without any preparation... *I'm sorry I behaved so badly before. By the way, have you heard from Lizzie?* That wasn't going to happen, was it?

And there were other questions I wanted to ask besides: how was she feeling, deep down? Had the ache ever stopped? Did she still think about Lizzie every day, every night, like I used to think about Jenny? I needed to explain to her that I'd allowed Lizzie to take Jenny's place, and that I knew it wasn't right, now that it was all too late. And then I realised something else: that before I could even think about making any attempt to contact Mrs. Brown, there was someone else I needed to make it right with first.

Jenny 2

If Dave was surprised when he opened the door, he didn't show it. We had kept in touch sporadically after the divorce, to begin with because of the practical matters that had to be sorted, and then out of a sort of habit. My sister had contacted him when I became so depressed, perhaps thinking he might be able to persuade me to seek help where she had failed, and he added his voice to Laura's. I felt in a way that I owed it to him to let him know how much it had already helped; I also felt I owed him an apology, although that seemed too small a word for what I really owed him.

'Rachel!'

He smiled, which was kind of him since I'd arrived unannounced on a Saturday morning when he probably had other plans.

'Come in...come in.'

He stood aside to let me into the hallway before closing the front door, and then led the way into his neat sitting room. A small vase of daffodils stood on the mantelpiece.

'Let me get you a coffee. Is it still milk, no sugar?'

I nodded, afraid to speak, and he disappeared into the kitchen. I looked around the room. He had never remarried, and everything about the room spoke of him. There were no papers lying about, although I knew he brought work home. Of course, he would have a little home office somewhere; it wasn't a big house, so probably in one of the bedrooms.

He came back with the coffee and seated himself opposite me. It felt a bit like being in the counselling room. I picked up my coffee but it was still too hot to drink, and as I was putting it down again he said,

'So how are you, Rachel? You're looking so much better.'

Jenny 2

'I've come to ask you something,' I said, nervously. 'It's a big ask.'

'So you'd better ask,' he said.

Cara seemed intrigued rather than surprised when I rang to ask if Dave could come with me next time, but agreed to the arrangement. When we got there, I saw that she had rearranged the chairs ready to accommodate the two of us. Once we were seated and the introductions made, Cara asked which of us wished to start.

I looked at Dave and he indicated that it was fine for me to go first. I felt he had given me his blessing; and so I began.

'I've told Dave about the things we've talked about in here. He knows how hard today is going to be for me, and I know how hard it will be for him, too.' I turned to look at him at this point. 'That's something I should have recognised a long time ago.'

He reached towards me and laid a gentle hand on my arm, in unspoken acknowledgement of what I had said. I remembered with such sadness how we had once had this kind of easy, non-verbal communication. Dave kept his hand there a little longer. It gave me the courage to continue.

'I know it's too late to make amends. I can't change the past, but I need you to know how sorry I am for all I did to bring about the end of our relationship.'

He looked as though there was something he wanted to say, but I carried on before he could speak.

'I behaved as though the loss of our child was my loss alone. I didn't listen to you, to your grief, to your sense of how we might have handled things differently, together...'

'Rachel...' He shook his head, lost for words.

'Perhaps you would find it helpful to tell the story together?'

Jenny 2

I found myself wondering why I'd had to bring him here to communicate in this way. It just felt easier, safer, somehow, to talk with a third person present. It also felt as though our words were being validated.

I had already told Cara once about the day we lost our baby. Now I wasn't sure I had the courage to go through it all again, but I knew that was why I'd asked Dave to come along. In any case, it wasn't my story alone; that was the mistake I'd made before. It wasn't that there was any chance of us getting back together, not this time, but I felt somehow that he needed to be part of this.

When I moved jobs soon after Lizzie's disappearance it was because I couldn't bear the idea of staying on at that school, where it had all happened. It must have been the same sort of feeling Dave had, when he couldn't bear to stay in the house that had never been Jenny's home. At the time I thought he was simply running away, but I could see now how hard it had been on him, especially with me in the irrational state I was in. This was another apology that I owed.

Together we recounted the story of our loss; at times we both cried and reached for the tissues. But it worked: the telling and the tears eased the pain, and at last I felt the healing had begun.

One more thing happened, afterwards. Dave felt in his pocket and produced an envelope.

'What?'

'Go on, open it. I thought this might help.'

It was the photograph he'd taken the day Jenny was born. There she was. I'd forgotten how beautiful she was, and in the photograph there was no way of knowing that she wasn't breathing.

'Oh, Dave...!'

I couldn't find any words.

Jenny 2

He held my gaze for some time. 'Was I right? Does it help?'

As I went to give it back to him, he stopped me.

'It's all right. I made a copy. We should both have a picture of her.'

Chapter Nineteen

Hannah - Rachel

Hannah

It had been a shock, seeing her in the street like that. I hadn't thought about her for years, not since that awful time...

When Elizabeth first disappeared there was a flurry of activity; the police quickly concluded that she was just one more missing person, a disaffected teenager who had simply left of her own free will and would be sixteen before anyone found her and therefore free to leave home. Jono blustered and shouted as usual, first at the police and then at the school. I tried asking around at the recreation area where she used to hang out, but none of those youngsters really wanted to talk to me, and if they wouldn't talk to me in my pathetic state, I knew Jono's approach wouldn't work.

Then there were the rows at home. They'd started when Jono didn't approve of Theo's choice of A Levels. In the end Theo gave in, but then later he dropped out of University. And Miles didn't even apply for Uni... Jono took it as a personal insult. We were just falling apart as a family.

Gradually, we got used to her not being there. She'd been wrong in what she said to Miles, though: we were not better off without her. So much time and energy had gone into worrying about her, and now there was just this awful void where nothing was resolved.

There was no way I could put things right, but eventually I realised I could make a start by trying to fix myself. The tablets the GP gave me weren't helping, so I agreed to see the therapist he recommended. With perfect irony the first session was arranged for Elizabeth's birthday. That was too much, and I cancelled it. Then I was sorry, and rang to make

Jenny 2

a new appointment. The receptionist didn't seem fazed by this and gave me another one a couple of weeks later.

I was nervous enough anyway, and still thinking about Elizabeth's birthday, and all the past birthdays, not all of which had been bad, I suppose. Then I started thinking about her future birthdays, and whether there was any chance I would ever get to celebrate one with her again... and I found I'd walked way past the house and had to retrace my steps. Then seeing *her* in the street made me almost turn back. I was already late, so what difference would it make if I didn't turn up at all? But somewhere deep inside something was telling me this was my only chance, so somehow I managed to put Mrs. Daniels out of my mind and carried on. I'm not even sure that she saw me, or if she did, she wouldn't have recognised me. I didn't recognise my own self most of the time.

'Hello, Hannah. Take a seat.'

The therapist gave what I'm sure was meant to be an encouraging smile. I fell clumsily into the chair: it was lower than I'd expected. She moved across to sit in her own chair and then asked, gently enough, what had brought me. I'd arrived late, of course, and was embarrassed and flustered, and then before I could get a whole sentence out I was weeping and sobbing and reaching blindly for the box of tissues, and then it was empty and she had to go and find a new one. Eventually I calmed down enough to talk, although my nose was throbbing; must have been as red as Rudolph's. Remembering the little toy reindeer Elizabeth had treasured set me off again.

'It's all right, Hannah. Take your time.'

Before I knew it, I was pouring it all out; it was like flood defences giving way. And what a flood!

'I don't know where to begin. Everything's such a mess. From the outside we don't look like the sort of people

Jenny 2

who need counselling – sorry, no offence. Or social services, come to that, but we did. Need them, I mean. Couldn't manage our own child. We're supposed to *succeed*, you know? I mean, we're well-educated, we have a nice house in a good area, our lifestyle, background, everything... And our family... well, that's another story. The truth is...we're a mess. *I'm* a mess. I'm such a failure as a mother... I've made a mess of everything...'

'*Everything* is quite a lot to talk about. Why don't we start with something smaller? You mentioned your family. Would you like to tell me about them?'

I breathed a very deep sigh. This was so much harder than I'd expected. She told me again to take my time. I must have looked such a fool, sitting there with my Rudolph nose, screwed up bits of soggy tissue raining down like a cartoon snowstorm.

'Well, that's the biggest mess of all. When the children were little we seemed to have everything going for us. And they're bright, or at least the boys are.' I knew I was pulling what Jono called my Anguished Mummy face. 'Elizabeth, though, she's something else altogether.'

For a few moments that felt like years, I couldn't go on, but the therapist waited as though she had all day and no other clients to worry about.

'There never used to be rows, but over the past few years...'

'What are the rows about?'

'It started with Theo's choice of A Levels. Jonathan thought he'd made the wrong choices.'

'Jonathan is your husband?'

'Yes. And Theo's our eldest.

'What happened over Theo's A Levels?'

'Oh, Theo found it easier to give in, in the end, but now he's dropped out of University altogether. And Miles - he's three years younger - didn't even apply for Uni...

Jenny 2

Jonathan had been academically very successful, so he seemed to feel personally insulted by that.'

The therapist calmly pushed the box of tissues in my direction, averting her gaze as I blew my nose loudly and wiped my eyes with the resulting screwed up mess. I didn't feel like me at all. I didn't even know who that 'me' was any more. I felt so weary, and the armchair was so comfortable. I found myself sinking deeper and deeper.

'I'm so tired.'

'I can see that,' she said, with a gentle smile. 'I can see how much you need rest, emotional as much as physical. But if you go to sleep here and now it might not be the best possible use of your time or your money.'

I did my best to sit up and pay attention, while she continued in her gentle voice,

'I understand that you feel you have failed your children in some way, but I'm wondering what it is that prompted you to seek help now, at this particular time.'

I tried to put some words together, but all I really wanted at that moment was to disappear into the depths of the armchair. I began to wonder if I would ever find the strength to leave it.

'Am I right in thinking you had some doubts about coming for counselling?'

I must have looked blank, because she went on, 'You cancelled your original appointment and then rebooked.'

'Oh, yes, yes I did …' I was going to have to tell her why, say it out loud.

'It clashed with a… family birthday.'

She waited, so I knew I had to say something else. This was hard. I was going to have to admit to myself that Elizabeth had been gone for two whole years.

'My daughter's.'

'And how old is she?'

Jenny 2

'She would have been eighteen.' I steeled myself not to think about the celebration that might have been.

'Would you like to tell me about her?'

I felt my guts twist with real, physical pain. No words came.

'Perhaps you'd like to begin at the beginning. What was it like eighteen years ago, when she was born?'

Could I do that? Drag myself through those fears all over again? I shook my head.

'I'm sorry… I'm struggling a bit today.' I was just about holding back the tears, although my eyelashes were thick with them.

'Is there anything in particular that has made you feel this? Apart from the date?'

'I…I saw someone in the street… someone I used to know. I don't think she saw me. It's been a while…'

'Do you want to tell me a little more about that?'

After some sighing and snuffling, I did my best to explain. 'Well, yes, OK. She was one of Elizabeth's teachers, from Hillmore High: the only teacher Lizzie ever really liked. And this teacher, she…she had a real soft spot for Lizzie. I got so jealous; she seemed to be closer to her than I was…than her own mother.'

I was still now, a block of stone; the waiting tears fell unimpeded.

'Take your time, Hannah.'

'Thank you.'

Another pause, more swallowing. I was a complete wreck.

'Things had come to a head at school. Lizzie was always in trouble; she'd been excluded a number of times; she'd been put in isolation endlessly; we knew she was mixing with the wrong crowd – their parents probably thought *she* was the wrong crowd; we didn't know, but we suspected, that she was using drugs, drinking…'

Jenny 2

I had to cover my face for a while as I burned with shame. 'She'd have been out on her ear a long time before that, if it hadn't been for Mrs. Daniels, but I hated the woman for having so much influence... She was spotless, nothing could touch her, and all the while she was judging me, making it clear I was a bad mother...'

'From what I've heard today you are doing a pretty good job of judging yourself, Hannah.'

That was a new one: judging myself, instead of being judged by others. Could that be true? Had my mother been wrong about me all that time?

'Would you like to tell me a little more about what happened?'

'After Lizzie took the rat to school – it's a long story - anyway, after that happened, it was a kind of last straw, and we were assigned a social worker. The EWO – Education Welfare Officer, it stands for - had been round a few times, mostly after Lizzie had played truant, but she and Lizzie didn't hit it off. The social workers were a bit condescending, I thought, but at least they got things moving. So there was this case conference, with everybody there, to decide what to do about the problem that Lizzie had become.

'We knew it was her last chance at an education. Jono was big on education; it was really important to him. I used to think that was all he cared about, but I think now it was all he could think of as a way of helping her. He wanted her to have something behind her, something that would enable her to be independent. If the school threw her out then, in her GCSE year, she had no hope. That's how he saw it. She didn't have much hope anyway, realistically; her writing and spelling were awful, and she'd missed so much... Anyway, the day of the case conference came, and he tootled off to work as usual. I couldn't believe it.'

I found myself staring at the wall behind the therapist's head, at and through the carefully-chosen neutral

Jenny 2

shades of the counselling room's decor. Then I remembered something.

'Actually, to be fair, he did turn up at the last minute - but I had needed him with me beforehand, needed to *know* he'd be there. But he looked terrible. Looking back I think... no, I *know*... that he loved her as much as I did. I think we just loved her in different ways.'

I saw her, the teacher, several times after that, always managing to avoid her, but one day, when it was pouring with rain and I was dashing, head down for cover, I ran straight into a woman carrying a takeaway coffee.

'I'm so sorry – I've spilt your coffee.'

It was seeping into her jacket, and I didn't know what to do.

'Don't worry,' she said, and then she looked at me properly. 'Oh – you!'

I looked back and echoed her cry of surprise.

'Oh! Yes... I'm afraid so.'

We stood there, frozen to the spot; the moment lasted several centuries.

Finally she said, 'Don't worry. I'm sure it'll be OK.' There was a bin next to where we were standing and she dropped the remains of the soggy cup into it.

I took a deep breath.

'No, look, the least I can do is buy you another coffee...'

She looked undecided.

'Come on, we're both getting soaked.' I felt I was bullying her a bit, but it felt good to be the one in charge for once. 'Let's go into Gino's and we can sit down for a bit... unless you're on your way somewhere?'

'No, I've just come from... from somewhere.' She paused, and I thought she was going to refuse, but as the rain grew heavier, she gave herself a sort of shake and said, 'Yes, OK. Thank you. A coffee would be nice.'

Rachel

It was like that time in her kitchen: the practicalities of finding seats and ordering the coffee took over for a while, and then suddenly, there we were, face to face, and I was consumed with guilt and wanted to apologise and didn't know how, and then she said,

'Have you heard from her?'

I was stunned. She was asking *me* the question I wanted to ask *her* but had no right to. Speechless, I shook my head.

'Well, if you're wondering: she's never come back.'

I babbled my... what? Apologies? Condolences? This meeting was nothing like the one I'd imagined. This was not going to be a time of reconciliation and forgiveness. She continued, in the same detached voice,

'I don't even know whether she's alive or dead.'

I held back my own tears somehow, afraid to speak, afraid the tears would fall despite myself. To cover the awkwardness, I began to drink my coffee, and she did the same. After a while I asked after her family, and she told me about the boys, and mentioned the disagreements and the difficult times they'd had. I told her about my change of job, and a few other trivia, and then tentatively asked if she would like to meet again the following week. No idea why I did that, but to my surprise, she said that she would.

Hannah

The next time we met it wasn't raining, but it was overcast, a dismal day more like October than early Spring. I arrived

Jenny 2

first, wondering if she would come, and then when she did, I wondered why I'd said yes. She looked better than the last time, more composed. It must have been as much of a shock for her as it was for me, that first time.

We drank our coffee for a while without speaking, and then she said,

'How are you?'

I looked at her blankly.

'Sorry,' she said, Silly question.'

'To be honest, I don't know how to answer it.'

'You don't know how you feel?'

'No.'

More silence.

Then I said, 'Sometimes I'm completely numb, no feelings at all. Then, other times, I feel so many different things at once I can't name them all.'

She murmured something. Sounded like: 'Yes, that's how I was.'

Was she comparing her feelings, her sense of loss to mine?

'What? How *dare* you...?'

She looked stunned.

'No, you misunderstand...'

'How can you compare a mother's feelings to a mere teacher's? You really are something else.'

I stood up to leave and she placed a hand on my arm to stop me, but I brushed it off.

I got as far as the other end of the High Street before she caught up with me. She was panting a bit.

'Mrs. Brown wait! Wait, please.'

I was a bit out of breath myself, so I stopped and turned to face her.

'Mrs. Brown...' she said again.

Jenny 2

'Oh for goodness' sake, we're not in your classroom now. My name's Hannah.'

She nodded. 'Rachel.'

We were standing outside another coffee shop. She indicated the doorway with her head.

'Shall we?'

Over extra large mugs of coffee she explained.

'I wasn't trying to say I miss Lizzie the way you do, of course I wasn't. I mean, I do miss her, but...'

She was getting all tangled up. It was strange to see her struggling to find words.

'So what *were* you saying, then?'

That was when she told me that she too had lost a child, a daughter. She didn't seem to want to say any more, and I didn't press her.

Afterwards, we parted with a tentative hug. Was it possible that we weren't enemies after all?

PART FOUR

Chapter Twenty

1998

Beth

Beth

That last time I left home - I didn't know then that it was going to be the last time, of course...Anyway, when I left home that night, I didn't really know what I was going to do. I just knew I had to get away. The family would be better off without me causing trouble all the time. The social worker got me some help with my spelling and stuff - seems I wasn't stupid after all, just dyslexic. Well, what do you know? And with my computer, and spellcheck and all, you'd hardly know I had a problem.

But I'm getting ahead of myself. There had been so many bad things, and I'd let so many people down... the last straw was losing Rory. He was the only one who never judged me. He depended on me to feed him and clean out his cage and stroke him and hold him until he felt safe. It made me feel good, as though I actually mattered to someone. When he went, I felt there really was nothing and no-one for me.

Over the years I've missed my family, of course, and I've often wondered if I should get in touch, but the longer I've been away, the more I thought it would be too much of a shock if I just turned up, out of the blue. They wouldn't want their lives messed up again.

Jenny 2

It was pretty grim at first...no, it was very grim. That first night, I walked until I couldn't walk any further, and finally I lay down, somewhere on the other side of town, all scrunched up in a shop doorway, shivering with cold and desperation. I wanted sleep to bear me away from reality, but I was still awake when the sun came up. I was so close to despair that day.

I was better equipped that time, though, in practical terms. I'd learnt from my previous attempts to run away, and I'd packed a bag properly, but it's hard, trying to carry enough stuff around with you, and I'd overlooked some things. It's laughable, but the thing I really wished I'd brought was a toothbrush! After a few days of eating rubbish and handouts, my mouth tasted like a dustbin. Bet my breath smelled pretty ripe too.

I'd taken a comb, funnily enough, although my hair was so short it didn't really need it. I tried looking at myself in shop windows, but all I could see was this stranger...filthy, too, even though I went to the toilets in John Lewis, early, before there were many people about, to try and keep myself clean. They have nice soap dispensers there, but the smell of my unwashed clothes was stronger than the smell of the soap. I tried washing a few things through, but I had to push them back into my bag, and they dried all smelly because I had no way of getting the air to them.

The thing I needed most, though, even more than food, was sleep. There's hardly anywhere to sleep rough these days: the seats in the bus shelters slope downwards, so if you try to stretch out on them you roll off. I was too scared to try sleeping in the park: there are some very weird people around, and it's very dark there at night. Most of the warm spaces round the shops have these spikes, to stop people like me, I suppose. Well, people like I used to be...I did one or two things I'm not proud of, to get food, or to get myself out of a tight situation.

Jenny 2

I thought about going back to the hostel where I'd spent a night, ages ago, but I remembered how the policeman had come and taken me back home, and I didn't want to risk that happening again, so I carried on for a while, roaming the streets, a bit of begging, a bit of shoplifting. I said I'm not proud of myself.

Then one night I decided - don't ask me where the idea came from - to tuck myself up in the porch at St. Mary's. I remembered it from when I was a little girl, and I used to go to Sunday School there with my brothers. It was out of the wind, and I had this kind of superstitious idea that no-one would hurt me there, with it being a church. I thought God would look after me. Well, it turns out I was right. He did – or someone did.

There was a light on inside, but so low I thought it must have been one they left on at night, like the big shops, for security. I spread out my duvet – I didn't have a sleeping bag, so I'd just brought my bedding with me, although I'd already ditched the pillow by this time. It was too much hassle carrying it around. The duvet was starting to get quite smelly, but I was past caring, so I smoothed it out and lay down. I rolled myself up in it, with my bag under my head. You have to sleep on top of your possessions, otherwise people steal them as soon as you're asleep.

I'd been given a Mars Bar by someone earlier that day. She thought she was being kind, although what I really wanted was a wholemeal cheese and tomato roll. Why that? Perhaps my body was crying out for some proper nutrition. It was the sort of thing Mum would have given me. Anyway, I lay there fantasising about this cheese and tomato roll and trying to decide whether to eat the Mars Bar. My belly was rumbling and grumbling so loudly I thought the whole neighbourhood would hear. I was on the point of ripping off the wrapper when I heard footsteps. They were crunching a bit, because the path was gravelly stuff, but they were a bit random, as though the person wasn't too steady on their

Jenny 2

feet. I lay still as a board, and then there were more footsteps, and voices, raggedy voices, a bit aggressive, a bit slurred. Next thing I knew was the sound of breaking glass, not the windows, but bottles smashing against the wall. Then a sort of hissing sound: someone peeing up against a wall. The voices were getting closer. They were angry. I thought I heard punches being thrown. I was so scared, and without thinking, I tried the door of the church, even though I knew it was empty, and it flew open and next thing I was in there. I had my bag with me, but I'd left the duvet outside. And the Mars Bar. I only remembered that afterwards.

'Hey...what's all this? Can I help you?'

The voice came out of the darkness at the far end. For a moment I wondered if it was God speaking.

The man who stepped out of the shadows was tall and quite well built, which I remember thinking was just as well, if the men outside were going to follow me in. He wasn't God, although he might as well have been.

When he looked at me, I didn't see the usual look of aversion. He didn't look through me, or look away. He spoke to me as though I was a real person.

'Are you all right? Can I do anything?'

'There are some men outside,' I said, lamely. 'I was frightened.'

'Wait there - here, sit down. You look exhausted.'

He walked to the door and stepped through without a moment's hesitation. To my amazement, I heard him calling to the men by name.

'Come on, you two, break it up. Jim Rawlins, what do you think you're doing? You know Angie's going to be waiting for you. You'll regret this in the morning. And you, Andy, I'm surprised at you, getting yourself in this state....That's it, off you go...And you...'

He came back in and approached me gently, as if I was some sort of timid wild animal, the way I'd have

Jenny 2

approached Rory. He sat down a couple of seats away from me.

'Are you lost? Do you need help to get back home?'

I stared at him for a bit. I was lost, oh so very lost, but I definitely didn't want help to go back home, and so I was stuck for an answer.

'What's your name?'

There was no harm in telling him, I thought. But which name? The name I'd been baptised with in this very church? Not that I remembered it, of course, but there were pictures at home: Mum in a big hat, the boys all done up in shirts and ties, the vicar – not this one – standing behind the font, smiling benignly. Dad wasn't in the pictures. Perhaps he was behind the camera. Poor Mum: she looked so happy in those pictures. She didn't know, yet, what a disappointment I'd turn out to be.

He asked again, and I wondered whether I was still Lizzie, the troublemaker, or was I Elizabeth, Mum and Dad's little girl?

'Well? What should I call you?' He hesitated. '*My* name's David. I'm the vicar here.'

'I'm… Elizabeth. But you can call me …' I hesitated for a few seconds. 'You can call me Beth.' I wondered if I should shake hands or something.

'Are you hungry, Beth? My house is next door and my wife is great at rustling up food at all hours of the day and night. Would you like to come and see what she can do for you?'

I felt as though I should say no. What right did I have, after all, for people to be kind to me? But David had a warm smile, and he was already standing. He reached for my bag, and I thought how nice it would be not to have to carry it, and to look forward to something proper to eat.

Jenny 2

I was early for my meeting with Social Services. I knew how I looked: grubby and tired; hungry too. Gloria, the social worker, turned to her colleague and asked her to find some coffee and sandwiches.

'So, how's it going at the hostel?'

'OK, I guess.'

'Just OK?'

'No, of course, it's great not to be on the streets any more.'

That was an understatement: sleeping in a bed, after all those weeks of never being warm enough, or secure enough, or comfortable enough to sleep more than a few minutes at a time: there just weren't enough words to express what it meant. To think I had lived a life once where I slept in a bed every night. What a lot I had taken for granted.

My mind went back to the awful moment when I emerged from the church with the vicar, to find my duvet a soggy mess. I wasn't sure whether it was just beer, or beer that had already passed through the body of one of those men in the churchyard.

'Have you decided yet whether you are going to let us contact your parents?'

I looked away. I know what Gloria was thinking: she wondered whether I was fleeing some sort of abuse or neglect. I suppose she could tell I was from 'a good family' although I'd already been told, over and over, that that was no guarantee. She decided to try another tack.

'How old are you?'

I just looked at her. Was this a trick question?

'It might make a difference, you know,' Gloria went on.

I replied grudgingly. 'I'm sixteen. I left home two days before my sixteenth birthday. What difference does it make?'

Jenny 2

'Well, it means I don't have to call the police, for a start. There now...'

I found I had slumped forward, tears squeezing from the corners of my eyes.

'Is that a relief?'

'Yes.'

'I'm not going to force you to go back home, although I might try to persuade you.'

I felt the corner of my mouth twist into the semblance of a smile. 'You can try, but you won't succeed.'

'It must have been pretty bad, huh?'

'Yes. Well, no...Yes. It was. I can't go back.' In all honesty I had to recognise that, after some of the things I'd seen on the streets, and some of the stories I'd heard, it would sound a bit lame to admit that my parents' crime had been to expect too much of me, while feeding, clothing and attempting to educate me to the best of their abilities.

'I know I was lucky really. I know, in comparison with some people....' I faltered to a halt.

The social worker responded quickly. 'I'm not here to judge. But we do need to start looking at what you're going to do next. The hostel is only a short-term solution.'

Handing over the plate of sandwiches, she added, more briskly, 'Now come on, get these inside you.'

I picked up the sandwich nearest me. It was cheese and tomato.

Chapter Twenty-One

Beth

Beth

Gloria was a whirlwind of energy. Within days she had organised a trip to the council housing office, checked out my eligibility for benefits, telling me pointedly that my eligibility would be enhanced if I was in full-time education, and from somewhere she found a fund that would provide me right away with the change of clothes and toiletries I needed so badly.

'So, were you doing GCSEs?' she asked, innocently enough. It wasn't her fault, but her question touched such a raw nerve that I burst into tears.

'I can't go back to school. You don't understand…I just can't.'

Gloria gave me a few moments, making soothing noises and patting my arm.

'OK, I understand you don't want to go back to the same school, but at your age you could go to college to study…do a vocational course if you can't face taking your exams. Is there anything you've always wanted to do?'

Between snuffles, I explained, 'All I ever wanted was to be the academic success my parents expected me to be. Instead I always made a mess of everything, I was so stupid and naughty at five years old that my teacher taped me to a chair…

'What?' I saw Gloria's eyebrows shoot up. I told her a bit more about school, and home-schooling, and Hillmore. She interrupted me before I'd finished.

'Did anyone ever test to see if you might be dyslexic?'

Jenny 2

The Educational Psychologist worked from an office in the centre of town. I said I could get myself there, but Gloria said she would drive me. I guessed she wanted to make sure I actually kept the appointment, and I suspect she could also see how anxious I was.

We had to park a few minutes' walk from the office block. Gloria was muttering about the parking and was trying to hurry me along, but I was dragging my feet. In the past few days I hadn't been out and about much, and the world looked different now I'd been hauled up from street level. We passed a girl of about my own age, shivering on a threadbare blanket, a little paper cup in front of her. I wished so much that I had some change to give her: I could remember all too well the forest of legs hurrying past, the withdrawn glances, the sense of being invisible. I smiled awkwardly at the girl, who scowled at me in return.

There was one of those telephone entry things on the rather forbidding front door, and Gloria was clearly out of puff as she explained breathily to the voice at the other end that she was there with the three o'clock appointment. The office itself, when we finally reached it, was on the third floor; there was no lift, or if there was, Gloria made no attempt to use it, so she was even more out of breath by the time she handed me over to Mrs. Finkelstein.

Mrs. Finkelstein was efficient, but friendly, and I actually found myself co-operating for once with the business of writing and responding to various tasks. At the end Mrs. Finkelstein called Gloria back in from the outer office, where she'd been enjoying a cup of tea with the secretary. She had, she said, taken the opportunity to make several phone calls to and about some of her other clients, and I realised just how busy she was, and how lucky I was to have so much of her attention.

'Right,' Mrs. Finkelstein said, as Gloria stood up. 'Well, I'll get the report written up properly, and let you have

Jenny 2

it in a few days, but it's clear we have a very intelligent young lady here...'

She smiled at me, and I was so stunned that I made a noise that was a cross between a hiccup and a choking sound.

'She tells me no-one has done any of these tests before. Such a pity!' She shook her head. 'Such a pity....'

As Gloria turned to go, motioning me to follow her, Mrs. Finkelstein added: 'One good thing is that she'll get help at the College. They're very hot on special needs down there. Very hot on them. Well, goodbye. It's been a real pleasure meeting you, my dear.'

When we were back in the street, and heading towards the car, I asked, a bit narked, 'Did you tell her I was going to College?'

Without warning, Gloria steered me into a small café that we happened to be passing, and ordered tea and sticky buns. It reminded me suddenly of the times when Mum had taken me out, during the home-schooling period, and done things like this on the spur of the moment. I felt suddenly sad and ungrateful.

'Thank you,' I said, as I licked the last crumbs from my fingers. 'That was really nice.'

'You do know, don't you,' Gloria asked, 'That even though dyslexia isn't curable, as such, you can learn all sorts of strategies to get round it? Mrs. Finkelstein will make lots of recommendations. It doesn't have to hold you back.'

'That's easy for you to say...you haven't been called stupid all your life.' There was an odd look on Gloria's face, and I realised I had been rude.

'I'm sorry. I shouldn't have said that.'

'But you see it *is* easy for me to say, because I've been there and done it and I'm still wearing the tee shirt.'

'What?'

'Yes, I'm dyslexic, and I know exactly what it's like to be called stupid.'

Jenny 2

'But you're a social worker!'

'Yes. And...?'

'Didn't you, I mean...how did you, I mean....' I gave up trying to put my thoughts into words.

'I went to College and I got help, basically. So, shall we go over to the College and get a prospectus now, or would you like another bun first?'

Once the College place was secured, I needed a plan. The start of the academic year was months away, and the question was: what was I going to do until then? A job and an address seemed a good idea, and the thought of actually earning money, paying my way, filled me with unexpected feelings of self-worth. On the other hand, a totally unqualified and inexperienced sixteen-year-old wasn't going to land a secure, high-paid job in a hurry. And how to find somewhere to live?

'Don't you worry your pretty little head about that,' Gloria said, putting on a funny accent - I thought it must have come from a film or something – as she scrolled through her contacts list. 'Ah, here we are – Mrs. Green. She's the one!'

'The one what...?' But she was already talking to someone. I caught the words 'soon as possible' and a few 'nos' and 'yeses' and then Gloria swung round in her chair – I could see she loved doing that. She was like a big kid sometimes.

'Done!' she said. 'Let's get you back to the hostel to pick up your things.'

I loved the way Gloria walked. It was like nothing could ever possibly stop her. I watched as people leapt out of her way, although I'm sure she would never have barged into anyone, not deliberately, anyway. She was so positive, so sure, and I wanted to be like her.

'Where are we going, Gloria?' I was a bit worried; there were parts of town I wanted to avoid.

Jenny 2

'Don't you worry, girl. It's nowhere near your old school, if that's what you're afraid of. You won't be bumping into anyone you don't want to, that's for sure.'

'So, where...'

You'll love Mrs. Green. She's an older lady, very *respectable*...' She said 'respectable' in a funny way that made me laugh. I think she meant that Mrs. Green was no-one to be frightened of. 'She regularly takes in social services clients.'

I was a bit nervous of asking my next question.

'So does she know I don't have any money yet, to pay the rent?'

'That's all taken care of, Beth. Given your circumstances and the fact you will be returning to full-time education...' She turned and raised an eyebrow at me; the education thing was clearly the deal-breaker. I nodded, meekly.

'...Given that, the housing benefit will cover the rent.'

We crossed the road and turned into a pleasant little street of terraced houses, each with a neat front garden.

'And...' Gloria continued, 'If you can find yourself some part-time work, you'll have enough for a few other essentials.'

'Yes. Thank you, good idea.'

'Such as a decent haircut, for instance,' Gloria said pointedly.

I moved my few possessions into Mrs. Green's spare room the following Saturday morning, and gratefully swallowed the thick and wholesome leek and potato soup set before me. The house was orderly, clean, but so different from the spacious and unwelcoming house of my upbringing that I wondered how people could live so differently from one another within the same universe.

Jenny 2

I excused myself as soon as I could without seeming rude, and set off down the street, looking for all the world as though I had somewhere to go. At the corner I paused for a moment:

'58 Lilac Court. I must remember how to get home again.' Home! The word had a nice sound to it today.

Turning left into Willow Street I wandered past a small row of shops. Perhaps I *would* find a hairdresser's here: the rebellion had to end somewhere. At one end of the row was a proper old-fashioned baker's shop, tumbling heaps of rolls and buns crammed into the tiny window space. I was transported back to another happy interlude during the home-schooling phase, when Mum had taken to visiting our local bakers, the one with the 'artisanal bread.' I'd never been sure, then or now, what that meant exactly, but the smell of baking bread was tantalisingly the same. A row of gingerbread dollies danced across the front of the shop window. This would be a place to come back to.

Next door was a florist, and it evoked more memories of childhood: the vases of flowers, bought by my father in some extravagant gesture, wrapped in cellophane, all colour co-ordinated and tastefully tied. As often as not Mum would thrust them hastily into water 'to arrange properly later,' only for them to languish unarranged for weeks, drooping through lack of water until Mrs. P, the cleaner, took pity on them and threw them out.

As a very little girl I used to fish them out of the bin and play florist's shop, or bride and bridesmaids, out in the garden, with buckets of water and bits of string. I would be so totally absorbed that the game only ended when my fingers were cold and wrinkled and I was called in to have my hands wrapped in a warm towel. Until this moment I'd forgotten those happier times. As I passed the doorway I

Jenny 2

inhaled the scent of lilies, and noted the lack of spikes to deter rough sleepers.

It was a bright, sunny day and the little fluffy white clouds scudding along made me feel all clean and new. Everything about this part of town was a delight. I wondered again about finding a hairdresser's, but drawing level with the next shop window I stopped in awe.

It was not as smart as its neighbours, the paintwork scuffed and the smell more earthy, but the contents of the window made my heart leap. Cages and glass-fronted vivariums jostled for space at the front, while behind, on wooden legs, hutches protected their shy inmates: rabbits of all sizes and colours, their ears wondrously varied as to length, floppiness and general fluffiness. It was old-fashioned, chaotic, and deeply appealing. Before I knew what I was doing, I was inside.

I hardly knew where to look first. The tanks of gaudy tropical fish lining the walls was beginning to have a mesmeric effect, until a lazy movement near the floor drew my attention to a tortoise, surveying the world lazily from hooded eyes. Next to this pen were some strange, prehistoric looking lizards, striking poses that made me laugh out loud.

There was no-one else in the shop, and as I stood there alone I was swept back to the heart-pounding moment when I sneaked off to buy Rory. There had been a tank containing several rats, eyes and whiskers alert as they reared up inquisitively at my approach. They were all sleek and well-cared for, but I had known instantly that Rory was the one for me: love at first sight! Today though, the nearest thing was a family of white mice, busily twitching their whiskers in a cage near my feet.

Even without a Rory substitute, I felt somehow at home here. I knew instinctively that Mrs. Green's neat house

Jenny 2

was not somewhere I could take a pet of any kind, especially of the rodent variety. That didn't seem to matter, though, and besides, in my heart I knew I could never replace my old pet.

While the shop was very full indeed of animals - were those *hens* scratching about in a pen over in the corner? - it seemed singularly lacking in any sort of human occupant. I found I was becoming mesmerised again by the soothing backward and forward motion of the angel fish in a tank at the exact level of my eyes, when a voice behind me startled me, and then startled me all over again as it began apologising for startling me.

Someone emerged from the back room in a flurry of sorries, a gleaming length of snake dangling from his shoulder.

'I'm sorry!' he said again, at the very moment I also said, 'Sorry, I...' and then both of us laughed at the absurdity of it. Everything was making me laugh that day.

'I'll be with you in a sec - I just need to put Buster here back in his tank.'

The young man, tall and lean with a halo of auburn hair, stretched perilously across a row of tanks and raised the lid of the farthest one, deftly depositing the snake inside. It slithered into a corner refuge made of tree bark, to which was attached a kind of ghost snake.

'I just love it when they do that!' He pointed to the ghost. 'Have you ever seen it?'

I shook my head. I really didn't know what he was talking about.

'The old skin starts to become detached, and they sort of hook the front of it on to a rough bit of bark, and then, ever so slowly and steadily, they move forward, out of it.'

I stared at the snake, but it was still as a statue.

'It's like peeling off a tight tee shirt - they leave it inside out.' I thought it had to be a bit more dignified than that, but didn't say so. He seemed so taken with the snake.

Jenny 2

'When they're ready to shed, they start to look all dull and dusty, but when they come out of the old skin - well...' He gazed fondly at it, and I followed his gaze.

'Yes,' I breathed. 'All clean and new.'

There was silence for a few moments, but it wasn't uncomfortable. In fact, it was very comfortable, and I was content to stay there to enjoy it. We watched the snake for some minutes; it was doing nothing at all.

'I just love taking them out and looking at them when that happens,' he said. His tone was sort of reverent. 'People expect them to be slimy, but they're dry and smooth, and it's a nice feeling, when you hold them. Would you like to have a go?

'Ye..es, I think so.'

Was that his sales pitch?

'But, er, I'm afraid I'm not going to buy one.'

'That doesn't matter. Here...' He was already raising the lid again, and then with great tenderness lifted the coiled snake from the tank. It brought a few wisps of straw with it, as it began, slowly, to uncoil.

I reached out a finger and touched it gently. I couldn't imagine stroking it the way I used to stroke Rory, but I let the assistant transfer the weight of the snake gradually from his hands to mine. It stretched out and curved round, and I had the oddest feeling that it was observing me.

'Will it bite?'

'No, it's not poisonous. It's a constrictor.'

'Oh!' I began to push it back towards him, but he retreated, laughing.

'It's a North American corn snake. That's how it catches its prey - but look at it. How long would you say it is? Two feet? Two and a half? I think it would struggle to constrict you!'

'Did you say his name was Buster?' I asked, once the snake was back in his tank.

Jenny 2

'Oh, no, we don't give the individual animals names. It would be too hard to sell them if we did that. I just call all of them Buster.'

'Ah' I wasn't sure what to say next. Truth to tell I was feeling a bit of a fraud. I thought perhaps I should go, even though I really didn't want to.

'Well, I...' I began, at the same moment he said something.

'Sorry?'

'Sorry?' That made us both laugh again.

'I was about to feed him. Would you like to see? If you're not in a hurry?'

The snake's food was kept in a freezer in the back room, which he showed me, although I stepped back in horror at the sight of the packs of tiny frozen creatures. He took out what looked like a small mouse and placed it in a bowl of hot water to defrost. I watched, fascinated, as it became more mouse-like as it warmed. I couldn't help turning my head towards the cage of white mice at the front of the shop, and he said, quickly,

'Oh no, we buy them in, ready frozen.'

While we waited, we chatted. It felt so good to be talking to someone who knew nothing about me, who had no connection to my old life. I was reluctant to say anything about myself, but it seemed rude not to respond when he said,

'I've not seen you around before. Where are you from?' It was an innocent enough question.

'I've just moved here.'

'Right.' It was an invitation for a little more.

'I'm in digs. On Lilac Court.'

'Oh, I know it - just round the corner. You working, or what?'

211

Jenny 2

'Well, I could do with finding something. I'll be starting college in the autumn.'

He pulled a face. 'Rather you than me. I never got on with school much.'

That made me smile, but I didn't say anything more. It seemed I had found a kindred spirit.

As he was placing the now defrosted mouse in the tank, the doorway suddenly darkened as a large woman in ill-fitting trousers filled it.

'Have you got my bale of straw yet?'

'It's in the back, Mrs. White. I'll just go and get it,' he called, murmuring as an aside, 'Don't go anywhere. I'll be back in a minute.'

My eyes were still on the snake. I marvelled as I watched it pounce on the mouse, attacking it and dislocating its jaws in the process.

'It's OK, that's normal - they're made that way.' He was back from dealing with the other customer. 'Look - you can see the bulge as he swallows it.

Chapter Twenty-Two

Beth

Beth

That night, snug in my clean, warm bed at Mrs, Green's, I hugged to myself the memory of the day. I had ended up staying at the pet shop for most of the morning, while Patrick - I found out his name when Mrs. White said 'Bye, then, Patrick. See you next week,' as she bustled out with her bale of hay - while Patrick served customers and fed animals and in between we talked pretty much non-stop. I found out he was holding the fort for his uncle, who was the shop's owner. Like me, he wasn't sure what he wanted to do long term.

'But you're a natural in here,' I said. 'You look as though you belong; you're so confident!'

He looked pleased when I said that.

'Ah, well, that's the trick, isn't it? If you look confident the customers place their confidence in you. And then you become confident. Easy!'

Everything seemed easy to Patrick. He was so different from the people I'd hung around with at school.

'So, what do you do when you're not minding the shop?'

'Ah, well...' For the first time he appeared hesitant. 'That's a moot point.' He sat on a packing case and motioned me towards the only chair in the shop. 'To be honest, not a lot! I sort of more or less dropped out of Sixth Form...My uncle thinks I should go to College and improve my grades...redo my A Levels, maybe...'

'What about your parents?' I asked this a bit warily, knowing how much I hated that question. That's when his face clouded over, and for the first time he seemed uncertain of himself. Then his words came out all in a rush, and he didn't look at me as he spoke.

'They died when I was twelve. Car accident. It's OK, truly,' he added, when he saw how awkward I felt. 'I got used to it a long time ago. My uncle took me in. He's my Mum's brother.' He was quiet, then, and I knew not to say anything.

'He looks like her, as far as I can tell from the photographs. To be honest...' he met my gaze, and I saw that his eyes were an unusual shade of green. 'I can't really remember what she looked like. Just before I go to sleep I try to sort of conjure up her face, but she's become a blur...'

He bent down and picked up a piece of straw that had dropped from one of the cages and I watched him twisting it between his long fingers.

'Is there just you?' I asked, after a bit. 'I mean, no brothers or sisters?'

'No, just me and Uncle Tony.'

Later on, I found myself confiding things that I'd always intended to keep buried. It seemed only fair, though, after he had shared his painful memories. When I mentioned College again, he said,

'Is that right? Maybe I'll come along too if you're going to be there.'

I blushed, although I don't think he really meant anything by it. I said it was time to go.

He called after me as I was leaving.

'Beth...' I liked the way he said my name. He wasn't to know how new it was. 'What are you doing this evening? Maybe we could meet up after I finish here?'

That's how we became friends. A few days later he introduced me to his Uncle Tony, a smiling giant of a man with faded hair that must once have been the colour of

Jenny 2

Patrick's. I told them about Rory, but I had to decline Uncle Tony's offer to source a new rat for me.

Patrick showed me his prized possession, a motorbike that looked oddly small for his tall frame, although he assured me it was a perfect fit. He spent hours polishing and tending it, and I suspected that it played something of a similar role in his life as Rory had in mine. I wondered if he talked to it, the way I used to talk to Rory.

One day a card appeared in the window of the florist's shop: Assistant wanted. No Experience Necessary - Training Given. Trembling, I went in and asked about the job. The next week, I began work, and the week after that I spent some of my wages on a pot plant for my landlady, who said it was one of the best presents she'd ever had, although I seriously doubted it. I also bought a box of chocolates for Gloria, and the two of us devoured them surreptitiously in Gloria's office while we were supposed to be discussing how I should budget the rest of my wages.

It was cool in the shop, even when the weather outside warmed up. Ellie, the florist, explained patiently why the flowers needed to be kept at that temperature, and eventually I got used to it. I'd got used to so many things in the past sixteen years.

I saved up and bought myself a padded jacket to put on when I entered the shop, and I took it off when I left. For some reason it brought back memories of shopping trips with my parents, although I was quick to suppress those. I also knew with certainty, before many weeks were out, that it was not what I wanted to spend the rest of my life doing, and so I told Gloria that I was looking forward to the college course. She gave me a broad smile and said I'd made her day.

To Uncle Tony's delight Patrick enrolled for his A Levels, while I was persuaded by Gloria to visit the Special Needs

Jenny 2

Department, although that's not what it was called at the College, a few days before the end of term.

'Here we are.' Gloria glanced at the sign above the door. 'Student Support.'

Her smile of encouragement urged me through the door. 'I'm right behind you. Come on'

The receptionist took my name. 'Oh good! We're expecting you. Ginny will be out in a moment.'

Ginny turned out to be every bit as warm and welcoming as the receptionist as she ushered us into her cosy office.

'Would you like tea or coffee?' she asked with a smile.

A few minutes later it was brought by one of the College catering students, all done up in her chef's whites. This definitely wasn't like school.

The student placed the tray on the desk

'I've brought some cookies too, Ginny,' she said, 'Fresh from the oven!' Then she smiled at me, as though I was a real person and not some weird outcast.

After the cups had been dealt with, and while we were still making crumbs as we devoured the cookies - they were still warm - Ginny got down to business. It was clear that she had been well-briefed.

'I know you've not had a very positive experience of education so far, Beth, and I'm really pleased you've decided to trust us to try and give you something better. We do know how hard it can be to ask for help sometimes, but, you know, support is available here whenever you need it.'

'What…how…?' I noted that Ginny didn't pounce on my hesitation and fill in the blanks, as all the teachers used to; she didn't talk over me or roll her eyes. It even occurred to me that she might be someone I could trust.

'I mean, how is it organised? Are there classes and form tutors?'

Jenny 2

Ginny explained that the structure of the College was much less formal than that, at the same time emphasising the various levels of support. She talked about inclusivity, said there was a whole range of different needs. She made it sound like pretty much anything could be catered for.

'What about sanctions?' I was a bit nervous about this. 'I'm not living at home, so who will you contact?'

Ginny was so patient with me, like she really understood. She explained that any problems would first of all be discussed with the student concerned.

'We usually find that difficulties can be sorted out fairly easily. You will be developing as an independent learner, so we hope you will come to us if you have problems.'

'What about…detentions?'

Ginny actually laughed when I said that, but not unkindly.

'Heaven forbid!' was all she said.

Then Gloria leaned forward, placing her cup on the desk with a bit of a clatter. She had clearly enjoyed that cup of tea, her first since breakfast, she said.

'I understand there are counsellors here, to help with non-academic problems?'

'Oh yes. We try to cater for the whole person, not just the brain. Although I gather…'

She gave me a serious look, and I began to wonder if I'd got the whole thing wrong after all. I had taken an assessment test the previous week, even though I was sick with fear, but I'd forced myself to complete it. Now was the moment of truth.

'I gather you have a very good brain.'

'Oh! I…I…' Did I really just hear that?

I looked at Gloria, who did her eyebrow-raising thing again.

Jenny 2

By the time we left the campus I was clutching a pile of leaflets detailing all the student resources, including the courses of study. I had also been taken to see the academic tutor, who explained how courses could be tweaked and tailored so that I could do enough in one year to prepare for A Levels the following year. I doubted that, but didn't argue. I was still speechless from the interview with Ginny.

Gloria had to hurry off to deal with a crisis involving one of her other clients; I got the impression she would have preferred to stay with me. As she left, she gave me a great bearhug, and a suggestion.

'Why don't you have a wander round and see everything before you go?'

It was big, much bigger than school, a world within a world, and little worlds within that. Although I wasn't allowed in - safeguarding rules - I could see into the Nursery. Small children on tap for the Child Care course! I wondered where they got them from. One of the staff asked if was doing the course next year, and didn't mind that I wasn't. She told me something about it anyway.

'The children belong to members of staff or students, or sometimes members of the public if we have spare places.'

I really liked the idea of that. It felt like being part of a family.

And then suddenly it was autumn, and the start of term. True to his word, Patrick was there along with me. I often wonder whether I would even have got over the threshold if I'd had to go to the College alone that first day. Even after all Gloria's careful arrangements, and Mrs. Green's nurturing, and even with Patrick's encouragement, it was only because he held my hand - literally - that I made it into the building.

Jenny 2

At lunchtime we met up in the canteen and I watched with amazement as he polished off pizza and chips as well as some unidentifiable pudding drowning in slick yellow custard. I couldn't eat a thing, even though the waves of nausea had faded somewhat once I discovered that College really wasn't School. I'd had an absolutely absorbing English lesson that morning that reminded me a bit of my time with Mrs. Daniels, and a talk with Ginny about strategies for coping with dyslexia, and now I was content to just sit with Patrick.

'So,' he said at last, licking the back of the spoon and pulling a face at his reflection in it. 'How was your first morning?'

'Blissful! I can't believe this is me.'

'What have you got this afternoon?'

'Study Skills. You?'

'Chemistry.' Patrick had already told me that he'd chosen science subjects at random when he was at school and had left because of what his teachers had described as a 'relaxed attitude to formal learning'. There hadn't seemed much chance of a career at the time, but as his interest in the pet shop had grown, he realised that the subjects he had abandoned might after all be helpful in furthering a career, one that involved animals.

'I could do with coming to a Study Skills class. I think I've forgotten how to!'

'And I never knew in the first place!'

We laughed together so easily.

I caught sight of the giant clock high on the canteen wall. There were no bells here.

'Nearly time.'

Patrick disentangled himself from the stool and picked up his bag. 'You're doing amazingly. I'm proud of you.'

That made me catch my breath. I wanted to hold on to this moment. I stood on my tiptoes and gave him a hug.

Jenny 2

'It's all thanks to you.'

We had arranged to meet outside the main door and walk back together after classes. Because I was still rather scared of that roaring monster of his, Patrick's version of Rory, and not at all sure yet that I wanted to risk being Patrick's pillion passenger, he had willingly agreed to forsake his beloved bike that day in order to walk into College with me.

Before we were due to meet, I had an appointment with the Health and Beauty Department, which offered its services, under tutor supervision, in much the same way that Hospitality and Catering supplied food to the canteen. Now that my hair had grown to a more respectable length, after the frenzied hacking I'd given it before I left home, I wondered if it could be shaped into something a little, well, more feminine. It made me blush to use the word, even to myself. My hair was blond again now, the pink dye and dreadlocks a thing of the past, things that belonged to Lizzie, not me. But how would Patrick like me to look?

I was a few minutes late. The supervision process had slowed down the haircut unbelievably, but then I was glad the tutor had been there to ensure it was done properly. This was an important haircut.

I wasn't sure what Patrick's expression meant as he saw me. I felt exposed, no longer hiding behind a defensive shield of rebellion. Up until that moment I'd felt there might be a sort of glow and an energy about me. Now it faltered. He just stood there, looking at me, and I began to turn away.

So he didn't like it? He didn't really like me: perhaps he was only being kind, seeing me into College on the first day. He was a kind person; maybe he saw me as he saw the animals in the shop, interesting, cute, even, needing a bit of attention.

He caught up with me, took my arm, turning me to face him.

'You're looking pretty good, Buster!'

That was too much for me after the emotions of the day, and I found myself shedding the tears I'd promised myself would not be shed, no matter what.

'Hey, what's wrong?'

He placed his hands on either side of my shoulders. They felt warm through my sleeves. My head was level with his chest.

'I'm not a pet.'

'No, you're not. You're an amazing person.'

His tone was gentle, and it wasn't the tone he used to the animals in the pet shop.

'You've gone through so much and you've picked yourself up and you've carried on. You've helped me get back on track. Honestly, Beth, I'd never have made it to College without you. I can't bear to think of you being alone any more. Come here.'

He hugged me then, and I let the remaining tears soak into his shirt for a while before I looked up at him. He dropped a kiss on my head.

'So, what do you think of my hair, then?'

'Your hair? Have you done something to it?'

I mock-punched him then, laughing as much as he was, and it was all easy between us again. I really didn't mind being teased in this gentle way.

Chapter Twenty-Three

Rachel – Hannah

Rachel

Over the next couple of years Hannah and I continued to meet for coffee from time to time. She was working again, and things seemed to be getting better between her and her husband. I was glad for them, glad that their loss was no longer forcing them apart as had happened with me and Dave.

Most of the time we only talked about safe topics, like the weather and the price of petrol and how there was nothing worth watching on TV these days. In some ways it was almost as if the past had never happened; we were just two people passing the time of day, but always beneath the surface was that largely unspoken connection between us that had lasted since Lizzie was five.

There was one day when she seemed down.

'What is it?'

'I keep thinking about how Lizzie didn't know that we loved her. I just wish it wasn't too late to tell her.'

'It might not be too late. You can still have hope.'

I had tried to keep the bitterness out of my tone. Then I looked up and saw she was staring at me, in a very concentrated way. She spoke hesitantly.

'I used to hate you, you know.'

I didn't know what to say.

'You were always so sure of yourself, so... in command.'

That took me by surprise.

'No, you are so wrong. That's not me at all. It's never been me. I was a failure, teaching other people's children because I didn't have – couldn't have - my own.'

Jenny 2

Hannah

That was when she told me about her own lost child, about what had happened at the hospital that day.

'She'd have been twenty this year.'

'Same as Lizzie.'

'Twentieth of April'

'Same as Lizzie,' I said again.

We put down our mugs and stared at each other for long minutes. After all this time I was face to face with the distressed woman whose howl of anguish still sometimes haunted my sleep, only to discover that I had known her all along.

Finally, I managed to say, 'I wish I'd known that, back then. I thought you were judging me all the time. You seemed to know my daughter better than I did.' I pressed my lips together, trying to supress the words, but they came out anyway, along with a sob. 'She liked you so much better than me.'

Rachel looked nonplussed and made a half gesture towards me, then changed her mind. Instead, she said, 'In a way I *was* judging you, I suppose, because you seemed to have everything: so smart, so sure of yourself, with your brood and your nice house...'

'So you hated me too...'

'No, not hated. I was jealous. Jealous of all you had. You had everything and I had nothing, but still you were unsatisfied. You had *Lizzie*...'

'Sometimes I wished I didn't.'

She looked up at me and I saw the glint of tears. 'Are you shocked?'

'Not now, no. I would have been then.'

Jenny 2

Rachel

I decided it would be OK to tell her something truly shocking. Taking a deep breath, I began to tell her about Jenny, how she had continued to grow in my mind after we lost her.

'When I started working with Lizzie – she was Elizabeth then, of course - well she sort of became Jenny for me. I had been carrying around in my head a vague image of a little girl, and then suddenly she was there, real and alive. I could put a physical form to my lost child … in time I think Lizzie did become Jenny for me…'

I couldn't go on then. I remembered how angry she'd been, that time at her house when she told me to leave. Here I was, taking over her child again. I looked up.

'I'm sorry. You must think that's awful. Do you still hate me?'

Slowly, she shook her head. 'No. It explains a lot that I couldn't understand before.'

'I do understand how hard that is, the not knowing. I at least have certainty. I know I can never have Jenny back, but that's all right, now.'

'Is it? All right?'

I thought for a moment, and discovered the answer. 'Yes.'

I knew somehow that it was. Lizzie had never been Jenny, and I had wronged Hannah by allowing her to be, but I still had hope for myself, and had begun to find healing and wholeness.

A little later she said, 'Tell me about Jenny. If that's all right?'

I found I could, after all, talk about it. She knew about the ward, and Sister Stevens, of course. I was still getting used to the fact that our connection went back far beyond Hillmore High, before the dreadful TA, right back to the very beginning.

Jenny 2

I described what it had been like for me, being in hospital, how it wasn't the first time. I told her about the terrible moment when they told me my baby had died inside me, the photograph Dave had taken, how I had failed to see how lost he was too…

I thought it would probably be the last time that I told the story, and the last time that I would need to.

I continued to see Cara for some time, but less and less frequently, and the day came when we both knew it was time for me to strike out on my own.

"When you first came here,' Cara said, 'You were feeling very stuck in your life. You'd been through a great deal, a lot of changes, but somehow you couldn't let go of the past. You were nearing the age at which most women are facing the menopause, but I know it wasn't quite like that for you…'

'Not with my medical history.' It surprised me that it didn't hurt any longer to acknowledge that.

'Yet something brought you here.'

I tried to remember how it had been then. I wasn't sure I was the same person. Recalling that time was like looking in from the outside at another person's life.

'My sister was fed up with me. After she'd chivvied me and told me to pull myself together, and after she'd tried being really sympathetic and treating me with kid gloves, and after she'd suggested seeing the doctor, and taken me on trips to take me out of myself, she sort of threw up her hands and told me I'd have to do something myself, because she had no idea what else to do.'

'So coming to see me was a last resort?' Cara laughed.

'No! It's been what saved me! It's true that I couldn't let go of the past…well, you know all about the past now.

Jenny 2

Lizzie's disappearance triggered feelings about the loss of Jenny, and...'

There was a silence, but I no longer found the silences uncomfortable.

'I don't think my age had anything to do with it; I had known for years that I would never have children.' I paused. Cara was looking at me. 'Have more children,' I added.

'That's important, Rachel.'

I looked up, surprised.

'What is?'

'That you can acknowledge that you did have a child of your own.'

And I knew she was right. 'Yes, and that child was Jenny. However much I cared about Lizzie, however much it triggered memories of my own loss, she was never my child.'

I paused to allow the truth of that to sink in. Cara allowed the silence to continue.

'And... I have finally managed to separate Jenny and Lizzie in my mind.'

Sounds floated up from the street below: children playing, a dog barking, a car engine starting up, footsteps. Ordinary sounds, bringing me back to the everyday world I was about to re-enter. I had already told Cara about the tentative friendship I had formed with Hannah.

'I finally told her...about Jenny, about...you know...being haunted by her, seeing her grow. *Imagining* her.'

There was a longer pause this time.

'That's all it ever was: my imagination. How could I possibly know what she would have been like?'

Cara said: 'Was it all bad, the imagining?'

'No...no, it wasn't bad, not entirely. It helped me to survive; it led me into the teaching profession...but I wish I hadn't driven Dave away because of it. It took me a long time to see that it was his loss too.'

Jenny 2

I glanced at the clock. I knew our time was drawing to a close.

'You know, Rachel, you have repeatedly spoken of yourself as someone who isn't, and never was, a mother. But you were, however briefly. You were a mother. You carried a child to term, and you gave birth. And you loved Jenny.'

She allowed this thought to hover in the air.

'And because of that experience, you were able to harness your maternal feelings to help the children and young people in your care. You can't turn back the clock, but you can learn from the past: you can see the past differently, and you can feel differently about it.'

'And I do.' I realised in that moment that I'd forgiven myself at last. 'Would you…would you be offended if I said that I don't think I need to come any more?'

Cara smiled. 'I'd be pleased, not offended. I'm glad you feel that things have shifted for you, and that you can now get on with your life.'

Cara stood and gave me a hug. I felt the tears welling, but they were no longer tears of pain.

'I can't promise that everything will run smoothly for the rest of your life,' she said, as I moved towards the door, 'but I do know that you are stronger than you were and, now that you've faced the past, you have what you need to face the future.'

Hannah

I had found a strange comfort in my relationship with Rachel. At first it was because she was the final link with the past, with Lizzie. Later, when she told me about her own lost child, I understood how much sadness she too had experienced, and somehow that made a difference.

Jenny 2

Sometimes we met at the coffee stall in the park. There was a bench where we could sip our drinks and watch the ducks and the small children feeding them totally unsuitable things and squealing with excitement. Despite the noise it was peaceful sitting there in the open air with the spring sunshine on our backs. It seemed to make talking about the past OK. Then she said,

'I was so much in the wrong.'

'What?'

'With Lizzie. About Lizzie. About you...'

'No, I don't think so. None of us had the whole picture. And Lizzie learned a lot from you. She enjoyed your lessons – '

'When she was in them...'

We both laughed at that. Rachel added, 'True, she did spend a lot of her time in Learning Support – '

And then we discovered the final link in our chain of connection. I had talked a bit about my own regrets, and she mentioned again her husband. He sounded a very kind man, very patient. I said as much.

'Oh, he was,' she said. 'And I took it for weakness, or not caring. I was stupid and stubborn in refusing to countenance the idea of moving on after our loss.'

'But loss isn't something you choose to feel or not feel, is it? You can only move on when you are ready, I guess. You lost such a lot, didn't you? You lost not just the child you gave birth to, but all your hopes for the future.'

'You sound like my therapist!'

I was horrified she should think I was pretending to be something I'm not.

'Oh, look, no, I'm sorry, I'm really sorry...I didn't mean to sound as though I was, you know, taking on a role or anything...'

I wanted to bite back the words. Who was I to talk to her about her own loss? She was really no different from

Jenny 2

me: she was a human being who suffered pain and loss just as I did.

'No, I mean it. You sounded just like her then. That's just the sort of thing Cara says.'

'Cara?' There was a pause. 'You're seeing Cara?'

'Yes. Have you heard of her? She's really good. I'd recommend her. Actually, I think you'd find her really helpful...'

'I know. I do. I mean I've been seeing Cara too.'

We laughed about that then. It seemed inevitable that our lives, so long linked through unhappy events, should still be connected by the means we had both chosen to seek healing.

'You know you told me about how Jenny sort of lived on in your mind? Well after Lizzie left I used to have this dream – daydream, really. Elizabeth as a serene young woman, carefully dressed and smiling, walking towards me. She would tell me she was so glad she took my advice about her choice of University, that she'd enjoyed every minute of her course, and was now ready to take on a responsible job.'

Rachel smiled sympathetically.

'I know all about those sorts of dreams.'

'And she would say how glad she was that I stopped her from doing those silly, adolescent things she wanted to do, and ask where she would be now if she'd gone ahead and had a tattoo? Or a nose piercing?'

'That was never going to be Lizzie, though, was it?'

'No.' I shook my head to banish the thoughts. 'It was a nice day-dream, but it didn't work. You know what? I actually found myself longing for Lizzie as she really was, dreadlocks, piercings, rat and all... I love her so much and I want her to know that, but it's too late now. It's all too late.'

Rachel held me as I sobbed. I think she was crying too. Then we walked around the lake in peaceful silence for a while.

Chapter Twenty-Four

Beth

Beth

Mrs. Green was very dubious about it and said she would need to contact Gloria.

'It's just, you know, we really can't bear to be apart.'

My landlady gave a sigh. 'Young love. Yes, I know, I do, believe me, Beth, I do understand. But listen…' She sat heavily on the threadbare sofa, motioning me to sit beside her.

'You've done so well, haven't you? Did you ever imagine you'd get all those GCSEs in one year?'

I pointed out that I'd had to resit maths. Mrs. Green waved that aside.

'But you passed second time, didn't you? You stuck with it and you got the grade. And that's the point, isn't it? You're halfway through your A levels and your tutors are pleased with you. Don't jeopardise that now by letting yourself be distracted.'

'But I wouldn't. I won't be. We'll be able to revise together. It'll save time: at the moment we spend half our time travelling backwards and forwards to be together.'

'Save time? Or be a distraction? Come on, Beth! After all you've been through, did you ever imagine you'd be applying to University? You have your whole future ahead of you and a real chance to make something of your life. Don't risk all that…'

'My whole future, yes, and I want to spend it with Patrick.'

Jenny 2

She sighed again. She really did care about me, but she must have forgotten what it was really like to be young and in love.

Gloria did a lot of sighing too, a few days later, when I was summoned to her office. Then she did something much worse: she insisted on seeing Patrick's flat. He, of course, was charm itself. He opened the door and greeted her with his best smile.

'Do please come in.'

'Thank you. It's good to meet you at last.'

'And you, Gloria. I've heard such a lot about you from Beth – all good, by the way.'

She laughed. She knew when she was being charmed, all right. However, her face fell as she examined what passed for a kitchen, and she was clearly horrified by the shared bathroom on the half landing, with its mouldy walls and stained enamel bath. Pat took us back upstairs quickly and offered Gloria the comfortable end of the sofa.

'I understand from Beth that you were living with your Uncle, Patrick,' she said as she settled herself. 'Was it your own choice to leave?'

'Oh yes. He didn't throw me out or anything. I still go round there and see him. He's very supportive.'

'So, if you don't mind my asking, why the flat?'

Pat gave a shrug and another of his smiles. 'Independence? Spreading my wings…?'

He had moved out of Uncle Tony's the minute he knew he had his deferred place on the animal management course. It was at a Uni some distance away from the town we had both grown up in, the place where bad things had happened to both of us. The plan was for me to get a place at the same Uni.

Jenny 2

Gloria stood up then and paced the cramped living room. I could see she was trying to keep her thoughts to herself, but her face was screaming 'not suitable'!

'May I see the bedroom?'

'Of course.' He leapt up and opened the door with a sweeping motion and a little bow, as though ushering her through the door of a stately home. I was cringing, but as the door opened fully I saw that for once he had actually made the bed.

'Hmm. Not much space in here, is there?'

I pointed out that we didn't need much space; neither of us had much in the way of possessions.

'Mainly books,' Pat said, which was true. Some of mine were in there, scattered about the floorspace amongst his discarded washing.

Gloria raised a lot of questions about housing benefits and other support I'd been getting, as well as putting hard questions to me about what would happen if we broke up. I refused to take that seriously.

'But we won't. Ask Pat if you don't believe me.'

There was more sighing. 'That is what you say now, Beth, and I know you believe it, but...'

'No! No buts. There are no buts with us two.'

Finally, she agreed to another meeting, this time at her office. Pat was again on his best behaviour.

'Look, I know you have to have Beth's best interests at heart. She's your client and I'm not. I realise that. But honestly, Gloria, we are committed to each other...'

'How committed?'

He looked startled. 'Like... for life? Is that good enough?'

He gave my hand a squeeze and I felt my heart squeeze with joy along with it.

'Is that true for you too, Beth?'

I nodded, too emotional to breathe.

Jenny 2

'Then why the hurry? You have your whole lives ahead of you, don't you?'

Technically, I didn't need Gloria's permission, but I really wanted her blessing, so I agreed not to move until my end of year exams were over. In July I said goodbye to Eileen Green, with some regrets because she'd been really kind to me. I got a holiday job at the florist's and with my first week's wages bought her the largest bouquet I could carry.

'They're like you,' she said. 'A bit spiky on the outside, before they open out, but then truly beautiful on the inside.' She gave me a hug, and I had to wipe my tears on my sleeve so she wouldn't see them. Then she straightened up and said, 'Now, remember: work hard and pass those exams, my girl.'

Gloria, like the miracle-worker she was, managed to find some money from a bursary for the final year of my education, and I settled down in the flat to make my Uni application. To think that this was really me: dropout, failure, no-hoper, poring over University prospectuses and looking forward to a whole new life.

I kept my promise to Gloria and Mrs. Green and worked hard at my A levels, only occasionally allowing Pat to distract me. On lazy Saturday mornings we would lie back in bed, gazing up at the yellowed ceiling and trying to find patterns in the network of cracks.

'Look! Over there!'
'Where?'
'Over towards the corner. Next to the one that looks like a map of the Underground.'
'What am I supposed to be looking at?'
'It's a chicken.'
'I can't see a chicken.'

Jenny 2

'Yes, look. See where my finger's pointing There, right there. See?'

'Doesn't look like a chicken to me. Where's it's head?'

'I dunno. They don't usually come with their head on.'

'What...? You're talking about a *roast* chicken?' I hit him with a pillow and some feathers came out, tickling my nose. 'Chicken murderer! And you an animal lover...'

'Well, you like roast chicken too.'

The pillow fight got fiercer and only stopped when I started coughing. Some of the feathers had got into my throat.

We had two gas rings and no oven, so a roast dinner was out of the question, except when we went to Uncle Tony's sometimes on a Sunday. That's when I wished I had a family to introduce Pat to, although I wasn't thinking of the family I'd actually had, more like a dream family.

'I'm your family now,' Pat said to me once when I was feeling a bit down about it, and I was thankful for that. 'And one day we'll have something better, you know, maybe a carpet on the floor and our own bathroom, little luxuries like that?'

None of that mattered to me.

'Yeah, one day, maybe, but this has everything we need.'

'Well, true: for a start it has a shed for my bike...'

'And we have a kitchen, of sorts...'

'And a fridge...'

'And a share in a bathroom...'

'And who needs to spend a long time in the bathroom anyway?'

Jenny 2

This was a reference to some of the other residents, who lacked both patience and consideration for the needs of others.

'Yeah. Who cares?'

Pat had gone back to his job at the pet shop once his exams were over: ideal experience for someone planning to study animal management at Uni. It paid for the rent and petrol for his bike. He also did shifts in the Students' Union bar at the local Uni. I think he secretly enjoyed immersing himself in the student atmosphere.

We talked about getting married, one day, but there was no hurry. We knew we were committed to each other, so what else mattered? Besides, who would we invite to the wedding? Pat had no family to speak of, and I certainly didn't want to speak of mine, although I did just occasionally wonder what they were all doing. Sometimes, just as I drifted off to sleep, I wondered if they ever missed me at all.

We talked idly about travelling, taking time out; sometimes we talked about running a pet shop of our own, but as my exams approached, we talked more seriously about my need to focus on revision. I still had to pinch myself to believe I had actually applied to University: Elizabeth Brown, lost cause, nuisance and black sheep of the family was going to conform at last! With the encouragement of my tutor, I was predicted good enough grades to end up with three offers, one of which I might actually achieve. Thankfully, one of them was at the Uni where Pat had his place. Now that I'd done it, I couldn't wait. I actually, truly, wanted to learn! Pat wasn't brimming with excitement in the same way, but then he didn't have the same need to prove himself. No-one had called *him* stupid when he was growing up, although he admitted that they had often called him *lazy*. That didn't surprise me at all; I loved his relaxed attitude to life, and the fact that he didn't feel the need either to rebel or to prove everyone else wrong. He just took life as it came. I wished with all my heart that I could do that.

The two minutes seemed to last a lifetime. I forced myself not to look, to fix my eyes instead on the ugly wall clock, mentally counting off the agonising seconds. Then I waited a bit longer, for luck. Finally, taking a deep breath, I looked. There was a blue line, clear as day.

How had it happened? Well, yes, obviously I knew how, in principle, but we'd been careful, hadn't we? I began to wonder what Pat would say. I imagined myself rushing down to the front door as soon as I heard his key in the lock, flinging my arms round him. 'Guess what?'

But was that the way to do it? I didn't doubt that he wanted children, eventually, but it might be better to wait for him to get into the flat, ease off his boots and sink into the low armchair, groaning as he usually did, before I hit him with the news. Then I could introduce the subject gently, without giving him a shock.

I glanced again at the clock. He was late back from the pet shop. That was unusual for a Friday evening. It was the night he worked at the Students' Union Bar, so he was usually home from work in good time so we could eat before he had to go out again for his shift in the Students' Union. I often went down there towards the end of his shift to drink a thrifty half pint and then walk back with him, our arms wound round each other as he told funny stories about his day, or about the customers he'd served that evening.

I thought I should really get on with preparing the meal, although I wasn't feeling particularly hungry myself. No doubt he'd be home any minute. He was on the bike, so it shouldn't take him long. As I opened the fridge, I realised how queasy I was feeling, and the thought of food, of cooking... I got to the shared bathroom just in time, thanking

Jenny 2

my lucky stars that Bill from next door wasn't in there with his hearing aid switched off.

It was as I came out, wiping my nose and mouth and reflecting that if there was one thing I really, really hated, it was being sick, that I became aware of the insistent knocking on the front door. The doorbell was broken, and the landlord still hadn't fixed it, despite all the tenants nagging him. The door had frosted glass panels in the upper part and through them I could make out two dark blue outlines. Whoever it was, they were clearly not going anywhere. Equally clearly, no-one else was going to answer the door. I descended the stairs slowly, feeling sicker than ever...

Because I was still a client of social services, and in receipt of benefits, the College contacted Gloria after I'd been absent without explanation for three days. I could see how worried Gloria was when she came round to the flat. Someone else had let her in: there was no way I could have dragged myself down the stairs, and I don't really know how I ended up flat out on the floor. Nothing seemed to matter any more.

'I knew there was something wrong,' Gloria muttered, as she heaved me up off the floor and got me onto the bed – our bed, where I would never again lie snugly next to Patrick making plans for the future.

By the time the doctor arrived, she had managed to get most of the story out of me, although I'm not sure how much sense I was making. I can see now that Patrick never stood a chance. The lorry had failed to stop at the Give Way sign and gone hurtling on to the High Street at the exact moment he and his precious motorbike were passing the junction. It would have been instantaneous, the police had said.

Jenny 2

And now I was pregnant, and on my own. And Patrick would never know.

Gloria sighed and muttered under her breath, 'Just when I thought things were moving forward...'

The doctor insisted that, in view of my condition - I was now being so sick I couldn't keep anything down - I should spend a day or two in hospital, under observation.

Gloria gave me one of her suspicious looks. 'Have you actually *tried* to eat anything?'

I didn't answer. I was finding it impossible to react to anything anyone said, until she told me she really needed to contact my parents, and that brought me to my senses. Gloria laughed at my furious refusal; getting a reaction out of me had clearly been her aim.

It was the day I felt the baby move – 'quicken' they used to call it - that the world somehow righted itself. The nausea was receding, and I had, reluctantly, started doing things again, attending classes, studying a little in the evenings, even shopping for food. Shopping for one. I was reaching up for a packet of cornflakes at the back of the little convenience store on the corner, when I felt a strange fluttering sensation. I was so taken by surprise that I exclaimed out loud, and several people turned to look at me before returning to their shopping baskets.

The cornflakes never got bought. I left the shopping and stepped out on to the street. It was a fine day in late spring, and somewhere a blackbird was singing. I walked, oblivious of my surroundings; as I gazed into the cloudless sky, up through the layers to where the air was so thin that it was no longer there, to the place where space itself began, I felt alive and at one with the universe. Women had done this, experienced this, since the beginning of human history. I was one with them, one with women all over the world. I was part of the greatest miracle I could imagine. I was carrying a living child inside me.

Jenny 2

The elation lasted until I got home. Then I sat down and wept because Pat would never know his child, never hold it, never watch it grow, never know its love, and I would have to be mother and father to our child. I slept in my clothes that night, and by morning the pillow was soaked with tears.

The light filtered through the undrawn curtains, waking me not long after I had finally succumbed to exhaustion. As I heaved myself out of bed I felt it again, that strange, hardly discernible sensation of the child within me. That was when I knew. I knew I must make plans. I had responsibilities now. But, the question was: what was the responsible thing to do: condemn my child to a life of poverty with one parent, or give it up to people better and wiser than myself?

'Beth!'

Gloria's cry of surprise showed she was both pleased and surprised to see me, in equal measure. She stood back to look at me: I had rounded out since the last time we'd met, and Gloria, apparently satisfied, breathed a sigh of relief. Sweeping her bag and a pile of papers off a chair in one of her grand gestures, she made space for me to sit down.

I launched straight in before I lost my resolve. 'I need somewhere else to live, somewhere where I don't have to share a bathroom; somewhere more suitable for a baby, without damp walls and peeling ceilings.' This was no time for small talk.

'I've been to the college, and my tutor is going to contact the exam board. Apparently they can make some special arrangements... I've been to the clinic this morning: everything is fine with the baby. He or she is growing nicely, and I'm feeling so much better since I stopped being sick.'

'Do you know what you're having?'

Jenny 2

'A baby?'

We both laughed. It seemed such a long time since I had been capable of making a joke. 'No, I didn't want to know the sex. It makes no difference; I'll love it to bits whatever it is.'

The solution Gloria came up with worked remarkably well. Within a week I was reinstalled in my old room at Mrs. Green's. My landlady was surprisingly happy to see me again, and not remotely fazed at the prospect of the baby. If anything, she was looking forward to it, she told me. She had a friend with grandchildren and an apparently inexhaustible supply of baby clothes, all clean and in very good condition. Social services had access to some of the other baby equipment, and once Mrs. Green had rearranged the furniture to make room for the cot beside my bed – my single bed - the room was very snug indeed.

During those months I was fussed over and fed and cared for, and treated with the greatest kindness. I wept over Patrick and the life we had planned together, but that was mostly at night, and I hid my tears at other times. Besides, I was busy. I had revision to do.

And so I completed my A Levels. Furthermore, I got better grades than Theo, although it was to be some years later before I found that out. He said then that his heart had never been in the science subjects Dad had persuaded him to choose.

On the day the results came through, I called Gloria to tell her the good news, and to thank her. I'd got a place at my second choice – the local University, which, ironically, now suited my current situation. Gloria congratulated me mechanically – I think her first reaction was relief; then gave a little yelp when she realised what it meant.

Jenny 2

'So you're in! You got your place at Uni!' She was almost more excited than I was. 'Wouldn't that be great news to tell your family?'

'Now come on, Gloria. That wasn't part of the deal. You know that.'

'OK, OK.' Gloria had calmed down a bit by this time. 'But seriously, Beth, wouldn't you like to see them, tell them about the baby? They could do a lot more to help you than Social Services can....'

'You're wrong, actually.' I knew my tone had darkened, but I had to be truthful. 'You and your team have done far more for me than....'

I didn't finish the sentence. At the other end of the line I knew that Gloria could sense the tears sliding down my nose. She made a soothing noise.

'So, how long is it now?' I could hear her mentally calculating the weeks.

'Any day now, according to the midwife.'

'Hmm. We haven't got long, have we? I wonder whether you would be advised to defer your course for a year?'

The next call I made was to my college tutor in Student Support, who advised me to accept the place, and to get in touch with the University Nursery. She then congratulated me warmly and wished me well. I knew she meant it too. Elizabeth Brown was a success story, as far as the college was concerned.

The twinges that I had taken to be indigestion earlier in the day seemed to be coming with increased frequency. At first I put it down to all the excitement, but after a couple of hours I had to admit that Something was happening. Something Big. It was time to call for help.

Jenny 2

'Eileen! Eileen!' It was the first time Mrs Green had been on first name terms with a social services client, but then she always said I was a very special one.

There was no reply from downstairs. Could she have gone out? The effort needed to get myself down the stairs felt like too much, and, suddenly exhausted, I lay down for a bit of a rest. I must have dozed on and off for a while, and when I came to, the light had faded, and still my landlady wasn't back from wherever she'd gone. The pains - they were definitely pains now - were much stronger, and coming very close together. I placed my hands very cautiously on my huge belly and felt it tighten under them. Things were happening over which I had no control. I knew vaguely that I should be phoning the hospital, but Eileen Green's phone was in the hall downstairs, and my own mobile was annoyingly out of charge. The contractions started to come so close together that they blurred into one another, and I started to yell. Then, out of my head with fright and pain I beat the bedroom wall with my fists, kicking and writhing in panic.

I had lost all sense of time, so I've no idea how much later it was that I heard the front door open, and the welcome sound of footsteps coming up the stairs. These were brisk, no-nonsense footsteps, not like Mrs. Green's more tentative ones, and for a moment I panicked, wondering who this could be. The next thing I knew, Miss Stevens, the neighbour on the right-hand side of Mrs. Green's house, came in without ceremony, and in one fluid movement removed her coat and smoothed out the tangled bedclothes, all the while speaking gently and reassuringly.

'Don't worry. It's all OK.' she said in her soothing tones while she reached gently for my wrist. Her hands were cool and dry.

'I'll call the hospital in a moment. Let's just see how far on you are. You know I'm a midwife, don't you?

Chapter Twenty-Five

Beth - Rachel

Beth

At first I would sit for hours, just holding her, gazing in awe, in absolute wonder. I remembered what I'd been told about supporting the baby's head. Miles and Theo had both experienced the arrival of a new baby in the family, but it was all completely new to me. My own child was the first small baby I had ever really seen, certainly the first I had ever held. It was like holding a bird. I could feel her fluttering breath and her tiny, regular heartbeat. As I gazed at the diminutive bundle that was by some miracle my daughter, one hand carefully beneath her head, I was aware of the enormity of the responsibility. If I removed my hand, the tiny neck would snap, the precious new life would be snuffed out. I was terrified.

I'd moved into my flat with help from Gloria – it had made sense to accept a place at the local Uni after all - and spent a lot of time in the early days just watching as my child slept. Mine and Patrick's; I tried not to cry. I loved the way she abandoned herself so completely in sleep, her arms thrown above her head, her tiny frame rising and falling to the rhythm of her breathing. That moment when I held her for the very first time is burned into my brain. Over the weeks that followed I tried to learn how to shape my life to hers, this tiny new being with so much life ahead of her. I wondered if I would ever learn how to be a proper mother.

It was such a struggle learning how to do everything on my own. I was exhausted from the night feeds and the endless washing and keeping up with my studies. Sometimes I'd forget to eat, although I never forgot to feed her, not once, not even at night when I was dog-tired; some sixth sense always woke me the moment she stirred.

There was that one, dreadful night, though, when I'd been slogging all day over an essay on the theme of appearance and reality in *Hamlet*. I picked her up from the University nursery and just about managed to put one foot after the other as I wheeled the buggy back to the flat. The stairs seemed steeper than ever that evening, and I made myself a cup of tea and some toast before I fed her. She grizzled a bit and didn't seem all that hungry. That panicked me a bit, but I remembered what the health visitor had said about 'calm mother, calm baby' so I forced myself to sit patiently with her, until we both nodded off in the chair. When I came to it was after seven, and she was sleeping soundly. I carried her into her little bedroom and didn't even change her or undress her for fear of waking her. She looked peaceful when I put her in her cot and tiptoed out, straight to my own bed.

It was a shock when I woke and it was daylight. I had slept so soundly that at first I couldn't think where I was, or why I was still dressed. Then suddenly I knew; my heart started pounding and I had to fight my way out of the tangled bedclothes to run to her door. She should have had a feed hours ago.

I stood in the doorway for so long that my left foot went to sleep. I could see her, a tiny hump beneath the honeycomb blanket, still as a stone. Parental negligence: that's what I'd be charged with. I had never felt fear like it.

I found myself standing beside the cot without knowing I'd moved. She looked so peaceful. What should I do? Ring Gloria? Ring an ambulance? My mother would have known what to do. Why did she have to come into my mind at this moment of crisis in my life, my new life, the life I had chosen?

Jenny 2

Then I heard it: the little snuffling sound she makes when she's ready to wake up. I leaned over the cot, and her eyes opened, clear and bright and fully focused on me, and for the first time, her little rosebud mouth formed a smile, a smile just for me, for her mother.

I missed my first lecture that day. It didn't seem to matter, not when I could be here, tenderly bathing and feeding my child. It was almost nap time when I bowled up to the nursery.

It was Bonnie on duty in the babies' room that day.

'Bad night?' Her tone was sympathetic.

'They're all bad nights at the moment.'

It was too much effort to explain that, paradoxically, it had been a bad night because for once she had slept through.

'It'll get better,' she said, as she took my child from me with all the expertise I lacked. For some reason I began to cry, and Bonnie put her spare arm round my shoulders.

'It's hard on your own, isn't it?'

That made the tears worse.

'Here, wait while I put this little one down and...'

She was tucking her into a nursery pram as she spoke.

'Now we'll put her out in the garden where she'll get some fresh air, and you and I will have a cup of tea, okay?'

As we sat in the cramped staff room I began to relax.

'She's doing really well, your little girl.'

'Is she?'

'Yes! You only have to look at her to see she's happy and well cared-for.'

'She smiled at me this morning. At least, I think it was a smile.' I was already beginning to doubt myself.

Jenny 2

'Beth...' She sounded tentative for the first time. 'Is there really no-one who can help you out a bit? No family? Lots of our mums find they really value having their own mothers around in the early weeks.'

I noticed the time and said that I'd better go: best not to miss too many lectures. Bonnie took my half-drunk mug from me and gave me a reassuring pat on the arm as I stood.

'Let us know if things get too much for you.'

Professor Chandler was lecturing on Shakespearean sonnets, but I hardly heard a word. Instead, I found myself wondering if my mother had ever felt afraid when I was little, and whether I had ever smiled up at her the way my daughter had smiled at me that day.

In theory, things should have got better once she was established in her new routine of sleeping right through, but I now found myself waking in the night when I would have been feeding her, sometimes even tiptoeing into her room to check that she was breathing. On one such night, as I lay alone in the darkness, it came to me: surely the best thing I could do for her would be to give her away, relinquish all claim on her, let someone else give her the life she deserved?

But even as I thought this, a shudder ran through me and I felt the milk in my breasts flowing in response. An unknown tenderness enveloped me and I knew: nothing must ever harm this tiny child, entrusted to me, to Elizabeth Brown, clumsy dyslexic, school truant and rebel. No-one must ever be allowed to hurt her, humiliate her, make her feel inadequate. She might not have a father, but she would have a mother who would sacrifice anything and everything to give her the life she deserved. My decision was made – for good this time.

Jenny 2

Rachel

For a couple of years nothing of note happened in my life. I got up and went to work each day. Sometimes I went out for a drink with colleagues. Mostly I stayed at home, reading, marking, and wondering where my life had gone.

Hannah and I continued to meet up from time to time, and it always felt good to see her, but we no longer needed to talk about the past. Jono was at a conference in New York when the twin towers fell, and she had an anxious few hours until he managed to contact her. Then the air space was closed and they didn't know how long it would be before he could get home. I had a minor health scare, and was considering applying for a promotion at work.

Hannah updated me on the boys: Theo and Jono were reconciled, and the photography hobby had grown into a business, with the other hobby, the jazz band doing well too. Miles seemed to have made a success of his life as a personal trainer, although Hannah admitted she still didn't really understand what it entailed.

Education was in a state of flux, with more funding, less certainty, endless new initiatives, changes to the national curriculum, the introduction of academies… I was tired of it all. The Labour government was returned for a second term; a disease of cattle caused devastation to farmers, the Queen Mother died; England didn't win the World Cup. Later, there was a massive protest in London against the Iraq war. Those were the things we talked about then.

The following year spring came early, and as I recovered from my lethargy I took to walking for miles around the town, filling my lungs with the scent of blossom in the parks and in other people's front gardens. I found myself revisiting parts of the town I had avoided for so many years that I'd almost

Jenny 2

forgotten they existed. One day my feet led me past a house with roses in the garden. Memories stirred, but the pain had gone. A young couple came out of the house, the house where Jenny never lived. They were carrying a baby, and began tucking the child into the waiting pram with such a look of tenderness that it made me catch my breath. The woman saw me watching and gave me a smile. I hadn't gone there deliberately, but I was glad that I had found the place. On the very spot where once white roses bloomed, new buds were breaking out, in April, too. That had to mean something, didn't it?

Beth

The local church ran a mother and toddler group, and I started taking Annie there during Uni vacations. She was reaching the stage where she needed to be with other children, and I made some friends there, too. In some ways we had more in common than the people on my Uni course, although there was nothing wrong with them. They just hadn't had much life experience, I guess, while I'd had more than enough. I was beginning to think about what would happen if and when I got my degree. I was determined to provide for my child, not just a home but a mother who would be a role model.

But as the course went on, it got harder. Annie didn't sleep so much during the day, and the nursery fees took a huge chunk of my grant. Bonnie had been on at me again about looking for further support. She meant family, but I closed that idea down right away.

I went to see Gloria.

'You're looking tired,' was how she greeted me.

'Not you as well, Gloria. I've had enough of that from the nursery.'

Jenny 2

'How's she getting on there?'

'Oh, she loves it. I'm so lucky, really.'

'But?'

'There's no but.'

'Yes there is.'

'Well, yes, OK, maybe a little one… it's hard juggling study and baby. I'm determined to do this, though.'

Gloria laughed. 'Oh, yes, I know all about your determination.' Then her expression changed. 'You're not… you're not thinking about adoption again, are you?'

I shook my head emphatically. 'No, we're sticking together, Annie and me.'

'You know, what Annie really needs is a surrogate grandmother.'

I laughed. 'Not sure where I'd find one of those.'

'There are schemes…' she said airily, 'Pairing up young families with older people.'

She wasn't selling it to me.

'Do you still see Eileen Green?'

'I've seen her a few times. She has two lodgers now.'

'Hmmn. Pity. And you've got your own life now. She's probably too busy anyway…'

Gloria was leaning over the buggy, willing Annie to wake up. I loved watching them together. She would have made a good surrogate Granny, but that wouldn't have worked. Professional ethics.

Chapter Twenty-Six

Rachel – Beth - Hannah

Rachel

'Mrs. Daniels?'

Like every teacher, I was used to being greeted by young persons, at the supermarket checkout or behind the counter at Boots or some such place, asking if I remembered them. They usually remind me gently that they were in my tutor group or enjoyed studying *Of Mice and Men* or that they used to have braces on their teeth. Sometimes there is exciting news: they've just finished a degree in Linguistics or landed a job abroad. I almost never recognise them, though, for while I have barely changed, young people grow and change at an alarming rate during those years.

This one, though… For a stunned few moments I stood, looking at her, while I struggled to find my voice.

'Lizzie?'

'It's Beth now, Miss.'

'And who is this?' I nodded towards the pram, where a baby nestled, her rust-coloured hair peeping from a hooded all-in-one garment the colour of spring skies.

A look that could have been sadness, or pride, or both, crossed her face.

'This is my daughter.'

I was at a loss. I wanted to ask how? What? When? But it was all too much.

'How…how are you?'

'It's a long story.'

Later, after several cups of instant coffee in her little flat, she began to tell me some of it. She was clearly very proud of

Jenny 2

that flat, with its rooftop view of trees, just greening into full summer leaf. Perhaps she didn't notice how shabby everything was, inside. It could not have been more different from her childhood home.

'I love sitting here,' she said, gazing out. 'I feel safe and settled and somehow in the right place, for once.'

She turned to me with a smile. 'You set us a writing task on that once: *My Special Place*. Well, this is my special place.'

I tried to say something about her writing, but she hurried on in a rush, as if it was something she needed to get out.

'I loved your lessons. It might not have looked like it, but I did. You probably don't remember, but you got me to start keeping a diary to get me expressing myself. It became a sort of friend when there was no-one else. I stopped for a while when I was with Patrick, and then, afterwards, well I needed a friend again, so I decided to write it all down, the whole story. There's another purpose to it now.'

She looked over to where the child lay, still sleeping peacefully.

'Now someone very precious will one day read it.'

I didn't know what to say.

'Anyway, as I said, I enjoyed your lessons, and when I got myself sorted out, with the dyslexia and all - '

I nodded. Of course; that had been the problem her parents hadn't wanted to see.

'Well, I got help at college with my GCSEs, and I enjoyed my English A Level, so that's why I chose English for my degree.'

I just shook my head in wonderment. It was such a lot to take in.

'You're doing a degree? In English?'

'Yes!'

Jenny 2

She was laughing now, and pointing to a somewhat ancient laptop on the little desk near the window. 'With the spell check and the strategies they taught me at college you'd hardly know I'd ever had a problem.'

She picked it up and stroked it lovingly.

'It's seen better days, but it works, and the thing I've learned over the past few years is that if something works, it's madness to attempt to fix it.'

She was laughing again, and I realised sadly that I had hardly ever seen her laugh in the old days.

The baby stirred, and our talk turned to more immediate topics. Lizzie - Beth – said best to wait and see if she would go back to sleep, but that had to be balanced against letting her sleep too long, or she wouldn't sleep at night, and that's the time she needed for reading her set texts and writing essays. These were things I knew little of; in my sister's house the children had been pretty free-range, and I just assumed it all happened without effort. I had only ever really seen babies from the outside, all clean and dressed and ready to go.

She asked me about school.

'Oh, I left Hillmore a few years ago, after… Four years ago.' I wondered if she would ask about her mother, but she didn't. Perhaps I shouldn't have been surprised.

'Where are you working now?'

'I'm at Grovewood High – not far from here actually. It's more relaxed there. Uniform isn't the be-all and end-all it was at Hillmore.'

She laughed again, and I wondered whether I should be the one to mention her mother, but something held me back. Then her expression became serious.

'If you're wondering about Annie's's father…'

'Oh, no… that's none of my business…'

'He was wonderful. He got me back into education. We had a little flat… we thought we'd be together for ever…'

Jenny 2

I thought back to when Dave and I had believed the same thing, promised it, in fact, in our wedding vows.

'These things happen,' I said.

'But it wasn't one of *those* things.' She took a breath. 'Patrick was riding home on his motorbike one evening when he was hit by a lorry that failed to stop at the junction.'

I didn't know what to say.

Beth

It was nice when Mrs. Daniels came to the flat that day. I had hardly any visitors, no time, really, between Annie and my studies. It felt good to have someone to talk to about what had happened since I left Hillmore, because she was the one person who had cared what happened to me at that time. When I told her about Patrick, and the tears came, she was kind and held me until they stopped. It was the first time in a long time that I'd cried, but I felt better afterwards.

My course was going okay, although I was tired all the time, and as Annie got older she was awake for longer and I worried about slipping behind with my work. There was another thing nagging away at me too: seeing Mrs. Daniels had made me realise how lonely I was. I would sit in the lecture theatre sometimes and look around at the other students. They were all a bit younger than me, and some of them were drunk with the freedom of being away from home, but there were a fair few who were still living with their parents. Sarah, who I often sat next to in lectures, used to say she didn't know how she would have coped with all the work without her mum to look after her, do her washing, cook her meals and so on. I didn't bother to say that in my home, I was mum! I also pushed away the thoughts about my own mother.

'Do you get on well with her?' I asked.

'Oh, yes, she always says we're more like sisters!'

Jenny 2

I tried not to pull a face.

'So what does she say about how you're getting on with your Uni work?'

Sarah shrugged. 'Nothing. I don't think she's that interested in it, to be honest.'

But she cared. She cared about Sarah's wellbeing; that much was obvious. I felt lonelier that ever.

Rachel

I bumped into Beth a few times after that. It was as easy to walk that way home as any other. Sometimes we went to her flat, sometimes the park. She let me push the buggy on one occasion, and I felt as though everyone was staring at me. I tried to offer helpful advice about her course, but I don't think that's what she wanted from me.

I raised the subject of her family only once, and saw a sudden flash of the old Lizzie.

'I'd sooner be back on the streets!'

'Beth, you have a child now.'

'I am not subjecting her to the childhood I endured. I don't want to talk about it.'

During half-term Beth asked if I'd like to go with her to the carers and toddlers group at the local church. It took place in a spacious room in the church hall, with room for little ones to run around, and shiny ride-on toys to play on. Beth asked me to hold the baby while she went to get a coffee and chat to some of the other mums.

'How should I hold her? Like this?' I was really nervous.

'Yes, that's fine. She'll soon let you know if she's not comfortable.'

I marvelled at the way she trusted me.

Jenny 2

One of the others – a grandmother, judging by her age – came and sat beside me.

'Aww, she's beautiful, your little granddaughter. 'What's her name?'

I opened my mouth to say that she wasn't my granddaughter, but the other woman was busy tickling Annie under the chin and making her giggle.

'How old is she?'

I made a guess, based on what Beth had told me about the circumstances of her birth. 'She's coming up to one,' I said proudly, as if she really were mine.

Afterwards, walking back towards the flat with Beth – she'd let me push the buggy again – I allowed myself the brief fantasy that we were mother and daughter, and Annie the first grandchild in our family.

I saw Beth and little Annie intermittently over the next couple of years, and marvelled each time at how much the child had grown. It was exciting to see her when she began to walk, wobbling alongside Beth, who had to bend nearly double in order to hold on to her hand. Then her first words came, and then more and more each time.

'This is...' Beth paused as she made the introduction. We had long since been on first name terms. 'What should she call you?'

'How about Auntie Rachel?'

Beth smiled.

'Yes, lovely! This is your Auntie Rachel, Annie. Say hello.'

The little one waggled her fingers at me. I don't think she had worked out the difference between hello and goodbye at that stage. I was enchanted by her impossible attempts to get her tongue round my name, warmed by the sense of family relationship it implied, and consumed with guilt when I thought about Hannah. I had to try again. It took two or three attempts before I got the words out.

Jenny 2

'Beth, do you ever think about your mother?' Although I already knew her feelings on the subject, I wasn't fully prepared for the strength of feeling behind her response; it was like seeing the fourteen-year-old rebel again.

'WHY?' She had stopped, right in the middle of the pavement, careless of who might be walking by. 'Why does everyone go on about my mother? Why should they all think that having a child of my own suddenly means I need my mother?'

I wanted to mother her myself then, give her a hug, tell her that it was all right, but she didn't look receptive to that. Instead, I said,

'You may not need her - you are clearly managing well on your own. But don't you think she should know that she has a grandchild?'

She unclenched her fists a little and mumbled an apology.

'They keep asking me at the nursery if I have any family, to help out, give me a break...' She looked at me through wet eyelashes. 'I really appreciate the help you give me...'

'I don't think I've done anything much, but I am amazed at how far you've come, on your own...'

'I wasn't on my own, to begin with.' Her voice shook a little. 'I had Patrick at first...' Tears were threatening again.

'I do know how hard it is to lose someone you love.'

'I thought your husband was still alive?'

'He is, although there is more than one way to lose someone. And...' I wondered whether to say it, after such a long time and so much buried pain, 'And he isn't the only one I have lost.'

Somehow, we were both hugging and crying after that. As I stood back, I said,

'Your mother doesn't know if you are dead or alive. Couldn't you at least give her that?

Jenny 2

Hannah

The boys had both been for the weekend, bringing girlfriends, flowers and chocolates, and news of their own worlds. Theo and I reminisced about the day he'd come home in his third year at Uni to announce that he was giving it up in favour of travel and taking photographs. That had been like a red rag to a bull as far as Jono was concerned. The row they had disturbed the neighbours, who actually came round to ask if everything was all right. But all that was so long in the past, like so much in our family life, and we found ourselves laughing uproariously at the memory. Miles was content with his life, helping couch potatoes to get fit, as he put it. When our visitors had gone, the house seemed very empty.

Jono was away on one of his trips, representing his company on the other side of the world, and when I hauled myself out of bed on Monday morning my mood was low. In order to escape the unwelcome silence, I left for work early, before the post had arrived, so when I got back at six and saw the card on the mat, with its familiar, wonky handwriting, I was so overcome with hope and fear that I couldn't bear to open it for a long time. It lay on the kitchen counter while I put the kettle on - the days of reaching for the bottle the moment we got in were, thankfully behind us – and it was only after my coffee had brewed and I was sitting down that I dared to open it.

Inside was a pretty card, the sort that comes from a high street chain. There was a printed message: *Thinking of you*, and below that she had written, *I thought you would like to know that you have a granddaughter. Her name is Annie.*

Jenny 2

My first instinct was to call Jono, to let him know that our daughter was alive, but it was the wrong time of day where he was, and so I sat there while my coffee went cold, shedding the tears of so many moments of regret.

When I rang Rachel to suggest we meet up she was a little offhand.

'Are you okay, Rachel?'
'Yes, fine. Sorry, I'm just a bit, well, preoccupied.'
'Do you want to come here for coffee?'
'OK, yes. Saturday morning?'
'Good, I'll see you then. I have some news.'

Rachel

Hannah's phone call, which once would have been so welcome, had caught me in something of an emotional turmoil. My invalid father's death the previous year had been followed shortly after, and unexpectedly, by my mother's. The brevity of her time free from the responsibilities of being a carer denied her the chance to spend time with my sister or me, as she had longed to do, and I grieved her loss of that as much as I grieved my own loss of two parents within a year. Of course, the emotional charge of the funerals inevitably evoked my other loss of twenty-two years ago, but it was a dead child I mourned now, not a child of my imagining.

Our parents' house sold for a surprisingly large sum considering what they'd paid for it as newlyweds, and so little money had been spent on it, or indeed on anything much, and my brother-in-law had offered such sound financial advice, helping them to invest their savings prudently, that we were left the kind of sum, even divided by two, that meant I could consider taking early retirement. Laura was happy to spend her share on helping her two youngest through University, and our shared loss brought us closer together. I saw more of her children – adults now – than I had for many years, and enjoyed the feeling of being part of a family again.

I was still seeing Beth quite a bit, occasionally babysitting when she wanted to slip out to the library in an evening, and everything in my particular garden seemed to be blooming. Then, a few days before Hannah's call, while I was still juggling numbers and plans and even drafting my letter of resignation from the school, Beth arrived on my doorstep, apologising and crying and blowing her nose.

'Come on, come in. Here, I'll take the buggy.'
'I'm sorry. Oh look, the wheels are dirty – your carpet!' and she was off again.
'Carpets clean, Beth. I'm more concerned about you. Come and sit down and tell me all about it.'
I discreetly removed a few ornaments from Annie's reach – we'd been caught out the week before – and put in front of her the little box of toys I kept for her visits.
'I don't know what to do, Rachel. I've been given notice.'
Notice: what did that mean? Was she in trouble with the University authorities? It took a while to sink in.
'I've had a letter from the landlord, look…'
She handed me a typed letter that had been folded and unfolded a number of times. It had been a long time since my own renting days, but it looked pretty clear to me. The landlord was not renewing the lease. There was nothing, legally, she could do.
'So what will you do?'
There were more tears.
'I've no idea. I'm coming up to my final year, and it's hard enough to fit in time to study, and the nursery fees are going up, even though they're means-tested, and rents round there are so high, and student flats get taken at the

Jenny 2

end of the summer term, you know, passed on by final year students...'

I passed her the box of tissues. It reminded me of my time in counselling, except it was now up to me to be the one keeping calm.

'Beth...' I began.

'No, don't. Don't go there. I've written to her, let her know I'm alive, like you said, just like you said. I even told her Annie's name... but I won't, I can't, don't tell me to go to her...'

'OK. I'm going to put the kettle on, and then we'll go for a walk and clear our heads and look at the options. All right?'

She nodded.

The options were not many, and the fact that Annie refused to stay in her buggy and kept wandering off towards the pond didn't help. By the time we got back, and I had put the kettle on again, I had made a decision.

'How would you feel about moving in here?'

'Really?'

'Yes. I have a spare room, and I'm taking early retirement, so I won't need my study any more: that can be Annie's room.'

The look of joy and sheer relief on Beth's face had me catching my breath.

'*And* I will be able to take care of Annie for you, once I'm not working.'

Hannah

I couldn't keep it to myself. I told Rachel the minute she stepped through the door.

'What did she say?'

Jenny 2

'Oh, it was just a card. To tell me I have a granddaughter! Now at least I know that she's alive... and maybe she wants to build bridges. I mean, why contact me, why tell me about little Annie if she isn't planning to bring her to see me?'

Rachel's reply seemed a little flat. I'd expected her to be as excited as me.

'That's really good news, Hannah. I'm pleased for you.'

Then I remembered what she'd told me about her own daughter, and I felt bad for thinking that.

'I'm sorry... I should have realised...'

'What? Oh no, don't be silly. Of course you're thrilled, and you know I'm OK about Jenny now.'

I made the coffee as calmly as I could. I'd made chocolate chip cookies, but Rachel declined.

'So, what's going on with you?' She didn't answer immediately. 'I mean, we haven't seen each other for ages. You must have some news?'

She told me about her inheritance. I'd known about her parents' deaths, of course, and had sent condolence cards, but we'd had little communication beyond that. Finally she put down her mug.

'Yes, I do have some news... I'm taking early retirement.'

Chapter Twenty-Seven

Beth - Hannah - Rachel

Beth

The doorbell rang. It made me jump, because I'd been deep in a novel I'd actually chosen myself, to read for pleasure, a joy after all those set texts in preparation for Finals. I could still hardly believe that I'd passed – not only passed but got what is termed a 'good degree.' My new course was starting in September, but for now it was the summer, and I had earned a bit of a rest. Rachel was out, somewhere or other; she'd been a bit vague, and a bit tense, I thought.

Annie was happy at the kitchen sink. She liked to play at washing up, with a sinkful of bubbles and a few carefully chosen, unbreakable utensils, so I put down my book and went to the front door.

'I'm sorry, I'm afraid Rachel isn't... Oh!'

The woman who stood there was as shocked as I was. I'm not entirely sure she even recognised me at first, but she must have done, because she said my name, at the exact same moment I said,

'Mum!'

There was a very long moment of not knowing what else to say, when a sudden crash from the kitchen set me running. Mum must have followed me in, because she was there with me in time to see Annie clinging to the taps and wailing.

'Mummy! Mummeee!'

I was just in time to catch her as she lost her grip on the taps.

Jenny 2

'You used to love doing that,' Mum said. 'Washing up. And I lost count of the number of times you managed to kick the stool away. Just like this little one.'

To hide the tears that sprang so unexpectedly at that, I turned away and filled the kettle. I knew that the anger, so long buried deep, would have to be addressed some time, but for the moment I was surprised by how calm I was. By the time I'd switched the kettle on, Mum had settled herself in a chair and was talking to Annie, very gently. It was the oddest feeling, seeing my mother and my daughter talking to each other, almost as though a broken circle had been repaired.

Mum looked up.

'Does she know about me?'

I shook my head.

She gave a sad little smile. 'Fair enough. I don't want to cause you problems.'

As we drank our tea, Annie playing with her little tea set at our feet and interrupting our conversation with instructions to 'drink this', Mum said,

'I had absolutely no idea you were here, Elizabeth, truly. I was supposed to be having coffee with Rachel.'

'She's gone out.'

'Do you know how long she'll be?'

I shook my head.

'She didn't say. She did seem a bit... well, on edge, when she left.' Then it struck me. 'Could she have set this up? She's been on at me for ages to get in touch with you.'

Mum's expression was hard to read. 'Has she now? So she persuaded you to send me the card?'

I didn't need to reply. Then another thought hit me.

'You said you were supposed to be having coffee together? So, is that something you do often? I mean, do you know each other, like friends or something?'

'It's something we've been doing for years.'

Rachel had never told me that.

Jenny 2

Hannah

I looked around Rachel's kitchen. The kitchen of a woman who lived alone and liked things neat and tidy had been transformed. Little Annie's toys lay scattered across the floor, with more spilling out from a basket beneath the table. The worktops bore a clutter of cheerful nursery cups and dishes, not all of them clean, and a pile of the child's clothing lay in a heap, presumably waiting to be ironed, on top of a laundry basket in one corner.

'So… you're living here?'

'Didn't she tell you that either?'

The answer to that must have been obvious, so instead I asked what she was reading. I had seen the book, left open face down where she must have left it when I rang the bell, but couldn't read the title from where I was sitting.

'*Never Let Me Go*. Kazuo Ishiguro. Shortlisted for the Booker prize.' Then she added, 'It must be funny for you to see me reading.'

'Was that Rachel's idea?'

'No, it was Patrick's.' To my questioning look she added, 'Annie's father. He got me back into education.'

For some stupid reason I felt the tears welling, and when I looked up I saw that her eyes were moist too. Then she told me. The story of the past seven years was a long one, interrupted several times by Annie's various needs: toilet, drink, biscuit, 'cuggle', as well as by a lunch that Elizabeth prepared effortlessly for the three of us. When Annie had gone for a nap she resumed the story.

'Don't count on peace for long – she's almost given them up' Elizabeth said, and then she told me about her degree and her plans for the future.

'A teacher! You? After hating school so much?' I couldn't take it in.

Jenny 2

'But that's why. I want to help people like me. You know what they say: no-one forgets a good teacher.'

Right on cue, almost as if she'd planned it, we heard Rachel's key in the lock. For a moment all my old anger and frustration boiled up, but the woman crept into her own kitchen almost as if she were the interloper. The silence was intense.

Rachel

I'd heard the last bit, about the teacher training course. Stupidly, without acknowledging Hannah, I said,

'You didn't tell me you'd applied, Beth.'

Hannah said, 'Beth, is it? You've given her a pet name, I see.'

I tried to decipher her expression. It might have been pure hatred.

'It's the name I chose, Mum. It's what I call myself now.'

Annie could be heard, shouting that she'd finished her sleep, and Beth went to see to her. Hannah and I stood on opposite sides of the kitchen, just looking at each other. I wondered if I'd made a colossal mistake. Finally, she spoke. Her voice sounded strained.

'What else haven't you told me?'

'Does it matter? You know now.'

She just stood there, looking at me. This hadn't gone quite the way I'd planned. My own voice sounded strained too as I replied, 'For heaven's sake, Hannah, I've brought you and Beth back together. Why aren't you pleased?'

She was angry then.

'You're doing it again, aren't you? You're doing what you've always done. The superior one, the one who knows best... who knows best about my own daughter.'

Jenny 2

That was the moment Beth re-entered the room, carrying a wriggling Annie.

'Stop it, please! I've just got my head round the idea that you two are friends, and now you're enemies again. Rachel has been more of a mum to me these past two years than you ever were...'

That was the moment when Hannah ran for the door. I took Annie from Beth and pushed her in the same direction.

'Go after her, Beth. Now! Believe me, you'll regret it if you don't.'

'I'll regret it if I do.' She stood there shaking her head from side to side. 'What on earth made you do it? You betrayed me.'

And then she went out.

I don't know what was said out there in the street. My focus was on Annie. Perhaps this was the last time I would see her...or Beth... or Hannah. It was quite some time before they came back in, and both their faces were blotchy. Hannah resumed her position on the opposite side of the kitchen from me and sighed deeply.

'All right Rachel. I guess this doesn't have to be Gunfight at OK Corral.'

I'd never seen the movie, but I got the gist, and it lightened the mood a little. I tried to explain.

'I'm sorry, Hannah. I can understand how angry you must be. We literally just bumped into each other in the street one day, and...'

'Why didn't you tell me she was alive?'

'I wanted to, believe me, but she was adamant.'

'I'll believe that. That's Elizabeth: stubborn to the last.' There was a slight smile as she said that, and she turned to look at Beth with warmth.

I continued my account.

Jenny 2

'Beth was being evicted and had nowhere to go and her exams were coming up and …'

I didn't know what else to say. There was an awkward silence.

'And today? I take it that was deliberate?'

'Yes. Stupid, I know, but I couldn't think of another way of getting you two together. And you did seem to be talking, when I came in….'

'Yes, it's quite a story.' She threw her hands in the air as if sweeping the past away, and when she spoke again her tone had softened. 'Well, come on: you invited me here for coffee. Do I have to make it myself?' and it was just a little more like it had always been these past few years.

Beth put her head round the kitchen door to say she was taking Annie to the park.

''Bye, Ganny Rachel,' the child called, and I cringed.

Hannah raised an eyebrow. I'd always envied her ability to do that.

'Sorry. I didn't ask her to call me that. I used to take her to the toddler group at the church, and there were lots of grannies and everyone just assumed I was hers and so she did too, and then it just stuck. We kept telling her to call me Auntie Rachel, but…'

'OK. That's not important now. The thing is: what happens next?'

That was indeed the question.

'I guess that's entirely up to Beth.'

She was silent for a few moments.

'I won't pretend that I'm not jealous that you've been living this cosy family life with my daughter and granddaughter all this while – '

'Only a few months, actually.'

'But being jealous of you and your relationship with my daughter is nothing new. And, if I am to be searingly honest…' A look of what I can only describe as pain shot across her face, 'To be honest, my own family life has been

Jenny 2

so much easier these past few years... even with the great, gaping hole at the centre.'

I struggled to find something to say, but she shushed me.

'Rachel, I know you have had a great, gaping hole at the centre of yours for the past twenty-two years, so I can't really be angry with you. Only sad.'

Over the following weeks I left Beth to herself as much as I could. She went back to visit them in the house she had left in anger and despair, and found parents overjoyed at her return, but she hadn't moved in. In the meantime she continued to fill my house with her young life and Annie continued to call me Ganny Rachel, absorbing without difficulty that she also had a Ganny Hannah and Ganpa Jono.

Of course I had come to care for her over the years, to love her as the adult daughter I had never had, and I would have been content to continue playing 'Happy Families' with her and Annie for years to come. There had been a time when she needed me, when she was a child and more recently, but that time was past, and my holding on to her would only cause division, as it had before. Dave had made me see, years ago, that loving and letting go are sometimes the same thing, and so I nerved myself to tell her that she

should choose the other one, her real mother. I was just waiting for the right moment.

One Saturday afternoon, Beth had arranged for Hannah to come over. I offered to go out, but she smiled and said that she wanted both of us there this time. What she actually said was 'both her mums' and I stowed the bittersweet phrase away in my heart for later.

'The reason I asked you both here,' she began as we cradled our mugs of coffee, for all the world as though she were opening a meeting, 'Is because both of you, quite understandably, have been asking me about my future plans.'

Hannah was looking quite pale that day. I wondered if she had a cold.

'Just a moment, Beth, before you say anything else. I have thought about this a great deal, and I've talked it over with your dad, of course. The thing is...' She paused to catch her breath, and her voice was husky when it finally came out. 'The thing is, that I want you to know how very much I love you, and despite what you may believe, I have always loved you. No, let me finish... I can see how happy you are here. You have found a new family and Rachel can give you unconditional love and support and...' She was sobbing now, but waved away Beth's attempts to stop her. 'If you want to stay here, you have my blessing.'

Now it was time for me to speak.

'Can I have my say now? Beth, I freely admit I have come to think of you as a daughter and would love to continue as we are, but I will not come between you and your mother any longer. You must go back to your family, your real family.'

Then I turned to face Hannah. 'I hope you can forgive me, and that, maybe, we can still be friends?'

'Oh for goodness' sake, stop this!' Beth spoke more loudly than I'd ever heard her. 'There is no need for any of this. I don't need to choose. I need both my mums.'

She'd already worked it all out. Her teacher training would be delivered within a school setting, so she'd be teaching almost from the start...'

Jenny 2

'Learning on the job,' said Hannah.

'That's right.' She gave an anxious little smile. 'And earning, although not very much. I mean, I won't be able to afford to pay rent until I have qualified teacher status.' She looked from one to the other of us. 'I will only manage to get through the next year if I have your help: help with childcare, and help with accommodation.'

There was a heavy silence. Eventually, Hannah spoke, slowly.

'So...are you going to stay with Rachel, if she's willing to keep you?'

'No...' I felt my jaw clench painfully as I said it, 'You should move back in with your parents.'

'I don't know.' She shook her head, as if to clear it. 'I don't know what I should do... I just know that the training, will be very demanding. I'm going to need a lot of support. Childcare, too, like you were saying, Rachel.'

Then she asked if we would keep an eye on Annie for a bit as she had some errands to run.

'A tactical withdrawal,' Hannah observed drily. 'Leaving us to fight it out between ourselves.'

'Hannah, I'm sorry, and I'm certainly not going to fight you. I offered to have her here, to look after Annie because she was distraught the day she came round, after her lease wasn't renewed...'

With a sigh, Hannah said, 'It's all right, Rachel. I know you didn't do it to spite me.'

'Anyway.' I looked round at the kitchen, with all the accumulated clutter of a small child's requirements. 'I'm starting to feel I need my own space back. I *want* her to move back in with you.'

It was one of the hardest sentences I have ever uttered.

Chapter Twenty-Eight

2021

Beth

Beth

My daughter was twenty in April. She enjoyed her first two years at Uni, but her final year was a bit of a disappointment, with all the lectures online. Still, at least she'd had two years in which to make friends, and they all kept in touch via Zoom, and then socially-distanced walks in the park, as soon as it was allowed. It was the same park where I used to take her in her buggy, back when I was a student myself. My experience was very different, though, and not only because there wasn't a pandemic then. I'm glad she is free of the burdens I carried, the shame of my teenage years, the feelings of being unloved, the grind of bringing up a small child on next to nothing, fitting in learning around a child's needs. I would never put it to her like that, of course; I would never want her to think I resent her, and she is such a reminder of Patrick, with her wild coppery curls and striking green eyes.

People sometimes get confused when I speak about my mum, because sometimes I'm referring to my 'real' mum, and sometimes to Rachel, who was a real mum to me too, for a time, when I needed her most. You might say that I was blessed to have had two mothers in my life, and in the end, is it even possible to say which one loved me more: the one who took me back, or the one who gave me up?

ABOUT THE AUTHOR

Carolyn Sanderson has dipped her toes into the world of academia, and worked in a number of fields including counselling, training and working for the Church of England. She has also had a number of years of being at the sharp end in front of a classroom full of adolescents!

She has written articles, reviews and a number of hymns, and lives in Milton Keynes, a surprisingly green city. When not writing, she loves tending her garden.

Also by this author:

Times and Seasons (in the Weidenfeld &Nicolson series Hometown Tales)

Women don't kill animals (in The Word for Freedom, Short Stories of Women's Suffrage, Retreat West Books)

The World Was All Before Them
© *Carolyn Sanderson* 2023

No Abiding City
© *Carolyn Sanderson* 2023

The Sacramental Garden
© *Carolyn Sanderson* 2023

Jenny 2

Printed in Great Britain
by Amazon